DEMETER'S DILEMMA

THE CROSSROADS KEEPER
BOOK 3

SAMANTHA BLACKWOOD

BARGHEST PRESS

ABOUT THIS BOOK...
DEMETER'S DILEMMA

When Zeus invites Alex to a dinner party with the gods on Mount Olympus, it's an invitation she can't refuse.

Busy juggling death magic training with the Fates, deleting ominous texts from her estranged mother, and fighting with an over-protective Hellhound lover, Alex doesn't have time for socializing, but she can't really say no when a cranky cherub delivers Zeus's dinner invite.

Before Alex can choose her dress for the divine dinner party, a goddess with a dilemma descends on the Crossroads, demanding that Alex skip the event because death is on the menu and the rebellion among the gods is heating up.

Demeter desperately needs Alex's help to save a demi-goddess daughter she's been hiding for half a millennium. Her daughter's Crossroads is under attack, and the rebel god Morpheus is up to his old tricks.

Olympe isn't just a goddess's daughter; she's also the only woman alive who can help Alex learn the truth about her unique divine heritage. Alex must risk Zeus's displeasure and rally her supernatural posse to take on an old enemy and save a new friend.

However, using her dangerous new death magic might just be the end of everything.

Mythical Greek gods, quirky supernatural creatures, a newbie Crossroads Keeper, and a sassy, snarky … and magical pink-eared poodle battle the forces of chaos in this urban fantasy series filled with adventure, humor, a smidge of romance, and newfound family ties.

CHARACTER LIST

MAIN

Alex Blackwood - A Crossroads Keeper with more dangerous powers and divine relatives than she knows what to do with.

Chronos - Greek Titan and Primordial god of Time. Husband to Rhea. This retired god has got some shocking news for Alex!

Conor - Barghest Hellhound shifter and Guardian of the Crossroads. Alex's overprotective boyfriend.

Demeter - Greek goddess and one of the Crossroads creator triune. Mother to Persephone and Olympe. A goddess with a dangerous dilemma.

Hecate - Greek goddess, Alex's boss, and head of the divine triune that created the Crossroads.

Larry the Kibble Guy - Sassy magical Familiar and Alex's partner.

Maia Blackwood - Alex's ghostly aunt and the former Crossroads Keeper, until her untimely death. Alan's girlfriend.

Nyx - Greek goddess of Chaos. Daughter of Chronos, mother of the Fates, grandmother of the Oneiroi, and related to Alex. Always trying to make bad things happen.

Olympe - Mother Superior and Crossroads Keeper. Warrior nun. Semi-divine daughter of Demeter and magical mentor to Alex.

Persephone - Greek goddess. Demeter's wayward daughter. One of the divine triune who created the Crossroads.

The Fates - A trio of Greek goddesses and Alex's quirky divine relatives. **Atropos:** Dangerous mean girl and scissor-happy lifeline cutter. **Clothos:** Mother goddess and weaver of the Web of Life. **Lachesis:** Nuttiest of the lot. Measurer of the span of each life ... and everything else.

Vincent Ianotti - AKA Vinnie the Vampire. Former New York City mob boss and current restaurant owner. He's Maia's friend and Alex's honorary uncle.

Zeus - King of the gods. Brother to Demeter, husband to Hera, and related to Alex. Finally admits he's got a divine rebellion on his hands.

MINOR

Calliope - Servant to Clothos and friend to Alex. Descended from a no-longer-so-dormant Keeper family line.

Chion - Calliope's handsome older brother. Restaurant owner and a bit of a lady's man.

Crazy Sam - Wild West cowboy ghost. And yes, he's pretty darn crazy, but not a bad ghost, really.

Grenoble/Nitus - Former Goblin King on a mission to free his people—or die trying. Larry's best friend and partner in crime.

Grigory - Hellhound Barghest Shifter and the Grenoble Crossroads Guardian. Friend and protector of Olympe.

Goblin Royal Family - **Yima:** Grenoble's evil stepmother. **Methol:** illegitimate king and half-brother to Nitus (now Grenoble), whom he deposed and left for dead more than a decade ago. **Modi:** Grenoble's feisty sister.

Hades - Greek god and Persephone's husband. Finally steps up and brings his war-dog, Cerberus, with him.

Helen Grimby - Wannabe Crossroads Keeper. Alex's birth mother and Maia's older sister. A nasty piece of work.

Heli - Human daughter of Zeus. Demeter's rude assistant.

Hera - Greek goddess and wife of Zeus. Not a nice goddess, at all.

Icelus - Greek god. One of the Oneiroi, three divine brothers with powers over sleep and the unconscious. Brother to Morpheus. He's a wolf shifter who might must be a good guy.

Leonard Allard - Revenant and Alex's friend.

Lir - Kelpie shifter. Olympe's handsome friend with benefits. He and his herd are a big help, in more ways than one.

Momus - Zeus's cherub messenger. Truly a nasty little dude.

Morpheus - Greek god. One of the Oneiroi, three divine brothers with power over the unconscious. God of nightmares. Alex's nemesis. Brother to Icelus. Always up to no good.

Queen Elizabeth I - An ancient Tudor ghost. A bit of a royal snob.

Rhea - Titan and wife of Chronos. Close relative of Alex's. Very close.

Sister Reine - Strict head nurse of the convent's infirmary. Not a nice nun.

Sister Zoé - Olympe's right-hand Crossroads priestess. Demi-goddess daughter of Aphrodite.

Talon Grimsby - Necromantic mage and Alex's sort of and very-much-more-than-dead father.

Sundry other bit players.

1

FAMILY TIES THAT BIND

Alex rolled out of bed quietly, trying not to awaken the snoring Hellhound shifter sleeping next to her. As she slid her feet into slippers, a soft snicker sounded. She rolled her eyes and mind-spoke to her magical partner, who was currently crawling out from under the bed. *"I thought you agreed to make yourself scarce when Conor and I ... uh, spend time together."*

The small white poodle with bright pink ears grinned up at Alex knowingly and replied the same way. *"When you two get it on? When you do the horizontal mambo? When you—"*

"Oh, shut up, Larry. I get the picture," Alex whispered, hoping her magical mutt couldn't see the fiery blush staining her cheeks in the shadowed room. Her romantic relationship with Conor was so new that she was having trouble adjusting to it herself. Dealing with the sly looks and teasing comments from Larry and the rest of her heart family was even more difficult.

Conor snorted and readjusted his position before settling back onto the mattress with a soft snore. Alex slid quietly from the bed and shuffled toward the bathroom. She threw Larry one last glare over her shoulder and mind-spoke a firm request. *"Why don't you go find your goblin buddy and bug the chef for breakfast? Whatever you do, just get out of here and give us some privacy, for deities' sake."*

Larry snickered and headed toward the newly installed dog door. *"Don't forget, you've got that last training session with your cousins this morning. They say you're as ready as they can get you with your death magic. They plan to head back to Mount Olympus soon, after reporting in to your grandfather."*

Alex breathed a sigh of relief. Her three cousins, the Fates—yes, those ones, had recently returned to the Crossroads and worked her hard over the past month, helping her master her newly discovered death magic. She now had a handle on using it—or rather, on not using it. Frankly, the Primordial divine powers over life and death she had inherited from her grandfather, Chronos, terrified her. She had no intention of using her death magic, ever. Or—well, never again since the last time she'd used it and almost killed a Fae prince. Granted, he'd been trying to kill her at the time, but still.

Resting her hands on the sink, she grimaced at her reflection in the mirror. Memories of when she had both discovered and used her death magic for the first time filled Alex's mind. She remembered her undead father's agonized screams when she had inadvertently destroyed his borrowed body—and his soul. Of course, he'd been trying to kill her at the time, so there was that. She was beginning to sense a theme...

"Sweets, are you up?" Conor's rough voice questioned her from the other room, pulling Alex out of her dark musings.

"Yep," she replied. "I'm gonna take a shower, then I have a final training session with my cousins." She dropped her head, avoiding her reflection in the now-steamy mirror. Her divinely dangerous cousins were leaving soon, but the rest of her heart family, including Conor, would still be close. Sometimes too close. Then there was her newly discovered divine family to consider, as well.

Thank goodness my crazy—and freaking dangerous—cousins will be on their way back to Mount Olympus in a couple of days, she reflected with a sigh of relief. During their second visit to the San Antonio Crossroads, the divine trio had fulfilled Chronos's orders to train Alex to control her death magic. Hopefully, she could now keep her head down and avoid any more dealings with her divine family. Dealing with one family at a time was more than enough.

2

THE FICKLE FATES

Alex dodged another shadowy bolt of death magic thrown by her loving cousin, Atropos. That bitch was definitely trying to kill her. Breathless, she tucked, rolled, then shot to her feet, arms outstretched. A powerful stream of death magic shot from her fingers, hitting her snarling cousin square in the chest. The powerful blast threw Atropos backwards, and she landed on her ass in the dirt several yards away. The powerful goddess of death let loose a foul string of curses, then an uncharacteristic grin split her long, thin face.

"You'll do, Cousin Alex. You'll do," Atropos crowed as she climbed to her feet, her long legs and arms spider-like. "If *I* can't kill you with death magic, and *you* can throw me off my feet with yours without killing me, then my job here is done."

Alex nodded at Atropos, being careful to keep her pleasure at the goddess's unlikely praise off her face, then turned to face her other two divine cousins. Clotho and Lachesis both clapped madly in support. *Thank all the deities*, she thought. She'd lived through the intense bootcamp of death magic training from her trio of divine cousins, also known as the Fates, albeit with more than a few cuts and bruises, along with a concussion or two, along the way. But she had made it! *And* she had taken her most powerful and annoying divine cousin down a few times in the process. Yay!!!

While she wasn't pleased when her newfound grandfather, Chronos—yes, that Chronos, the Titan god of Time—had tasked the Fates with training Alex to control her death magic, she had understood the reasons behind it. He was right, dammit. Without control over the Primordial magic she had inherited from her divine ancestor, she could easily kill someone in a fight ... alright, a whole lot of someones. Okay, maybe even a small country or two full of someones. Or a world. *Sigh.*

Clotho's plump cheeks quivered as she nodded her head and smiled at Alex. "My dear, you have mastered a divine power that no other demi-goddess has ever manifested. Your control over your death magic is commendable," the motherly goddess complimented her. The stout goddess flicked an apprehensive glance at her sister, Atropos. "In fact, I think you're almost a match for my most powerful sister."

Atropos snorted and tossed an angry glare at her sister. Before she could unleash a blistering rebuttal at Clotho, their third sister, Lachesis, cut in. "Now, now, sisters of Fate. Alex's accomplishments do not lessen our own power over death." The tiny, bird-like goddess tilted her head. "In fact, I'd say that, all things considered, having a fourth family member with death magic is a good thing. After all, four is an even number, and everything is always easier with even numbers." The goddess of measuring the span of each life nodded, smiling happily.

"We all know how much you like measuring all the things, dear sister," Atropos snarked. She pursed her thin lips, then admitted, "However, perhaps you are right this time. With our *dear* mother, Nyx, still plotting her escape from the Underworld so she can bring her unique brand of chaos to all the realms, having another powerful cousin with death magic in the family is probably a good thing." The arbiter of death sniffed and turned away. "I'm going to write up our report for Chronos, then pack my things." She threw a scornful glance at her sisters. "I suggest you two morons do the same."

Lachesis eyed her sister's retreating figure with a tiny sigh of relief and then flicked a glance at Alex. "Cousin, we have done all we can to prepare you for the battles coming your way. Please use your death magic wisely, cousin."

"You'll need it soon, dear. Best to be prepared," Clotho murmured as she hugged Alex gently. "You're more than welcome to come and stay with us anytime, you know. And don't forget, there's a Divine Council meeting coming up sometime soon. If you need a place to stay when you visit Mount Olympus, just drop us a line and we'll prepare one of the guest rooms." The motherly goddess patted Alex on the cheek, then trudged away after Atropos.

Alex gave her remaining cousin a finger wave and a small smile. "Bye, Lachesis."

"Farewell, dear. We'll see you soon," Lachesis replied, then she scampered after her sisters.

"Not if I can help it," Alex muttered as she watched the three Fates wend their way through the gardens. She had no intention of visiting her divine cousins or Mount Olympus anytime soon. Nor did she have any plans to use her death magic—wisely or not. She'd spent the past month learning how to control it, and control it she would. She planned to stuff that sucker into a large box and relegate it to a tall shelf in the back of her soul closet.

Alex shook her head to clear it, then ambled down the garden path in the opposite direction of her deadly cousins. She planned to begin her avoidance of all things divine immediately. No more death magic. No more worries about her demi-goddess status or her divine cousins and certainly not her Titan grandfather.

Really, Chronos, why couldn't you listen to your wife and just keep it in your pants, dude? She muttered to herself dryly.

ALEX'S STEPS took her where they often did: to the small Greek temple nestled in a clearing just outside the estate gardens. The pale stone of the temple's Doric columns reflected the early evening moon's pale silver light.

Lowering herself wearily onto the low stone wall surrounding the temple courtyard, Alex sighed in pleasure. The sun had set recently, so the stones still held the heat of the day, and the warmth felt good on her overworked muscles. Death magic training was a real bitch.

Nope, not going there again. Alex yanked her thoughts back to the Crossroads. The Crossroads was usually quiet at this time of day, as most travelers used the ley line crossings either early in the morning or well after dark, depending on their species. Vampires, of course, always took the night train ... er, ley line.

Speaking of vampires, here comes one now, Alex mused. She rolled her shoulders and pasted on a welcoming smile. "Hi Uncle Vinnie. It's good to see you."

The stocky vampire approached smoothly, his gait more of a glide. As usual, Vinnie wore an expensively tailored, midnight-black Italian suit. When he smoothed back his thick, ebony hair, the rings on his fingers and the heavy gold watch on his wrist glittered in the moonlight.

"Hi sweetheart. How you doin'?" Her adopted uncle smiled at Alex, his full lips showcasing very white teeth—with very sharp and very pointy canines. His eyes glowed silver-red, almost exceeding the just-risen moon in brightness.

If anyone fit the traditional image of a mobster—and of a vampire—it was her Uncle Vinnie, Alex thought. And tonight, his vampire was on full display. Typically, vampires retracted their fangs when not feeding. Or at least that's what she suspected, since she'd never actually gotten a closeup of them before, and had no desire to do so.

"I'm good, Uncle Vinnie, thanks." Alex patted the wall next to her, trying not to stare at Vinnie's full-on vampire glory. "Uh, you can have a seat, if you like."

Vinnie plonked himself down on the wall and gave Alex a narrow-eyed examination. "I take it you passed your last death magic class with those fucking crazy cousins of yours?"

"How can you tell?" Alex grinned. "Oh, that's right. I'm still alive."

The vampire snorted a laugh and gave Alex a one-armed hug. "I never doubted you'd make it through in one piece, my dear."

Alex held back the first thought that came to mind. But *I had my own doubts about that very thing.*

As if she'd spoken her thoughts out loud, her adopted uncle grinned at her. "I didn't have any doubts, dear. You're more powerful than you know." He frowned and added, "Or than you're willing to admit to yourself."

Rubbing her hand across the wall's rough stone surface nervously, Alex glanced away from her uncle's knowing gaze. "Well, it's all done now. I'm all trained up on my death magic. The Fates leave soon, so I can get on with my life ... and with my real job as Crossroads Keeper."

Vinnie studied Alex for a long moment, then he gave her a sly smile and changed the subject. "Speaking of getting on with your life, how's things going with Conor? I haven't seen you two at the restaurant in a while." The vampire's eyebrows lowered. "He's still treating you good, right? If not, you just let me know—"

Alex interrupted before her uncle's temper flared further. "Things between us are good, Uncle Vinnie. Real good. No worries there, bud, so just calm your vampire self down." She patted his hand reassuringly. "We've both been really busy, is all. I've had the death magic training, and Conor's been dealing with some trouble brewing amongst the ghost community, from what I hear."

"Whaddya mean, 'from what I hear?' Hasn't he been helping you with your death magic training?" Vinnie barked, his crimson eyes glowing brightly, rivaling the sun he'd never again see. "I told that mangy Hellhound ... Barghest ... whatever he is, shifter—"

"I know what you told him, Uncle Vinnie. Conor told me." Alex rolled her eyes and huffed in annoyance. "You told him to stick to me like glue during the death magic training. Not that he needed to be told. He's been trying to do that, anyway."

She heaved a sigh. "Like I told Conor, it's as if you both don't trust me to handle myself. Dude ... it's my life. Let me handle things my way. You can just chill your vampire and Hellhound selves out. I'll let you both know if or when I need help. I promise."

An uncomfortable silence descended between the pair; their absent gazes followed the fireflies flitting across the courtyard.

Finally, Vinnie roused himself and spoke. "Okay, doll. I get it. We're both crowding you a little."

"*A little?!*" Alex growled. "Conor won't even let me leave the grounds without him escorting me. We had a big fight about his overprotectiveness again yesterday—oh wait, you know about that, don't you? I'm pretty damn sure he told you."

Alex realized why her uncle's vampire mode was so evident. The poor undead man was just as worried about her as Conor. She knew both men only wanted to support and protect her, especially now everyone knew about her true heritage. After all, a Crossroads Keeper who also happened to be a newly discovered demi-goddess with unheard-of powers over death magic that rivaled the Fates was pretty unique. Alright, totally one-of-a-kind.

A lightbulb went on in her head.

"Wait, it's not just *me* you two want to protect, is it? You think I could lose control of my death magic and hurt ... uh, kill a lot of people. Am I right?" Alex's head fell back, and she gazed unseeingly at the moon. "I'm not gonna let that happen, Uncle Vinnie. I've got the training now to control my death magic, and that's exactly what I plan on doing. If I never have to even think of freaking death magic or being a demi-goddess again, it'll be too soon. I'm a Crossroads Keeper. I've accepted that. It's my job, and I'm damn good at it. Isn't that enough?"

Alex realized her voice had risen and ended in a whine. She pursed her lips and nodded once. "It's enough for me, anyway."

Vinnie snickered. "So flamingos aren't the only ones who bury their heads in the sand, huh?"

"Oh, shut up, you. I'm not avoiding anything." Alex chuckled despite her anger. "And it's ostriches who bury their heads in the sand, not flamingos, Uncle Vinnie."

"Whatever. You know what I mean, doll." He grinned indulgently at her, then leaned forward, his gaze intense. "Anyway, how about that Divine Council meeting I hear is coming up soon? I heard you'll be on the guest list. Right at the top, in fact. You can't avoid your divine family—or the duties such a heritage provides —forever, you know, no matter how much you'd like to." The vampire gave his recalcitrant niece an amused side-eye.

"I'm skipping that meeting," Alex stated, smacking the rock wall with finality. "And I'm turning down any other divine invites or demands that come my way from now on."

"Should I get you a pink flamingo feather boa?" Vinnie replied with a smirk. "Or is it a chicken you're imitating now? Bukk, bukk, bukk—"

"Cap it, Uncle Vinnie." Alex heaved an aggravated sigh and shoved to her feet. "I'm gonna go hang out in the In-Between with Hecate for a while. At least *she* understands what my real priorities should be. After all, she's the one who made me one of her priestesses and oath-bound me as a Crossroads Keeper. Remember?"

"You can't avoid your demi-goddess status or your death magic by pretending they don't exist, niece."

Alex shrugged off her adopted uncle's words and walked faster.

"Bukk, bukk, baaaalk." Vinnie's chicken sounds followed Alex as she jogged across the courtyard and climbed the marble steps leading to the Crossroads temple. Her Crossroads temple.

3

TEXTS & A TELLING OFF

As Alex reached the temple portico, her cellphone pinged with a text message. She paused as a feeling of dread pulsed through her chest. *Not another one.* Despite her urge to ignore it, she pulled out her phone and gazed at the screen. *Yep, it was another text from the homicidal ice queen, also known as her mother.*

"Hello Alex. Stop avoiding me. We need to talk."

Alex pursed her lips and turned off her phone. She had no desire to speak with the mother who had abandoned her as a baby, then kidnapped her as a pre-teen and hidden her from both the magical world and those who truly loved her for decades. Oh, and then there were the times *mother dearest* had attempted to kill her and take the Keeper's role she so coveted for herself. There was that, too. She didn't know what her mother had planned for her this time, but she was *damn* sure it wasn't good.

Slipping her phone back in her pocket, she rolled her neck, trying to ease the tight muscles the stressful day had caused. She touched the cool marble of the closest Doric column, determined to escape for a while. Immediately, her stomach pitched as the temple's magic pulled her into the In-Between. She closed her eyes for the brief journey; it helped with the nausea.

Once Alex smelled the wood doused in musky incense Hecate liked to burn in her living room, she opened her eyes, hoping the goddess was present and not off visiting another Crossroads somewhere around the world. Hecate had been spending a lot of time visiting the other Keepers now that Alex and her supernatural posse had this Crossroads in hand, after the gruesome attacks earlier in the year.

"I see you have decided to visit me, child. And about time, too." Hecate's low-pitched voice soothed Alex's soul, but as the goddess's sharp words registered, a frisson of fear caused her heart to skip a beat. She needed to remember that goddesses, especially the powerful creator of the Crossroads system, did *not* like being ignored. *Oh shit. Maybe coming to the In-Between for a stress break wasn't the best idea.*

"Uh, hi Hecate." Alex tried to swallow around the tight ball of fear in her throat. "Um, it's just that I've been really busy with death magic training. Plus, we've had a lot of visitors through the Crossroads, since it's high season—"

The beautiful but deadly goddess fixed Alex with a narrow-eyed glare. After several minutes, which were filled with dangerous possibilities, Hecate's lips curved in a thin smile. She gestured to an empty couch and bade Alex to sit.

Discreetly wiping away the sweat that beaded on her brow, Alex hastened to obey. *Whew. That was a close call. She reaaallly didn't want to get on Hecate's bad side.*

"Wine?" Hecate raised a wineglass and poured it full of a thick crimson liquid.

Knowing the goddess's favorite alcoholic tipple tasted rough, bitter and nothing like modern wine, Alex bit back a reflexive 'no'. *Yuck.* Instead, she suppressed a grimace and reached for the glass.

"Thank you, Hecate," Alex replied politely. She knew the sly goddess was needling her by offering wine the woman knew she disliked. As long as that was the only 'punishment' Hecate meted out, Alex would be a happy camper. Unfortunately, she sincerely doubted the goddess had finished messing with her. She sipped her wine and waited.

"I understand you have successfully completed your death magic training." Hecate gazed inquiringly at Alex. "The Fates leave soon, yes?"

"Um, yes," Alex stuttered a reply. "Once they leave, I'll definitely have more time to dedicate to my Keeper duties." *Oops, she'd just used her divine cousins as an excuse for not visiting Hecate more often.* "And, uh, to visit you here in the In-Between and learn more about my responsibilities as your Keeper."

As the fraught silence lengthened, Alex decided today had been a no-good, rotten day. She had woken up that morning with the realization that, while make up sex was great, she and Conor had not actually resolved their issues. She needed him to tone down his overprotective tendencies, but he resolutely refused. Then she'd almost gotten killed by her craziest cousin during their last death magic training session. To top it off, her Uncle Vinnie had ambushed her just to hassle her about wanting to avoid her newly discovered demi-goddess powers and status, along with the divine family that accompanied them.

Alex kept her face blank as she sipped the revolting wine and resolved to pacify Hecate as quickly as possible, then go hide under the bedcovers for the rest of the evening. Why couldn't everyone understand she was still dealing with the massive changes in her life wrought by being dragged back into a magical world and into a heart family she had been spelled to forget? Discovering less than a year ago that she was heir to a goddess's creation, then being bound as a Crossroads Keeper, had been a LOT. The battles that followed to protect her Crossroads and the wider magical world that, until recently, she had not known existed—well, that had been a LOT, too. She thought she'd been coping pretty damn well, considering. She neither needed nor wanted any more status changes, deadly powers, or divine family members. *So there.*

Hecate's thin smile widened as she studied Alex, who hastily gulped her wine and choked, spluttering a cough. The goddess now resembled a cat that had found a nice, frightened mouse to toy with.

"Let's make a deal, Keeper," the goddess purred. She leaned forward, pinning Alex in place with her powerful gaze. "You will visit me every new moon to work on your Keeper abilities. You will meet with your aunt weekly to learn Keeper history, rules, and customs. You will train with Conor daily to improve your physical fitness and fighting ability. And you will continue to perform your role as Keeper of this Crossroads and Protector of Sylvan City, no matter what other responsibilities come your way."

The goddess paused and Alex hurriedly interjected. "It's a deal. I promise to do all of those things, ma'am." She hesitated, then added, "I *want* to do all those things."

"And the rest?" Hecate queried.

"Uh, what rest?" Alex finished the last of the nasty wine, then placed the glass on the table at her side and gazed fearfully at the expectant goddess. "Isn't learning to be a good Keeper exactly what you want me to do?"

"Don't play dumb with me, child." Hecate's tone was sharp, angry. "You have recently discovered your demi-goddess status and gained control of the Primordial death magic that is your rightful heritage."

Alex merely shrugged, unable to argue the point.

Hecate huffed in frustration. "You are a descendant of the most powerful Titan—Chronos, the Father of all Time. You are related to the deadliest and most devious of goddesses, Nyx, and your are a cousin to the Fates." Hecate showed her teeth in a cat-that-caught-the-mouse smile. "You *do* realize that also makes you kin to Zeus? To Demeter? To most of the Olympians, and, yes, even the

Oneiroi? And that last divine trio I mentioned includes your arch-enemy—you know, the rogue god who has promised to kill you—your cousin, Morpheus."

As the goddess recited the many relatives on her divine family tree, including the one who had vowed deadly revenge, Alex sank lower in her seat. She kept her face neutral, hoping the goddess didn't realize she'd made a direct hit with her sharp speech.

Of course, Hecate knew she'd hit home with her terse words, Alex realized. *She was an ancient and powerful fucking goddess—one who could read minds and hearts, at that.* Alex's fingers curled into the cushions on either side of her as she fought the childish urge to drop her head and hide behind her hands. It wouldn't help.

"What exactly do you expect me to do about my divine heritage, Hecate?" She demanded. "I can't help who my biological family is. After all, *I'm* not the one who slept with a Titan. That was my paternal grandmother, remember?" Alex's voice sounded both thin and defiant, even to her own ears. *What was she thinking, challenging a freaking goddess?* She straightened her shoulders and suppressed a groan, awaiting punishment for her blatant disrespect.

After a dangerous pause, Hecate replied, "I expect you to embrace your new role as a demi-goddess and make us all proud, child." The goddess grinned evilly, then reached out and patted Alex's clenched hand. "Including me. After all, we're family now."

Ah, fuck. Yep, Hecate sure knew how to contrive a just punishment. Crap on a stick.

4

DATING & DECISIONS

The candle's flickering light reflected off the planes of Conor's face. Conor's extremely furious face. "I told you, Alex. I'm a Barghest, descended from generations of Hellhound shifters. Hecate created my breed to guard both Crossroads AND Keepers. It's not just what I do, but who I am. You can't expect me—"

"I'm not expecting you to stop doing your job, Conor. Just, maybe..." Alex sputtered to a stop.

Conor's lips curved into a reluctant smile that didn't quite reach his eyes. "Maybe just not to do it so well, right?"

Alex signaled to the server. If they were going to have this conversation, she needed something stronger than wine. "Hi Gus, can I please have a mojito? Heavy on the mo."

The server grinned and bobbed his head. "You got it, boss."

"For the umpteenth time, I'm not your boss, Gus." Alex smiled and shook her head at the tall, thin man. "My Uncle Vinnie may own this place, but I'm just a customer."

The server shrugged one shoulder in disagreement. "That's not what the Big Boss says. He says we need to treat you like we treat him. Which is as the boss, so there you go."

Alex caught Conor's eye, and they shared a mutual grin, their disagreement forgotten for the moment. She wouldn't win her ongoing battle to convince her Uncle Vinnie's employees to relax and treat her as any other customer—at least, not this evening.

"Whatever you say, Gus. Just bring me a mojito and keep them coming."

"Sure thing, boss."

Sigh.

Once the server hurried off to fulfill Alex's drink order, an uncomfortable silence descended. They both filled the awkward pause by picking at the garlic-scented appetizers spread across their table.

Finally, Conor broke the tense silence. "Look, I understand where you're coming from, Alex. You weren't raised in the supernatural world. Your idea of being a strong, independent woman means not relying on others, not needing help and protection—"

"Let's just get one thing straight, bud. I *am* a strong, independent woman," Alex interjected, giving Conor a narrow-eyed glare.

Conor patted the air and opened his mouth to speak, but that just made Alex angrier. "Don't you try to tell me that women in the magical world all need big, strong men to protect them, because I know damn well that's not true. Just look at—"

"Oh no, you don't, sweets. Let's not make this a 'who is a stronger supernatural' contest." Conor shook his head and eyed her ruefully. "You'll win that one, every time. You're a demigoddess with death magic, for fuck's sake. You've got me beat by a mile."

"Then why—"

Conor gently placed his hand over hers. "Alex, the ancients built the supernatural community on interwoven abilities, duties, obligations, and alliances. Mutual support of others is hard-wired into most supernatural species." He captured her gaze, his eyes filled with both apology and intensity. "Hecate created my species to protect her Crossroads creation and to guard its Keepers. I can't help that. What I *can* do is try to give you space when you need it. But we're a team, Alex. There's no getting around that."

Alex searched Conor's eyes for the truth. Would he really step back and give her space when she asked for it? When she needed it? It was the only way their romantic relationship would work. Otherwise, they'd have to revert to being just magical coworkers, not lovers. Her heart dipped. She didn't want that, but time would tell.

During their intense conversation, Alex's drink had arrived. She caressed the ice-cold glass. Boy, she really needed a gulp ... er, sip of one of the bartender's amazing mojitos. The cocktail looked perfect; just the right amount of fresh mint, not too much ice, a frosted glass ... and a garish, fluorescent pink, flamingo swizzle stick. *Now wait just a damn minute.*

Alex's gaze searched the restaurant until she spotted her dapper Uncle Vinnie. The fool was standing near the bar, miming a furiously clucking and flapping chicken. He had a fluffy pink boa slung around his neck, which swung in time to his flapping wings—er, arms. Despite herself, Alex burst out laughing, and Conor joined her.

The evening's tension quickly disbursed, leaving Alex feeling lighter than she had in a while. Objectively, she understood that she still had a lot to learn about the supernatural world and her place in it. Reluctantly, she also admitted to herself that she couldn't—and shouldn't avoid her new demi-goddess status, powers, or divine family, for long. One step at a time, though.

Alex waved her uncle over to their table. The vampire clucked and flapped his arms a few more times, then regained his suave dignity and glided over to their table. She watched his approach and snorted a laugh; the pink feather boa did rather interfere with the whole mobster vampire thing he had going on.

"Yes, my dear? How can I be of assistance this evening?" Vinnie solemnly bowed his head, the twinkle in his eyes belying his serious demeanor.

"First of all, gimme that damn boa. It looks ridiculous on you," Alex said, grinning up at her uncle. "I, however, have a couple dresses it would look amazing with."

The vampire slid the feathery boa off his neck and gently placed it around his adopted niece's. After fluffing and adjusting it to his satisfaction, he stood back to admire his handiwork. "You are correct, my dear. The boa suits you better than it does me. You can keep it." Vinnie shook his finger in mock warning. "As long as you don't use that pink feathered monstrosity to justify continuing to bury your head in the sand regarding your new semi-divine status."

Alex rolled her eyes. "Ostriches are the ones who bury their heads in the sand, Uncle Vinnie, not flamingos, and I'm darn sure you know that." She knew her adopted uncle was only teasing her ... well, semi-teasing her. He had a serious motive, and he'd just made sure she knew it. Patting the chair next to her, she said, "Why don't you join Conor and me, since what I have to say next involves both of you dipsticks?"

Both men sputtered protestations at her insulting description, but Alex knew they understood it was her way of gently rebuking them for their recent behavior toward her.

As the last of their objections died down, Alex fixed both the men in her life with a serious look. "Listen, guys, I get your point. I'm still new to the supernatural world, and I don't understand yet how everything works. I also know that I can't ignore the whole demi-goddess with divine death magic thing. But gimme a break. Sometimes I just need a little time to myself, so I don't lose ... well, me."

Despite her best intentions, her eyes filled with frustrated tears. "I mean, sometimes I just want to head to a coffee shop alone. Do some shopping—also alone. Or maybe with a friend. You know, have some me-time or some friend-time." Speaking of friends, her mind filled with an image of a small, pink-eared poodle. After all, Larry *was* her first magical friend; she'd met him before she knew anything about her supernatural heritage.

Gazing pleadingly at the two men, she asked, "Do you both understand?"

After a tense moment, Conor grinned at her, his amber eyes glittering in the candlelight. "The last time you visited a coffee shop alone, sweets, the henchmen of an evil Fae prince kidnapped you and spirited you to the prince's lair in the Fae realm."

Vinnie snickered. "There is that, doll."

Alex huffed and threw her arms up in despair. "You get kidnapped from a coffee shop by *one* Fae prince, and suddenly *every* coffee shop visit is out of bounds. Remember, guys—that was before I knew about my death magic, and how to use it." She grinned in triumph. "If you recall, once I got to the Fae realm, I used my death magic on Prince Cair's ass, escaped his evil lair, *and* rescued his imprisoned royal sister, as well. I'm capable as fuck. Capisce?"

Conor and Vinnie exchanged a loaded look. They couldn't argue with her words. She *had* rescued herself from that fiasco. When Conor and the rescue team had finally arrived, they had found Alex and the princess free and miles from the prince's hunting lodge where they had been held captive.

Vinnie nodded reluctantly. "That you did, hon. That you did. However, when you first disappeared, you gave us both a heart attack." He curled his lip and added, "And, if memory serves, Larry had no small part in your escape or in helping Conor and his rescue team find you and the princess. You know, when you were both wandering around lost in the northern Fae woods."

Conor cut in. "All we're saying is that having a magical team supporting you while you get a grip on the supernatural world and grow into your demi-goddess status has gotta be a *good* thing. *Right?*"

After a long moment, Alex dipped her chin in agreement. Then she crossed her arms and gave the two men in her life a defiant glare. "But I'm still going out for coffee next week. By myself." She shrugged. "But maybe I'll bring Larry. You know, for moral support."

Vinnie suppressed a grin and gave a discreet signal to the server.

Gus quickly trotted to the table. "Yes, boss."

"Bring a bottle of the Domaine Leroy Les Beaux Monts, please. And three glasses."

The server nodded and darted away.

The vampire smiled benignly at Alex. His crimson eyes shining with pride, he took her hand in his and said, "You are an amazing, powerful, independent, and increasingly wise woman, oh niece of mine." He squeezed her hand, sadness tinging his gaze. "I just wish I—we could have been there for you as a child."

Alex's eyes widened as Vinnie's fangs lengthened in his distress. She placed her other hand over his, where it clasped hers on the table, and patted it. "It's okay, Uncle Vinnie. Let's not go there again. I'm here now."

"If that fucking mother of yours comes near you again, I'm gonna kill her this time, no matter what your Aunt Maia says," the vampire growled.

"Me too." Conor agreed.

Alrighty then, Alex mused. Now was probably not the time to tell these two that her mother had been texting her for the past several months, demanding they talk.

The expensive wine arrived at the table, and conversation devolved into ordinary matters, like the brewing ghost war.

5

GHOST WAR BREWING

lex blew out a slow breath and shook out her hands, then walked in circles on the gravel path near the massive barn.

Larry watched his magical partner pace, a frown creasing his doggie forehead. The magical connection they shared allowed him to feel his partner's anxiety and unease. Out loud, he asked, "Hey Alex, what's the problem? You and Conor have chaired posse meetings before. You both—"

Alex interrupted him. "That's just the thing, Larry," she moaned. "*Conor* and I have run posse meetings before—with the emphasis on Conor coming to the rescue when things go pear-shaped." She tilted her head from side to side, then rolled her shoulders. "I've told him I want to chair this meeting by myself."

"What the hell did you do that for?" Larry barked. "Conor's been running posse meetings here for almost a century. He's an old hand at it." Then understanding dawned. "Oh. Yeah. You want to show you can handle Crossroads duties by yourself." He snorted a laugh. "Queen Elizabeth's going to be there tonight, you know. Good luck, Alex!"

With a sarcastic tilt to her mouth, Alex nodded, acknowledging her Familiar's comments. "Thanks bud. You do *so* inspire confidence."

Larry grinned, a mischievous gleam in his chocolate-brown eyes. "You're welcome."

A stately, and only very slightly transparent, form hove into view. The ghost of Queen Elizabeth traveled down the gravel path soundlessly. Every inch of her slight form, from the tips of her gold embroidered shoes to the understated but elegant crown on her head, proclaimed her as Tudor royalty.

Alex suppressed a grin and mind-spoke to Larry. *"Speak of the devil."*

Larry mind-spoke back. *"Some have called her that in the past."* He snickered and added, *"But they rarely lived long enough to do it a second time."*

Alex dipped her chin as the ghostly queen floated by them and into the barn. Somehow, Larry's teasing had made her feel better. Like she could handle tonight's meeting, and even the haughty ghost queen, by herself.

WHEN ALEX ENTERED the massive arena, the restless posse members lining the bleachers immediately settled down and gave her their attention. After smiling at her aunt in silent thanks for her supportive thumbs up, she noticed Conor and Vinnie slouched in the back row. Conor caught her eye and gave her a slight nod. She heard his voice in her head. *"You can do this, sweets. I have faith in you."*

She tore her eyes away from her way too handsome Hellhound Barghest boyfriend and swept her gaze around the arena. It looked like everyone was in attendance except Billy the Squid, then she heard him approach. The heavy swish of gravel crunching under the massive squid's tentacles as he crawled along the path made her wince. They would have to rake the path tomorrow. Not really a surprise, though. A fifty-foot long squid could do a lot of damage to a nicely level gravel path. *Sigh.*

Billy tentacled his way into the barn, absently moving the tall sliding doors further open to accommodate his enormous size. The supernatural squid's deep baritone rumble filled the air. "Hi everyone. Sorry I'm late." Sidling along the arena until he reached the far wall, he stretched himself along the length of it. "I had to wait until the hatmaker finished my new hat so I could wear it tonight."

Murmurs of *'nice hat'* and *'it looks great on you, Billy'* floated from the audience. Indeed, Billy's new hat was something to behold. An excruciatingly bright blue, the cowboy hat sported a lime green braided leather band with a jaunty yellow feather tucked into the brim. Of course, as usual, the hat was human-sized and way too small for Billy's gigantic head. Like all its predecessors, the cowboy hat perched precariously on the tip of Billy's pointy head, continually in danger of falling to the ground far below, but the wearer didn't seem to care. No one had yet summoned up the courage to ask Billy why he didn't buy a hat that actually fit. After all, the hatmaker was used to making hats for all sizes and shapes of supernatural creatures.

Alex shook her head to break her fascination with Billy's fluorescent new headgear. She wondered what creature the scaly, lime green hat band had come from, but cut that thought short. She probably didn't want to know.

When Alex raised a hand, the last of the shuffling and muttering in the audience quickly died down. *Good start,* she reflected, careful to keep the surprise off her face. "Um, hi everyone. Thanks for coming tonight. It's so good to see all of you."

An unbelieving snort echoed from the middle of the bleachers, where the largest group of ghosts hovered. Alex took a deep breath and ignored it. She already knew what the cranky ghost of Queen Elizabeth thought of her. Not much. The woman had always made that abundantly clear. She decided she wouldn't give the salty, crusty, ancient—and very dead—queen the satisfaction of seeing her rattled.

Taking a deep breath to calm her nerves, she started the meeting. "As you know, there have been a few issues over the past month or so between several ghost, uh, factions." Alex eyed the two unhappy groups of ghosts in the audience. One group clustered around the ancient ghost queen, while the other, smaller group huddled near the grinning ghost of Crazy Sam. The two groups sat as far apart as possible and were each busy shooting chilly eye-daggers at the other.

Alex cleared her throat and continued. "Tonight, we're here to see if we can achieve a truce—"

Mutters, catcalls, and jeers erupted from the opposing ghost groups. The rest of the audience laughed, clapped, and heckled the angry ghosts.

Oh, shit. Alex quickly realized that attempting to negotiate a truce between the two warring ghost factions likely wasn't the best time to assert her independence by leading the posse meeting by herself. She strove to keep the nervous jitters she felt from showing.

Larry mind-spoke words of encouragement. *"Suck it up, Alex. You snuffed out your father's soul, and he was one of the strongest spirits in existence! Remember? You did it with merely a thought."* The little poodle snickered. *"He is now an ex-ghost. He is no more. He's stone dea—"*

Alex couldn't keep a low chuckle from escaping. She mind-spoke a reply to her supportive, if sarcastic, Familiar. *"Alright, I get it, bud. I get it. You can stop your freaking Monty Python impersonation now."* As she returned her attention to the restless audience, she found her nerves had steadied, admitting to herself that her furry Familiar may have a back-handed way of boosting her confidence, but it had worked.

Maybe it's time to show off a little, Alex mused. She called her Keeper staff from the ether, and the long wooden rod smacked into her palm immediately. She poured some of her mixed magic into the staff, causing the crystal at the tip to glow until a massive, colorful arc of raw power burst forth. The smell of ozone permeated the air as streaks of magical lightning forked toward the rafters high overhead. *Oops. Might want to tone it down a little.* Alex pulled back on her power until the magic settled into a whirl of red, black, and blue circling the staff's crystal tip.

Silence. No one dared move, and those who still needed to breathe held their breath. The wide-eyed audience gazed at Alex with a mixture of awe, pride, and fear.

"That's more like it. Pay attention to the demi-goddess, you supernatural yahoos!" Larry barked.

Her explosive demonstration of magic, along with her Familiar's stern rebuke, meant Alex now had everyone's very rapt attention. *That's more like it,* she mused.

A chorus of snickers sounded in her head, reminding her of the magical connection she shared with those oath-bound to her. As the snickers died down, Conor mind-spoke his encouragement. *"In the supernatural world, a show of magical power is often the best way to establish your right to lead. Good work, sweets!"*

Alex took a steadying breath, gave Conor a slight nod of thanks, and started talking. "Alright, everyone, now that I have your undivided attention, let's see if we can discuss the issues within the ghost community in a civil and productive manner." Her now-captive audience nodded quickly in agreement. Even the ghosts.

After several long hours of negotiations and with some help from her heart family, which Alex tried not to resent, the two ghost factions reached a compromise they could all live with. *Or be dead with,* Alex reflected wryly, considering their ghostly status.

DIVINE DINNER INVITATION

Alex sat at the long oak table in the manor house's massive kitchen, stirring her morning coffee and trying to focus her bleary eyes, and her sleepy ears, on Henri, the chef. The posse meeting the previous evening had dragged on into the wee hours, with a final truce agreed between the opposing ghost parties well after midnight.

"I said, do you want eggs or pancakes this morning, Keeper?" The little French chef raised his eyebrows at her. Alex realized this probably wasn't the first time the poor man had asked her this question.

Before she could respond, Larry and Grenoble raced into the kitchen, simultaneously growling their culinary desires. "Pancakes! Pancakes, Henri! Please!"

Wincing at the racket the duo made as they harangued the chef, Alex sighed and sipped her strong coffee thankfully. *Coffee must be the nectar of the gods,* she reflected. *No, wait, it couldn't be; nectar wasn't caffeinated. What exactly did the gods drink to wake up in the morning on Mount Olympus?* She wondered idly.

Focusing back on the still-bickering duo at her feet, Alex

exclaimed, "Oh, shut up, you two. I bet you've both already had your breakfast. You don't need anything else to eat."

"Are you *sure* I can't eat her?" Grenoble queried Larry in a pleading growl. "I know you made me agree not to eat her, but if she keeps limiting our other food options, maybe—"

Larry shook his head at the always-hungry goblin and placed a pleading paw on Alex's leg. "Just one pancake each, and I promise to keep Grenoble from snacking on you." The little poodle gave Alex his best 'puppy dog eyes' along with a canine grin to plead his case.

Heaving a sigh, Alex turned to the patient chef. "Alright, Henri. I guess it's pancakes all around."

The little man nodded once, then grabbed a large bowl along with a well-seasoned iron skillet and got to work.

Slowly sipping the last of her wake-me-up juice, Alex's mind returned to her earlier musings. *My Familiar might know,* she mused. "Hey Larry, do the gods drink coffee on Mount Olympus? If not, what *do* they drink to wake up in the morning?" Another thought occurred to her. "Or do the gods even need to sleep?"

BEFORE LARRY COULD REPLY, an unfamiliar, gravelly voice answered Alex's casual questions. "The gods drink whatever they damn well please in the morning, including that newfangled beverage you call coffee." A hacking cough interrupted the newcomer's explanation. "Coffee tastes disgusting, in my not-so-humble opinion. I stick to drinking the nectar of the gods. That stuff is the fucking bomb!"

Everyone gazed around in confusion, searching for the source of the voice. Thumping overhead, followed by a flutter of wings, drew all eyes upward. A chubby-cheeked baby with small, soot-gray wings peered down from his perch on one of the exposed rafters that crisscrossed the kitchen's high ceiling. The baby wore a grumpy expression, and his face also featured permanent lines of discontent etched deeply around his nose and mouth. Smoke wreathed around the baby's halo of golden curls from the cigarette clenched between his plump, pink lips.

An angry flutter of wings, just visible above the baby's shoulders, shook loose several small soot-covered white feathers, which floated lazily down toward the still-speechless gathering below.

"Whatcha all staring at, assholes?" The baby cackled a smoke-filled laugh. "None of you seen a freaking cherub before? Name's Momus, in case anyone's interested." The unlikely creature took a heavy drag from his cigarette and blew a series of perfect smoke rings, which wafted gently toward the room's high ceiling.

Larry gathered his wits first. *"Uh, yes, I have seen a cherub before, Momus, but never one—"*

"As good-looking as me, right?" The cherub cut in, giving Larry a smug grin. "I know, right? It's damn hard to be so good-looking. Alllll the girls want a piece of me." A rattling cough broke off the cherub's boasting. "Well, I better get down to business," he added, pulling what looked like a paper airplane from the small quiver on his back. He grinned down at Alex, then launched the paper into the air. "I have a message for you from the big guy."

Yep, definitely a paper airplane, Alex reflected. As the sleek plane circled its way down, her stomach clenched with anxiety. The last time a small supernatural had turned up at the house with a message for her, the missive had resulted in nothing but trouble, including unexpected royal intrigue and getting kidnapped by an evil Fae prince. Whatever message the paper airplane heading her way held, she was positive it was trouble. And who the heck was 'the big guy' Momus had referred to? *Sigh.*

Henri crossed his arms and frowned up at the cherub. "Don't cherubs normally carry love arrows in their quivers? Aren't you guys supposed to handle falling in lov—"

"What? I can't multitask?" The cherub shot back. He cackled and patted his quiver with a smug grin. "I've got all kinds of shit in here, bud." He rolled his eyes and added, "Including those stupid *arrows of love* everyone is always on about. Why? Want me to shoot you with one, tiny Frenchman? Who in this room would you like to fall hopelessly in love with?"

Aghast, the chef hastily replied, "No one! No shooting love arrows, please, Momus!" Relief flooded Henri's face as the cherub merely nodded and turned his attention back to Alex.

"I can see by your expression you understand that I'm here with an important message for you, Keeper." Momus hacked a cough and pointed at the floating missive. Ashes flaked from the cigarette still clinging to the cherub's lips, floating gently down in the wake of the paper plane, which was taking its damn time making several extra laps around the kitchen before finally reaching Alex.

Reluctantly, she reached out a hand, and the plane slid smoothly to a stop in her palm. She stared down at the missive, noting the creamy parchment and glimpsing the elegant script within. Her heart raced with a frisson of dread, and she hesitated.

"Go on, open it, idiot," Momus ordered. "I don't have all day, you know. Places to be, things to do and all that." The grumpy cherub glared down at Alex. "I'm supposed to take your answer back with me to the jerk-wad who sent that invitation. I'll catch hell in heaven if I don't." Giggling at his own crude joke, he gestured impatiently at Alex. "Stop fucking around and open the damn thing, lady."

Multiple points of consciousness awoke in Alex's mind. Those oath-bound to her had felt her sharp spike of anxiety and were checking in.

"Do you need my help?" Tyre, one of a trio of Indigo Fae pledged by their royal family to protect Alex, and her aunt Maia before her, mind-spoke to her. *"I can be there in minutes."*

Conor chimed in, concern clear in his voice. *"Me too. I'm on my way."*

Larry joined the mind conversation. *"I'm here with Alex, guys.*

Everything's under control. There's no need to come rushing over. An asshole cherub just showed up to deliver a message, that's all."

Both Tyre and Conor replied simultaneously. *"Oh, shit!"*

Alex reassured her wannabe magical protectors. *"Guys, I've got this. Independent kick-ass demi-goddess here, remember?"*

After a slight pause, everyone mumbled their agreement, along with a plea to mind-call them immediately if she needed help. Alex heaved a relieved sigh when Conor and Tyre receded from her awareness, taking their worry with them.

Time to make the donuts, she mused, glancing up at the impatient cherub. She unfolded the paper airplane and smoothed it on the table. The heavy parchment revealed unfamiliar Greek letters. At first, Alex panicked, wondering how she could tell the nasty little cherub she couldn't read the message, but the words slowly made sense. *Huh. Guess I can read Greek now.* She wondered if her new ability resulted from her Keeper role or from her newly discovered demi-goddess status. Both roles were rooted in Greek mythology ... but neither of them were all that mythological. It didn't really matter, she supposed.

As the words became clear, Alex sat up straight, all traces of sleepiness gone. *Oh shit, was right.* The missive before her was from none other than the leader of the Olympian gods, Zeus. It was an invitation to attend a banquet on Mount Olympus—and the date was less than three days away! *Damn it.* She chewed her lip in consideration. *Could she decline the divine invitation, or was this a mandatory-attendance type of event?*

Larry, still present in her mind, mind-spoke a reply. *"That's definitely a command performance, Alex."* He hopped up on the chair next to her and focused on the invitation. *"Ooooh look, it includes a 'plus one.' That's gotta be me, right? Oh, and look at those dinner choices! I think I'll have the filet mignon. And the shrimp."* Larry licked his lips, tail wagging in anticipation.

Despite herself, Alex grinned at her greedy Familiar and

unthinkingly replied aloud. "You'd attend your own funeral if there was food on offer at the wake, you little chowhound."

Grenoble snickered and Henri smothered a grin. Nonplussed, Larry sniffed and replied to the room at large. "You better plan on having decent food choices at my wake buffet. I'll definitely attend the whole shebang if you do ... and I'll haunt you forever if you don't."

Momus hacked a cough and clapped his hands sharply. "Hey! I'm not getting paid by the hour, you nitwits. Hurry the fuck up with your answer." Everyone grimaced at the cherub's harsh reminder.

Larry gave the rude dude a narrow-eyed glare and snarked, "Keep your wings on, bud. Alex is just making her meal choice, then you can be on your way."

Alex suppressed a groan, then pasted a smile on her face and accepted the inevitable. Gazing up at the cherub, she replied, "You can tell Zeus I'll be happy to attend." She pointed at her Familiar. "Larry here will be my 'plus one'. He'll have the filet mignon, and I'll have the vegetarian platter." She hesitated, wondering about the proper protocol when replying to a god's invitation. "Uh, do I have to write out a response, or is a verbal one acceptable?"

Momus pumped a plump little fist. "Finally! She gets off the pot and gives me a yes!" His pink lips curved in a wicked grin, the cigarette still clinging to them gamely. "Good answer, toots! Of course, yes really is the only answer. No isn't a wise option. And a verbal reply is fine."

Alex exchanged a nervous gaze with Larry, and mind-spoke a question. *"Wonder what happens if you say no? Or do I even want to know?"*

Correctly interpreting their mutual glance, Momus rasped a rough laugh and supplied an answer. "I got a couple death arrows in my handy-dandy quiver here for the 'no's'."

She kept a smile pasted on her face, but icy fear shivered down her spine. She gave the grumpy—and apparently deadly—cherub a polite finger-wave, and said, "Thanks for the information, Momus, but we have every intention of attending."

The cherub nodded, then flicked his cigarette in the air and disappeared with a ruffle of feathers and an evil cackle that echoed long after his departure.

Henri rushed over and stamped out the still-glowing cigarette butt, then gingerly picked it up and put it in the trash, his face a rictus of disgust. "Nasty creatures, those cherubs," he muttered. Shaking off the tense atmosphere, the chef rubbed his hands together and smiled. "Who is still in the mood for pancakes?"

Larry and Grenoble shouted an enthusiastic yes, but Alex's appetite had fled.

Well, fuck it with a cherry on top, she mused dismally.

7

DEMETER'S DILEMMA

Alex sat on the low stone wall next to the pond in the courtyard garden, absently trailing her fingers in the cool water and listening to the gentle splash of the fountain. Frogs chirped in the darkness, and the whirring of cicadas in the bushes drifted lazily in the night air.

She reflected on the hot mess of a day she had just about gotten through. First, she'd passed her death magic training, thank all the gods. Then, a foul-mouthed, chain-smoking asshole of a cherub had handed her an offer she couldn't refuse—not if she wanted to live.

After Momus's visit this morning, word had spread quickly about the divine dinner invite he'd delivered. The Crossroads gossip mill had certainly worked overtime today. Alex snorted and shook her head. Of course, those who shared a magical connection with her had immediately known something was up, sensing the spike in her adrenaline when the cherub had first appeared, as well as her fear when he had made clear the deadly consequences of refusing Zeus's dinner invite.

She had spent the rest of the day arguing with various members of her heart family, as well as with Tyre, the leader of the trio of Indigo Fae warriors assigned to protect both her and the San Antonio Crossroads. It seemed everyone had an opinion about Zeus's dinner invitation, as well as her decision to attend the event with only Larry as a magical back-up.

Her Aunt Maia's ghostly form had wavered between see-through and almost solid when she protested Alex's decision. "Alex, dear, I know you're a demi-goddess, and yes, Larry is a powerful Familiar, but you really should take some of the posse members with you, my dear."

Alex's mind had wandered, so she couldn't remember the rest of her aunt's vigorous and lengthy protest. Nor could she remember the varied arguments of the many others who'd questioned her decision. The one thing everyone had agreed on was that nothing good ever came of divine dinner invitations. You're definitely dead if you refuse—and possibly dead if you attend. The consensus was, as Conor so forcefully stated during his diatribe on the matter, 'reinforcements are mandatory' and 'how can you possibly think I'm going to let you go to Mount Olympus without me?' *Sigh.*

Shaking her head, she decisively slapped the rough stone of the pond's retaining wall. Then she told the frogs and cicadas, "I'm going to the dinner, dammit. And I'm going without a crowd of supernatural nannies. That'll just make me look weak. I'm a demi-goddess with death magic, for the gods' sake. Chronos, the freaking Primordial god of time, is my grandfather. Plus, Larry is one of the oldest and most powerful animal Familiars in history. Between the two of us, we can handle anything that comes our way. We'll be fine."

∽

"WILL YOU, THOUGH?" A deep, rich, feminine voice questioned Alex's emphatic statement.

Alex's gaze raked the area, searching for the speaker, and she suppressed a groan when she recognized the goddess in the garden.

A tall, willowy, and very beautiful woman stepped into the moonlight and approached the pond. She smiled at Alex and sat down on the stone wall next to her. Demeter glanced at the pond, her face impassive, then focused her penetrating gaze on Alex and repeated her earlier question. "Will you, though? Will you be fine at the dinner without your posse, Keeper?"

An uncomfortable silence stretched between them as Alex tried to formulate a sensible reply to the perceptive goddess. Her confidence plummeted. If Demeter, one of the oldest and most powerful deities on Mount Olympus, didn't think she could handle dinner with her divine relatives, perhaps she was right. She couldn't. However, as the obnoxious cherub had pointed out earlier, saying 'no' wasn't really an option, either. *Damn it.*

While Alex considered her response, Demeter smiled sympathetically at her and patted her hand. "Normally, I might agree with your statement, Alex. You *are* an extremely powerful demi-goddess." The goddess's long golden curls bounced as she shrugged and tossed her head. "With a divine level of death magic inherited from your Titan grandfather, plus your unique Keeper heritage, you're probably the most powerful demi-goddess in millennia, or maybe even ever."

Demeter gently squeezed Alex's hand in a silent show of support. "You have more divine power than many of the regular gods, dear." Then the goddess's lips turned down, and she looked away.

Frowning in thought, Alex considered the goddess's words. "I'm confused, Demeter. First, you say I don't have a chance of surviving the dinner on Mount Olympus, then you say I'm more powerful than—"

"It's not your magical power level that's in doubt, Alex. It is the combined power of those deities who plot against you ... against us," the goddess stated, her intent gaze probing Alex's. "You surely don't think that banishing Nyx back to her prison in the far mountains of the Underworld has put an end to her scheming, do you? Or that of her co-conspirators?"

Demeter heaved a sigh and rolled her shoulders. "While Nyx may be temporarily out of the game, thanks to your late father's Regenerant army, her conspirators amongst the gods—and their supernatural creations—are not. There are more than a few who'd be quite happy to see Nyx free and who would support her in a divine war to bring chaos to all the realms."

Alex closed her eyes and rubbed a weary hand over her face. "Haven't I done enough for you guys lately?" She asked rhetorically, no longer able to meet the intense gaze of the goddess seated next to her. She knew her newly loyal Regenerants couldn't contain Nyx forever, but she had really hoped to have more time to deal with that situation. Later. Much later.

Plus, it hadn't been long since her return from the Fae realm, where she helped depose a royal despot and install the current, much more benevolent, Fae queen on the throne.

She had even solved Persephone's problem. Her evil, plotting, princely Fae boyfriend problem. Alex admitted to herself that the prince's death in the battle for the throne likely solved Persephone's issue all on its own. Even so, Alex had helped. She flicked a glance at the ancient goddess seated next to her, wondering how much Demeter knew about her divine daughter's escapades.

Suppressing a sigh, Alex brought her mind back to the present. She returned her gaze to Demeter and was surprised to find the goddess stifling a laugh. "What is it? What's so damn funny?" Rethinking her abrupt and profane questioning of a goddess, Alex sputtered, "Sorry .... I'm so sorry, ma'am. Um, did I say something to make you laugh?"

"Oh, Alex, you are so transparent." Demeter snorted an ungoddess-like laugh. "Your face speaks volumes. I hope you never play poker at your aunt's weekly poker game. With such an expressive face, you will surely lose."

The goddess sobered, but a merry twinkle danced in her eyes. "I know all about Persephone's 'problem prince', my dear. And I know you helped solve the situation in the Fae realm that arose from her philandering ways." She gave Alex a conspiratorial grin. "I even know that *my daughter* was the driving force behind the whole Hades kidnapping escapade. I'm also very aware that eating those damned pomegranate seeds Hades gave her doesn't actually tie my daughter to the Underworld for half the year. I'm not a complete moron, you know."

"Uh, I never said ... uh, that you were—" Alex couldn't finish the sentence. How did you tell a goddess that you believed she was rather clueless about her scheming daughter?

Demeter's rich laugh filled the night air, momentarily silencing the frogs and cicadas. "I know you didn't actually call me a clueless mother—or worse, Alex. At least out loud." She gave an impish grin. "But your face says it all." With a sigh, the goddess added, "I know that others think I'm blind to my daughter's many faults, but I'm not. She's still my daughter, though. And I love her."

Alex nodded mutely. What she wouldn't give to have a loving and understanding mother like Demeter. She winced as thoughts of her own cold, calculating mother slithered into her mind.

"Alex, I need you to pay attention." Demeter's soft command penetrated Alex's dark musings. "We'll deal with your malevolent mother another time, dear. I know she poses a threat to you."

"Is there anything that you don't know?" Alex muttered, working hard to keep the sarcasm out of her voice.

"Not much, Alex. There's not much I don't know," the goddess replied calmly. "Which is why I'm here to tell you that you can't attend Zeus's damned dinner. If you do, you're very likely to wind up a brand-new resident of the Underworld." Demeter sighed heavily. "And I may join you there." She flicked a glance at Alex and added, "I mean dead, in case you didn't catch that, Keeper."

"What?!" Alex gasped. "I thought I—we had to go to the dinner. I was told refusing Zeus's invitation would mean death."

"Death is exactly what both of us risk if we attend, Alex." Demeter explained, smiling grimly. "My sources tell me there will be a team of divine assassins in attendance at the dinner. Their targets are you—and me—at the very least. And it could even be worse than that."

The goddess shifted her position on the wall so that she faced Alex directly. Capturing Alex's gaze, she pursed her lips and shook her head. "But that's not important right now."

Not important?! Alex's mind whirled. What could be more important than an assassination plot ... and what could be worse than that?

Before Alex could object, Demeter captured her chin in a firm grip. Her fierce gaze pinning Alex in place, she growled, "I said pay attention, Keeper!"

Alex gulped and nodded minutely. After a tense moment, Demeter sighed and released her. The goddess settled herself more comfortably on the hard stone wall, then met her gaze. Alex could swear she saw both abject fear and pleading in the powerful goddess's eyes.

As if reading her mind, Demeter raised her brows and gave Alex a small smile. "You're right, Keeper. I am afraid for someone, and I *do* need your help to protect them. You see, there's been a serious attack on a Crossroads under my aegis. Dealing with that situation is even more urgent than Zeus's deadly dinner date, which is why we both must skip the banquet."

The goddess sighed deeply, hands clasped in her lap, knuckles showing white. "I fear that the danger at the banquet and the attack on my Crossroads are most likely connected. However, my —our first concern is the dire situation at the Grenoble Crossroads."

A familiar sinking sensation settled in Alex's stomach as she fought to make sense of the goddess's words. Just over a month ago, another goddess had come to her demanding help. She had solved Persephone's problem. Now, it seemed that Demeter had a deadly dilemma, too.

"So, there's a team of divine assassins?" Alex queried the goddess in bemusement, even as she realized that may not have been the best choice for her first question. However, *'why the hell is there a team of divine assassins after us'* really was one of the more important questions, in her view. She had a *lot* of questions for this goddess with a deadly problem—which appeared to be Alex's problem now, too. How bad must the situation be at the Grenoble Crossroads for this powerful goddess to consider it worth risking Zeus's deadly wrath by missing his banquet?

DEMETER SHIFTED on the rough stone of the pond wall, as if settling in for a long chat. Alex hoped the conversation would include some answers, but the goddess's next words merely addressed Alex's initial question.

"Yes, of course the gods have teams of divine assassins, Alex," Demeter stated flatly. "How else would the gods keep everyone in line?"

Alex gulped. "Uh, teams?"

"Don't worry, Keeper. Most of the assassin teams are on our side," Demeter replied with a low laugh. She tilted her head in consideration. "Well, all the ones that are still alive, anyway. Except one."

"One what?"

"One team, Alex." Demeter's gaze narrowed, and she eyed Alex with concern. "Do keep up, dear. There is one remaining team of divine assassins that is in league with Nyx and her co-conspirators. As far as we can tell, this team includes at least one of the Oneiroi brothers, along with several lesser gods. They will almost certainly attack at the banquet."

Alex blinked, her mind returning to a dank prison cell in the

Underworld, where a divine enemy she had temporarily bested promised to kill her the next time they met. After killing one of Alex's rescue team, Morpheus had sworn revenge before escaping once he realized Alex and her team might prevail. All these months later, the god of nightmares still haunted hers.

"Morpheus," Alex muttered. "He's the Oneiroi you suspect is on this assassin team, right?" She stated it as a fact rather than a question. It had to be that slimy, divine relative of hers.

Demeter nodded approvingly. "I have always said you are smarter than you look, Alex. Yes, we suspect your cousin Morpheus is a member of this rogue team of divine assassins."

Alex opened her mouth, then snapped it shut, mentally slapping herself. As much as she wanted to, she couldn't ask with whom Demeter had been discussing her intelligence—or lack thereof. She really didn't want to know. Besides, that wasn't important right now. Instead, she asked, "What about his two Oneiroi brothers? We already know Morpheus is on Nyx's side. Do we know if his brothers are as well?"

Holy crap, Alex mused, worry curling in her gut. Not just one, but three divine beings with power over the unconscious. Gods who were powerful enough to influence even the strongest of their kind. That would be bad. Really, really bad. And those divine dummies were her cousins—nephews—whatever. Just another bunch of deadly relatives out to kill her. *Ugh.*

Demeter shook her head and shrugged. "We don't know, Alex. Since the battle in the Underworld, your other two Oneiroi relatives have made themselves scarce, so we don't know what their loyalties are. However, there has been a possible sighting of Morpheus in a cave system that contains a Crossroads in France. His appearance coincides with an attack on the Crossroads Keeper there, along with severe injuries to several of her priestesses."

Alex nodded, connecting the conversational dots. She asked, "The Crossroads that was attacked—it's the Grenoble Crossroads you mentioned earlier, right? And it's in France?"

Demeter nodded and pursed her lips. "Yes, and that brings me to my dilemma." The goddess narrowed her eyes, fixing Alex with a gaze that was at once commanding and pleading. "You see, I really need you to travel to the Grenoble Crossroads before the attacks get any worse. We simply can't have a Crossroads fall into our enemy's hands." She smiled grimly. "As I mentioned earlier, there are more important matters than Zeus's assassin-filled meet and greet dinner in honor of our newest demi-goddess. We can deal with that later, Keeper."

"To answer the question in your eyes, heed my next words," Demeter instructed. "Yes, I suspect Morpheus and his cronies are behind the attacks on the Grenoble Crossroads. I really need your help, Alex. That Crossroads is mine to guard, and the Keeper there … well, let's just say she's very special to me." The powerful goddess's eyes shimmered with tears as she gazed pleadingly at Alex. "I can talk to Zeus. Try to get him to reschedule the banquet. But I need you and your posse at the Grenoble Crossroads as soon as possible to help protect it—and her."

Alex mentally rolled her eyes but kept her face blank. Why couldn't she just have 'normal' relatives? You know, the ones you only had to put up with at Thanksgiving and Christmas when they would fight amongst themselves, shout, argue, and cry, their atrocious behavior a stark reminder of why you avoided them the other ten months of the year?

"Alright, I guess we're going to France, then," Alex muttered resignedly. She rose, absently brushing stone grit from the wall off of her jeans. "I'm gonna go pack and get some sleep. When do we need to leave?"

Demeter couldn't suppress a grin of triumph. "Excellent! I'll meet with you and your supernatural posse tomorrow. We can discuss the situation further and hash out which of your posse members would be best to accompany you." She rose gracefully and shook out her pristine, moonlight-white toga. "I'm going to the In-Between now to discuss strategy with Hecate and my daughter. We'll meet you and your posse at dawn in the training barn." The goddess smiled thankfully at Alex and then slipped away, her slim form retreating down the garden path leading to the Crossroads temple.

~

AS DEMETER DISAPPEARED FROM VIEW, the sound of pounding paws and scraping claws drew Alex's attention. She watched in wry amusement as Larry and Grenoble skidded onto the terrace in a tumble of fur and leathery green skin. Turning a resigned eye on the crafty-looking duo now ranged attentively before her, she asked, "How much of my conversation with Demeter did you guys hear?"

Larry and Grenoble shared a sneaky grin.

"We heard allll of it, Alex," Larry growled. "Why can't those damn gods sort out their own freaking problems? Why do we always have to..." His angry words trailed off and he snorted in disgust.

"Because Alex is one of them, Larry." Grenoble's rough growl countered Larry's complaint. "She's a demi-goddess now. Her grandfather is a Titan, one of the Primordial gods. Nyx is her aunt. Her cousins are the Fates, while their progeny, the Oneiroi, are her nephews—or second cousins. One of the two. Maybe both." The little goblin sneered, his razor-sharp teeth shining in the silvery moonlight. "Alex is related to all of those divine idiots in one way or another. Buncha' incestuous—"

Larry hastily interrupted his friend's incipient rant. "Um, okay, dude. We get it. But it's really not Alex's fault that she's related to most of the occupants of Mount Olympus. The question right now is 'what the hell is going on at your old Crossroads, Grenoble?'"

Alex's eyes widened. Larry's question reminded her that the goblin crouched before her bore the name of the Crossroads to which they would soon be traveling. "Grenoble, you're from Grenoble ... er, the Crossroads in France, right?"

The short, squat goblin eyed Alex as if she had just confirmed his suspicion that she was rather dim. "Yes, Keeper, I'm from that area. My chosen name is Grenoble. I took it after being nursed back to health by my good friend, Olympe, who is the Keeper of the Grenoble Crossroads."

A world of grief flitted through the goblin's eyes so quickly that Alex almost missed it. She recalled Larry sharing some of Grenoble's sad history with her. Exiled from his kingdom, cast out after fighting for his rightful leadership role, the royal goblin now eyeing her doubtfully had washed up on the banks of the river flowing through the cave system that contained the Grenoble Crossroads. Traitorous members of his former kingdom had beaten him, then cast his broken body into the river outside their nest, believing him dead.

Olympe, the Keeper of the Grenoble Crossroads, had nursed the seriously wounded creature back to health. Once recovered, the little goblin had cast away his former name, along with his kingdom, and pledged himself to assist Olympe in protecting her Crossroads in thanks for saving his life.

Years later, a visiting Keeper had befriended the still-despondent goblin. When the visitor offered him a place at her Crossroads, Grenoble had accepted, traveling to the San Antonio Crossroads with Maia, Alex's Keeper aunt, over a decade ago. Upon arrival, Grenoble had given an oath to protect his new Keeper and her Crossroads as he had protected his former ones.

Larry's worried gaze swung between Alex and his goblin best friend, and he mind-spoke a reminder. *"Um, Alex, remember what we talked about? What happened to Grenoble before..."*

Alex smiled at her Familiar and included the little goblin in her understanding gaze. "Grenoble, I'm sorry it took me a moment to remember your sad history. My deepest apologies." She hesitated before adding, "Maybe you should sit this one out, bud."

The goblin glared at her and bared his teeth in a dangerous smile. "I'll be accompanying you when your party leaves for my former Crossroads, Alex. Wild hell-horses couldn't keep me away." Grenoble flicked a glance at Larry. "Besides, you're going to need me. No one knows the cave system around that Crossroads better than me. Plus, Larry is small, so he can help with the smaller tunnels."

Alex's shoulders slumped in defeat. She sighed and nodded. "Alright guys, you're both on Team France. Can you please let everyone know about the planning meeting tomorrow morning?" An enormous yawn escaped her. "I'm off to bed. I need some sleep tonight if we've gotta plan yet another posse rescue tomorrow."

8

———

SOME TIME APART

Despite her resolution to get a good night's rest, Alex already knew she wouldn't sleep well that night. When she opened the door to her room, a glowering Conor met her gaze from the bed, where he lounged tensely against a mound of pillows ranged against the headboard.

Alex stifled a sigh. She knew that look. Conor was still royally pissed at her insistence that he remain behind at the Crossroads when she traveled to Mount Olympus for her dinner date with the gods. She fought a frown. How much more pissed would he be when he found out she planned to blow off Zeus's dinner invitation and travel halfway around the world to help defend an embattled Crossroads? *Ah, fuck.*

Judging by the figurative steam coming from his ears, and the dark muttering that drifted into her mind, she realized that Conor already knew about her change of plans. Damn that magical connection they shared. Of course, the magical connection wasn't all bad. Alex fought a rising blush when she recalled the amazing sexual experiences it allowed them to share, both physically and mentally. *Um ... just wow.*

Despite his simmering anger, a slow, knowing grin spread

across Conor's handsome face. "Hellhound Barghest here, remember? I can smell your desire, sweets." Muscles bunched and shifted under his smooth, tanned skin as he sat up and patted the bedcovers beside him. "Come and join me. We've got a lot to discuss."

Alex shook her head and headed for the bathroom, throwing a refusal over her shoulder. "No, we don't, Conor. We absolutely do not have 'a lot to discuss'. I'm exhausted and need to get some sleep tonight so I'm ready for the posse meeting tomorrow morning. We can all discuss things then."

The soft closing of the bedroom door signaled Conor's departure. Alex closed her eyes, drew in a calming breath, then blew it out slowly. *Men!* Especially overprotective 'Hellhound Barghest Guardian of the Crossroads and boyfriend' men!

As she worked her way through her nighttime bathroom routine, Alex smiled when she heard the flap of the dog door. At least there was one male she could always count on to have her back without trying to smother her. Of course, that male was a sassy, snarky, pink-eared poodle and her magical partner, Larry the Kibble Guy. But still, it worked for her.

"Oh goodie, the snoring bed hog is gone for the night. I get my spot back," Larry muttered happily.

In the mirror, Alex watched Larry jump on the bed and spread himself over the pillows, taking up much more space than a miniature poodle should. Her heart rose at the sight. She had missed the nighttime cuddles and soft snores of her furry friend, since he usually made himself scarce when Conor stayed overnight.

After finishing up in the bathroom, Alex turned off the light and slipped into bed, pushing Larry to one side so she had room. She laid her head on a pillow she reclaimed from under Larry's snoring head, smiling tiredly. It didn't seem to matter the size of the male, or the species. Bed hogs, one and all. Despite her exhaustion and the quietly snoring poodle next to her, sleep evaded her for hours. Her mind raced, turning over the day's tumultuous events. Considering scenarios. As the sky lightened toward dawn, Alex finally slipped into an exhausted sleep.

A ROUGH TONGUE licked her nose, then a wet nose snuffled into her ear. Alex frowned and clung to sleep, resolutely pushing her annoying Familiar away. "Larry, knock it off! Pretty sure I just fell asleep a couple hours ago."

"Be that as it may, oh Keeper of mine. If you don't get your lazy butt out of bed in the next five minutes, you're gonna be late for the posse meeting," Larry said heartlessly. He gave Alex one last sloppy kiss, then flew off the bed and hightailed it out the dog door. "Last one to the kitchen gets cold grits for breakfast!"

Alex pushed her head into the soft pillow with a groan. Damn it, the obnoxious poodle was right. She needed to get her rear in gear, no matter how little sleep she'd gotten. It would not do to keep a trio of goddesses waiting ... or her supernatural posse.

THE POSSE MEETING went just about as Alex expected it would. There was a lot of shouting and swearing from the posse members, a whole bunch of divine disagreement and threats of eternal destruction from the goddesses, and, toward the end, an angry giant squid knocked out several of the overhead lights with one wild swing of a massive tentacle.

After the meeting, Alex slumped at the kitchen table, eyeing Henri absently as he bustled around while making her a cup of his special super-strong espresso. When he added a shot of brandy, she almost protested, but thought, '*What the hell—why not?*' Instead, she dragged herself upright and thanked the rotund French chef when he handed her the potent brew.

"Drink this, Keeper," Henri said, smiling happily at Alex. "It will not only wake you up, but calm your nerves after that rather eventful meeting."

Alex grimaced as she sipped Henri's 'calming' rocket fuel. She understood the reason for the chef's happiness. Henri would be a member of the team heading to the French Crossroads with Alex to sort out the situation there. The head chef of the Grenoble Crossroads was one of those injured in the attacks, and the supernatural posses needed to eat. A lot. Henri was rightfully known as the best chef in the whole Crossroads network, and Alex's team needed his services to keep them properly fed and watered during their upcoming mission.

The bitter, alcohol-laden brew did its job and settled Alex's nerves. She grinned tiredly, recalling that morning's most vociferous arguing duo. Larry and Grenoble had shouted the loudest when demanding Henri's presence on the team. Those two miscreants were walking stomachs.

ALEX'S AUNT Maia drifted into the kitchen, approaching the table and hovering over a chair in a ghostly approximation of sitting, startling Alex into spilling some of her espresso.

The very solid-looking ghost smiled softly at Alex, and asked, "Are you happy with your chosen team, dear?"

"Um, I guess so," Alex said, avoiding her aunt's enquiring gaze as she mopped up the spill. "It's not like I really had much say in the matter. Demeter called all the shots last night." Alex tried to keep the resentment out of her voice. She knew the worried goddess was only trying to help. And it was Demeter who had asked for her help with the situation in the first place. The goddess with the dilemma should have a say in who traveled to Grenoble to help protect the Crossroads under her protection.

"Do you disagree with Demeter's choices for the team?" Maia queried Alex gently.

"No, not really," Alex mumbled, realizing she was being childish. The posse members Demeter chose were mostly the same ones she would have chosen for the team, if given the opportunity. She sighed and admitted, "Okay, yes, Demeter chose pretty much the same people I would have chosen."

"Pretty much?"

"Okay, okay. The exact same ones, damn it. I would have made the same choices." Alex buried her nose in her almost-empty cup and refused to meet her aunt's amused gaze.

Maia placed a chilly hand over Alex's and murmured, "Even the choice to leave Conor behind?" She didn't wait for her niece's answer before adding, "Oh, and language, dear. Don't think I missed that swear word."

"Sorry, Aunt Maia. And yes, I even agree with Demeter's decision to leave Conor behind," Alex replied firmly. "*Someone* has to stay here at the Crossroads to guard the place and make sure things run smoothly while I'm gone." She smiled and met her aunt's understanding gaze. "I know you'll help, too, Aunt Maia, but we need a strong presence, in case—"

"Yes, dear, I understand," Maia said, huffing a sigh. The ghost still pretended to breathe occasionally, despite not needing to do so. "I'll do what I can to help, but the Crossroads needs Conor here, despite his, ah, strong objections to remaining behind."

Despite herself, Alex giggled. "That's an understatement if I've ever heard one. I've never seen Conor's head shift into Hellhound Barghest form before, while the rest of him stayed in human form. I didn't know he could even *do* that."

Maia chuckled. "That was quite some howl, wasn't it, dear?"

"I thought Demeter was going to blow a gasket and smite him on the spot," Alex said, snickering. "Especially when he called her a divine pain in the as ... well, you know what."

Both women hooted with laughter. A while later, just as their amusement was reduced to sniffles and occasional giggles, the subject of their merriment strolled into the room.

"Having fun, ladies?" Conor's rueful grin told Alex that he had calmed down after this morning's flagrant display of power.

"Yep," Maia quipped. "We're having a blast." The ghost's knowing gaze swiveled between Alex and Conor, and she rose, nodded a farewell, and floated from the room, leaving nothing but a hint of her flowery perfume behind.

"It's funny how she still smells of lavender and citrus," Alex mused, eyeing Conor warily. "I didn't know ghosts could wear perfume."

"They can't," Conor said. "But that doesn't seem to stop Maia. She can do things I've seen no other ghost do." He tilted his head and studied Alex across the table, his grip tight on the coffee mug Henri had just placed before him. "You're just like her, you know. You can do things no other Keeper can do." He released his grip on the mug and placed his hand over Alex's. "I *do* trust you to take care of yourself, you know." He sighed. "It's just..."

"I know," Alex murmured. "It's your nature as Guardian of the Crossroads to protect both it *and* its current Keeper." She grinned and pointed at herself. "That's me."

"It's not just that, and you know it." Conor shifted uncomfortably in his chair, then grinned at her. "I'd want to protect your lovely ass—and the rest of you—even without the magical bond we share, and you know it."

"I know it," Alex replied softly. She turned her hand into Conor's and gripped it tightly. "I do know, Conor. But still. Sometimes, I just need space. If you always rush in to protect me, how am I ever going to stand on my own as Crossroads Keeper, let alone as a freaking demi-goddess? People need to see me taking care of things, not hiding behind—well, you."

Conor withdrew his hand and ran his fingers through his thick, black hair, his sensuous lips curving in a wry smile. "I get it, sweets. I do. But you'll have to bear with me. When it comes to you, I'm constantly fighting my protective nature." He rose with a fluid motion, then gazed sadly down at her. "And you're right. Maybe it's better to put some space between us for a while." He grimaced and added, "Plus, I should probably stick around to referee the truce between the warring ghost factions." After a final enigmatic glance, the Barghest shifter turned and walked purposefully out of the room.

Alex listened as Conor's footsteps faded away. Her stomach rolled while her heart pounded painfully. She knew he was right, but it still hurt. Hopefully, the time apart would help them sort out their feelings for each other—and give Conor a chance to realize that his overprotective nature was smothering her.

With a sigh, she admitted that involving romance in a work relationship might not have been the best idea. She and Conor would have to learn to work together over the coming years to protect this Crossroads and the supernatural city that had grown around it ... if they stayed together as a couple or not.

9

DEMETER'S OTHER DAUGHTER

"**D**oes everyone understand their roles and responsibilities during our upcoming mission?" Alex asked, stifling a yawn and glancing around the table at the attentive faces gazing back at her. It was nearing midnight on what had been a very long day. She was so ready to get a few hours of sleep before she and the rest of the team set off at dawn the next morning. "Are we all done with questions?"

General nods and mumbles of agreement greeted Alex's query.

"We got it, Alex," Larry replied.

"I'm ready to rip off some heads and bloody the ground with our enemies' entrails," Grenoble ground out, an anticipatory grin curving his thick lips.

Alex swallowed a queasy sensation at the goblin's blood-thirsty words, but admitted she and her team would likely spill blood during their trip. Probably a lot of it. The Grenoble Crossroads had suffered another attack a few hours earlier. This time, the attackers had critically injured the assistant Crossroads Keeper. The sooner Alex and her team deployed to protect the Crossroads and defeat its attackers, the better.

Demeter, seated at the head of the table despite Alex's intention to sit there herself, issued a final command. "Be ready to travel before the sun rises tomorrow, everyone. Bring your supplies and meet Alex at the Crossroads. You will travel the ley lines to England first, then spend the day there gathering the rest of the supplies. The following morning, you'll leave at first light and travel on to the Grenoble Crossroads in France."

Everyone started to chatter and rise from their seats, but Alex waved them back into place. "Let's go over things one more time, folks." She knew everyone understood their duties, but it would make her feel better to review everything again.

Grenoble spoke up first. He glanced over at the slight Frenchman seated across from him. "The Lieutenant and I have almost finished drawing maps of the cave system surrounding the Grenoble Crossroads."

Alex nodded at the goblin and turned a grateful smile on the short, lithe, and darkly attractive former police officer seated next to her. "Thank you for agreeing to accompany us, Leonard." She hesitated and added, "As long as you're sure..."

Giving Alex a wry grin, the elegantly dressed Regenerant replied, "Don't worry, Alex. Traveling the ley lines won't slice me to pieces, as it did many of my fellow Regenerants who journeyed here from the Underworld with ill intent several months ago." He chuckled softly. "Using the ley lines to travel from one realm to another is admittedly dangerous for my kind, but traveling the ones here on Earth won't kill me. Don't forget, I was one of the few who made it through the realms. A mere ley line jaunt across the pond holds no fear of death for me."

"That's because you're already dead, you idiot," Crazy Sam snarled from overhead. The ghost lazily circled one of the fluorescent light fixtures hanging over the conference table, his transparent body filtering the sickly yellow glow the flickering light emitted. "Ya can't kill what's already dead, bucko. Like you, Leonard!" The ghost cackled loudly, then seemed to lose interest in the proceedings. He landed on top of the long light fixture.

Raking it with his spurs, he shouted, "Yahoo, cowboy! Giddy up, you slowpokes."

Alex grimaced and hoped the aging light held firm. The electrical cords it hung from looked as if even the non-existent weight of a ghost cowboy might break them.

"I beg to differ with my esteemed colleague regarding the correct definition of death," Vinnie stated. "As a vampire, I may be undead, but I'm certainly far from gone." His thick eyebrows rose, looking like two caterpillars crawling toward the raven-black hair slicked back from his high forehead. "I'm having the time of my afterlife these days, and I'm sure the Lieutenant would say the same." The vampire grimaced and admitted, "Although, I gotta admit that neither of us would survive a thorough slicing and dicing, as happened to most of Leonard's fellow Regenerants when they attempted to travel here from the Underworld to attack our Crossroads."

Vinnie grinned fiercely. "Of course, the ones who made it through the ley lines to attack us met the end of our swords—and our fangs." He nodded politely to Leonard. "That's with the notable exception of Lieutenant Allard, here, who not only made it into our realm in one piece but helped us defeat his fellow Regenerants."

An excited murmur traveled around the room as the supernaturals debated Vinnie's afterlife comments and recalled their recent success in defeating the Regenerants, ending the threat caused by Nyx's army of criminal ghosts, housed in dead bodies resurrected by an evil necromantic mage.

My *army now*, Alex mused. Once Alex had destroyed the soul of their creator—her long-dead father, the Regenerants had immediately switched their allegiance to her when they sensed the powerful necromantic magic she had inherited from her newly nonexistent father. She stifled a wry smile. Her unwanted undead army currently held the goddess Nyx captive at the edge of the Underworld, on her orders.

Alex brought her attention back to the meeting and glanced at Demeter, not liking what she saw. Before the goddess reacted angrily to the team's excited conversations, Alex clapped her hands, the sound echoing off the thick concrete walls of the battle planning bunker. "Alright, everyone, that's enough. Let's agree to disagree on the definition of, uh, death. And if Lieutenant Allard is confident that he can safely travel the Earth leys, we must believe him."

The polite Regenerant, who before his first death over a century ago, had been a French police officer, nodded once, gracing Alex with a small smile. "Thank you for your trust, Alex. I won't disappoint you."

Everyone ducked when Crazy Sam jumped off the overhead light and flew erratically around the room. The light fixture swung wildly, splashing the room with shafts of sickly fluorescent yellow radiance. After a few circuits, Crazy Sam landed feet-first in the middle of the massive conference table, his metal spurs chinking on the polished wood. The ghost's form had grown almost solid in his agitation. "Listen up, Alex—and you, too, Demeter. We all know what to do. How about letting us get on with getting ready so we can 'git her done' and get some sleep before we have to roll out of bed too damn early tomorrow morning?"

There was a beat of silence while everyone recovered their breath, each of them thrilled that the irritated ghost hadn't chilled them on his wild journey around the room and concerned that an angry goddess might mete out a collective punishment to those present for the crazy ghost's disrespectful tirade.

After a fraught pause and a slight nod from Demeter, Alex sighed wearily. "Okay, everyone. That's a wrap, I guess." She rose and waved to her team. "See you all in the morning."

Before Alex could reach the door, Demeter called her back. "Keeper, we need to talk." With her back to the goddess, Alex rolled her eyes before strolling back to her chair.

"I saw that," the goddess said with a disapproving frown. "Don't you roll your eyes at me, Keeper."

Alex grinned. "No, you *did not* see that. You just guessed. It was a good guess, though." She lowered herself back into her chair, suppressing a groan.

~

"WHAT IS it you want to discuss, Demeter?" Alex queried, shifting in her chair and eyeing the goddess seated at the head of the table with resignation. The goddess was definitely sitting in her spot, Alex brooded with a spurt of resentment.

Demeter's eyes narrowed momentarily, then her lips curved in a reluctant smile. "You *do* have spirit, I'll give you that, Keeper."

"What? I didn't say anything!" Alex protested.

"You didn't need to." Demeter rolled her eyes and snorted. "I can read your face, remember?"

"Oh. Yeah." Alex lowered her gaze to the table and began playing with a pen someone had left there after the meeting. "Sorry."

Demeter chuckled and said, "No need to be sorry, girl. I *am* in your chair. However, for this mission, I'm afraid I'm ultimately in charge."

After several moments of silence, Alex looked up from her pen-nudging pastime. Her eyes rounded when she saw the goddess slumped over the table, with her head on her arms and her shoulders shaking silently.

"Uh, are you okay?" Alex asked, resisting the urge to go to the weeping goddess and comfort her. She wasn't sure how receptive Demeter would be to that. Flummoxed, Alex put the pen aside and smoothed her hands on the table. She'd never seen the proud woman show any sign of weakness. "Is there anything I can do?"

"Do you have any tissues?" Demeter mumbled, her voice muffled by her surrounding arms.

Alex grabbed a box of tissues and slid it across the table to a spot near the goddess's head. "There you go." She wrung her hands, not sure how else to help the bereft woman.

Demeter pulled a wad of tissues from the box without looking, then sat up. She wiped her eyes and blew her nose loudly.

Alex stifled a surge of jealousy; Demeter was one of those women who could have a good cry and still look stunningly beautiful. No red eyes or blotchy skin for this goddess, she mused wryly. "Is there anything I can do to help, ma'am?"

Smiling wanly, Demeter shook her head and said, "You're already helping, Alex. You and your team will restore order to the Grenoble Crossroads and save my—er, the Crossroads Keeper, as well as her acolytes." The goddess lowered her gaze to the messy wad of tissues still clutched in her hand and wiped her nose again. "I'll head directly to Mount Olympus and tackle Zeus to see if I can get him to reschedule the banquet."

Alex nodded absently in agreement. *Something's off here*, she mused. Why was Demeter so torn up about the attacks at the Grenoble Crossroads? This powerful goddess had been a paragon of level-headedness, competence, and calm when the world was crashing down around their ears several months ago during the violent attacks on the Crossroads here in San Antonio.

Admittedly, the disaster at the Grenoble Crossroads needed sorting out, and they must also investigate the potential involvement of Morpheus, and possibly other rogue gods, in the attacks. But why was *this* crisis so much closer to home for the usually competent and calm goddess? Alex frowned and flicked a curious glance at the woman seated across from her.

The goddess's grief-roughened voice interrupted Alex's musings. "Why am I so undone? Because she's my daughter, that's why."

Alex started and stared at the goddess. "*Who* is your daughter, Demeter? I thought Persephone was currently grounded in the Underworld?" Then, a sneaking suspicion arose. Demeter was an ancient deity; who was to say the goddess only had *one* daughter. "Is it the assistant Crossroads Keeper? Is she your daughter?" Alex remembered being told the poor woman was critically injured during the latest attack.

Demeter's lips pursed as her pained gaze met Alex's. "My daughter, Persephone, has indeed been restricted to the Underworld at the moment. However, while what happened to the assistant Crossroads Keeper is awful, and we shall avenge her, she is not my daughter." The goddess eyed the soggy tissues still crumpled in her hands and sighed. "It is Olympe, the Grenoble Crossroads Keeper herself, who is my biological daughter." Smiling wryly, she added, "Or should I say, my *other* daughter, because who can forget that flighty handful of mine, Persephone?"

Alex's eyes widened at the goddess's revelation. She nodded slowly, having oh so many questions. "Soooo, Olympe is your biological daughter ... by a human, I guess? Otherwise, she'd be a goddess, like you, right?" Her eyebrows rose at a novel thought. "And just how old is Olympe? I mean, you're ancient, so—" Realizing the conversational pit she'd just dug for herself, Alex clamped her lips shut, cringing slightly.

Demeter chuckled, a knowing smirk on her face. "You were about to intimate that a many-millennia-old goddess shouldn't still be ... what's the modern phrase ... 'getting it on' at this stage in her very long life?"

Alex grimaced. "Um, noooo ... no, that's not what I was about to say." Wilting under Demeter's disbelieving stare, she admitted the truth. "Okay, maybe that thought crossed my mind. After all, you must be..." She closed her eyes in despair. She'd almost made another comment about the goddess's extremely great age. *Sigh. I must have a death wish,* Alex reflected with mounting horror.

"I'm old enough to know better, you mean?"

At the suppressed laughter in Demeter's voice, Alex gingerly opened her eyes and risked a glance at the goddess, who seemed to take Alex's foot-in-mouth syndrome with good humor.

The goddess's lips curved in a salacious grin. "My 'other' daughter, Persephone, didn't inherit her extremely high sex drive from her father, Keeper."

A flush of heat swept up Alex's neck. Cheeks crimson, she muttered, "Uh, okay, thanks for that info. TMI maybe, though?"

The goddess burst into gales of laughter. "You humans are such prudes!" She smiled slyly, a wicked gleam in her lovely eyes. "Well, most of you, anyway."

Happy to see Demeter returned to good humor, Alex just smiled and shrugged.

Flicking a glance at the trash can across the room by the door, the goddess pitched her used tissues into it with perfect aim. By the time Demeter returned her gaze to Alex, her face had sobered. "Okay, enough with the wordplay, Keeper. There are some things you need to know, as they may have a bearing on your investigation into the attack on my daughter's Crossroads." She took a breath and began her explanation. "My daughter, Olympe, is the Abbess of the ancient Mère des Deux Abbey, which sits directly on top of the even more ancient Grenoble Crossroads, in the French Alps. She is also Hecate's head priestess at the temple there, and the Crossroads Keeper, of course."

Alex opened her mouth to ask a question, but then shut it again. Better to let the goddess continue. She would get answers to all her questions more quickly that way. Plus, she wouldn't risk the goddess's wrath by putting her foot in her mouth. Again.

Demeter grinned wryly at Alex. "In answer to your first unasked question: yes, my Keeper daughter is also a nun, as have been many generations of Hecate's priestesses who served the Grenoble Crossroads." She gave Alex a conspiratorial grin. "What better way was there to hide a Crossroads, with its Greek temple and cohort of priestesses, when Christianity came to Grenoble over two millennia ago?"

Alex nodded in acknowledgement of the wisdom behind Demeter's words, then eyed the goddess avidly. *What other secrets would she learn about the history of the Crossroads and about the trio of powerful goddesses who created them?*

"Olympe's father was a Catholic priest," Demeter said with a grin. "Oh, don't look so shocked, Alex. Priests *are* men, after all. And I can attest they have all the necessary equipment to satisfy a woman—or a man, under those heavy robes they wear."

"Remember what I said earlier about TMI?" Alex murmured, her cheeks on fire again.

The goddess winked and resumed her story. "Anyway, this priest and I shared a passionate summer in the mountains of northern Italy. Galileo was nice enough to loan us his summer cottage for the affair—"

Alex couldn't help interrupting. "Um, Galileo? *That* Galileo? The scientist and astronomer from five-hundred-odd years ago?"

"Yes, that Galileo," Demeter replied with a sigh of remembrance. "Such a kind man, and *so* intelligent." The goddess's lips turned down, and she frowned. "Such a shame what happened to him a few years after we met, though. Your Inquisition tortured the poor man until he denied his own discoveries, then the Pope kept him under house arrest until his death several decades later."

"Uh, it wasn't *my* Inquisition," Alex defended herself. "I'd just like to point out that I wasn't even born for another—"

"Oh, you know what I mean! You humans," Demeter snipped, wrinkling her nose in disgust. "The Inquisition was just *one* of the incredibly evil things you humans have gotten up to in the past several thousand years."

The words were on the tip of Alex's tongue, but she bit them back. She was pretty sure her face revealed enough of her thoughts, though: *speaking of evil, Demeter: who, exactly, did humans inherit that disease of the soul from? Can anyone say the gods, their creators? Anyone?*

The goddess sniffed disdainfully at Alex's unspoken criticism. "I never said the gods were perfect. Now, can I get on with my story?"

Alex waved her hand. "Absolutely. Keep on going, ma'am."

"Don't you ma'am me, you little..." Demeter's narrowed gaze pinned a wide-eyed Alex in place. After a moment, the goddess visibly composed herself and continued. "Anyway, there's not much more to the story. After our summer of passion, Olympe's father was called back to Rome, where he remained, eventually reaching quite dizzying heights of power in the Vatican."

"He became a pope?" Alex asked, dismayed, and a little impressed, despite herself. Demeter had had sex with a pope, albeit years before he took the oath of office, or whatever popes did when they took the reins of the Roman Catholic Church.

"No, silly, but he did become the pope's right-hand man. The top cardinal in the Vatican," the goddess replied, giving Alex a bemused grin. "Do you really think those prissy popes do all—or even most—of their own thinking, let alone dressing themselves in those ridiculous gold-embroidered robes?"

Alex kept her eyes studiously on Demeter's face. *Don't look at the goddess's well-draped, gold-embroidered toga, Alex, just don't look. Don't even think about making a smart remark*, she counseled herself silently.

"Anyway, as I was saying," Demeter continued, "I discovered I was pregnant after Giuseppe left, then traveled to France and stayed with the nuns at the Abbey in Grenoble until the baby was born." The goddess swallowed roughly and lowered her eyes to the table. "My daughter, Olympe, remained with the sisters ... priestesses, when I returned to Mount Olympus a short while after her birth."

"But why?" Alex asked, her voice sharp. She was just done with mothers who abandoned their children. After all, her own mother had rightly lost custody of her when she was a toddler. Helen had only returned when Alex's Keeper destiny became clear, stealing her away as an adolescent, jealous of the power her daughter would soon manifest.

Demeter smiled softly, her gaze filled with both pain and

understanding. "I'm not your mother, Alex. I did what was best for my child, no matter how difficult it was for me. Olympe was safe with the sisters, away from the treachery and calumny that often pollutes the very air on Mount Olympus." She hesitated and added, "Surely, you have read the Greek myths. You know how difficult it was—and still is—for humans with divine blood? Almost every god wants a piece of them, in one way or another."

Alex nodded reluctantly, suddenly realizing she wasn't much different from Olympe, herself.

"Anyway, in time, Olympe grew to be a kind and wise woman," Demeter said, her voice filled with pride. "My daughter was bound by Hecate as Keeper several centuries ago, when the Keeper before her grew too frail."

When the goddess's voice wavered, Alex said softly, "I understand, ma—er, Demeter."

Wiping away a stray tear, the goddess gave Alex a tremulous grin. "Good catch, Keeper. Well, there you have it. My sordid story of passion and pregnancy in Renaissance Italy."

Alex merely smiled and nodded. *Holy crap! With the emphasis on holy!*

Demeter met Alex's gaze, with the hint of a plea in her eyes. "So now you know my dilemma, Alex. I need you and your team to help save my daughter and make her Crossroads safe for her and her sister-priestesses."

10

TIME TO GO

Alex shoved the last item of clothing into her suitcase and zipped it closed with a sigh. She had taken her time packing, hoping Conor would show up so they could talk before she left. No such luck. She'd just have to wait until her return and hope distance truly made the heart grow fonder.

The dog door rattled as Larry dashed through it into the room. "Did you pack all my favorite treats?" Larry eyed Alex's small suitcase doubtfully. "No, you probably didn't. There's no way they would all fit in that thing, especially not with my special food and water bowls that better be in there. Well?" The pink-eared poodle gave Alex an inquiring look.

Despite herself, Alex smiled down at her demanding Familiar, then moved to one side and pointed to another, much larger suitcase behind her. "*That's* your suitcase, numb-nuts. It's got all your massive amount of gear, including your treats, kibble, bowls, towels, blankie, and even a pair of night vision goggles—although why you want those, I don't know, since you can't use them—along with everything else your highness requested."

Larry's narrow muzzle widened in a doggie grin. "You're right about the goggles, but they aren't for me. I promise you'll be glad I had you pack those suckers. The Grenoble Crossroads is located deep inside a cave system, remember? Everything else I asked you to pack is a necessity for me, of course." He jumped onto the bed and curled into a tight ball. "I think I'm gonna to take a quick nap before we go."

Alex checked her watch; it was three in the morning. They would leave for the Grenoble Crossroads in less than three hours. She dropped onto the bed next to her magical partner and closed her eyes. "Wake me up in a couple hours, Larry," she murmured.

"What do I look like, an alarm clock?" Larry muttered, giving Alex a serious side-eye.

"No, but I'm sure I could find a witch to turn you into an alarm clock, if you like," she replied. "Listen, bud, you and I both know you have a built-in supernatural sense of time. Just wake us both up in a few hours. Please."

"All you had to do was say 'please.'"

"Oh, shut up, you goofball."

"Anything for you, Alex."

She lay in bed listening to the soft snores of her furry Familiar. Despite her best efforts, she found it impossible to fall asleep. Instead, Alex's mind raced in anxious circles. Just when things had settled down, a divine someone had to drop another disaster in her lap. And this one was halfway around the world, for goodness' sake. She sighed deeply, recalling her dangerous journey to the Fae realm. And the journey to the Underworld before that. Each journey was necessary to avert a looming catastrophe. And the unacceptable behavior of various divine ding-a-lings had caused each disastrous situation. Godly antics were really none of her concern. Until they were. *Sigh.*

Darkness still ruled the sky when Alex and her team gathered on the Crossroads platform before dawn the following morning.

"You'll need this, dear. England is rainy this time of year," Maia said with a tremulous smile as she pressed a colorful umbrella into Alex's hand. The ghost wiped translucent tears off her face with a not-really-there tissue.

Vinnie chuckled as he hugged Alex farewell. "England is rainy at *any* time of the year, honey, so it's best to be prepared." The vampire patted Alex on the back. "Remember, if you need me, I'm just a phone call away."

Alex smiled affectionately at her adopted uncle, then her gaze traveled around the gathering of well-wishers, searching the crowd one last time for a glimpse of Conor. When she couldn't spot his distinctive figure, she brushed aside his absence, took a deep breath, and stepped off the platform into the ley line. The colors and sensations of ley travel still made her slightly dizzy, but at least she knew there would be a comfortable bed, followed by a hearty pub meal on the other side of this first leg of the journey. Larry had assured her they would arrive at the Crossroads in London in plenty of time to have a nice, long rest, then enjoy the best meal in England at a pub near the London Crossroads. *Yum.*

AFTER THE EARLY START, a missed breakfast, and an uneventful, if tiring, journey through the ley lines to the London Crossroads, Alex was very grateful to arrive and settle into her comfortable room at the Crossroads guesthouse. Despite leaving their home Crossroads before dawn, when you added in the three-hour ley line journey, plus the time change, they had arrived in London late in the afternoon, local time.

Exhausted, Alex and Larry had napped in their room for several hours before hunger drove them outside, toward Larry's promised 'best meal in London.' She opened her umbrella and held it aloft as she scurried through the rain toward the wooden pub sign swinging in the wind, glad she'd had the forethought to bring the umbrella on the journey. Well, glad that her aunt had pressed the sturdy thing into her hands when she wished her well early that morning. *Having a caring aunt was wonderful—even if she was a ghost,* Alex mused. *Heart family really mattered.*

Larry skittered ahead of her with a bark. "I'll meet you in the pub, Alex. It's too wet and cold out here for me. I gotta get inside soon, or I'll never get these damn curls out of my fur."

Alex grinned and picked up her pace. Larry was right about the weather, though. While weak late afternoon sunlight had greeted them upon their arrival at the London Crossroads, clouds, wind, and rain had rolled in before nightfall.

She hoped the food at the pub was as good as Larry promised, because she was famished. And soaked, despite her umbrella. Who knew England had sideways rain?

11

A FULL ENGLISH

Getting up the following morning was hard to do, especially at the butt-crack of dawn. For a second day in a row. Alex's jaw opened wide in a massive yawn as she brushed her teeth over the tiny sink in the small bathroom belonging to the guest room she and Larry had slept in for too few hours overnight.

Crap. Alex rubbed tiredly at the toothpaste drool that had dripped onto her shirt. Now, she'd have to change before they left for the second leg of their ley line journey. She sighed, hoping the day improved.

"Look at that mess you made, Alex," Larry commented from his spot on the bed, eyeing Alex's toothpaste-covered shirt in disgust. "Even *I* don't drool that much, and I'm a freaking dog!"

Glaring at her Familiar, she pulled the wet shirt over her head and donned a clean one. "It's toothpaste drool, you moron. At least I don't drool into my food every time I eat, like you do." She grinned at the little poodle, admitting their banter had helped cheer her up. She knew that was why Larry had started the mock argument so early in the morning, since he normally saved his snark until after breakfast, which, at this rate, they might miss if they didn't hurry.

"Come on, lazybones," Alex urged, "let's go get some breakfast before we leave for the next part of our journey."

Larry hopped off the bed and dashed to the door. "You won't get any argument about grabbing breakfast from me, Alex. But I positively resent being called lazy."

The two continued to bicker amiably as they made their way downstairs toward the guesthouse's dining hall, where, hopefully, a hearty breakfast awaited them both.

"BRITISH BREAKFASTS ROCK," Larry said as he surveyed his overfull plate. "Look at this! Eggs, bacon, toast, beans, grilled tomatoes — the works!" A bowl of kibble sat ignored off to one side.

"Don't complain to me if you get an upset stomach from eating all that rich food," Alex said, as she eyed her own heaping plate. Picking up her fork, she dug in with gusto. She'd probably feel sleepy after eating the enormous breakfast, but what the hell? She was *already* exhausted after two days on the go with very little sleep. Couldn't get any worse, surely.

Surely, they'd both work off the meal during the upcoming journey to the Grenoble Crossroads. Apparently, there would be a long hike uphill through the cave system under the abbey once the team arrived. *That's the excuse I'm going with*, Alex thought, as she wiped the plate with her last piece of toast and savored it.

Alex's culinary enjoyment ended at the soft ding of a text message. She refused to glance at her phone, knowing the message was from either her sulky lover or her crazy mother. Let 'em both stew.

Another ding a few minutes later weakened her resolve. She pulled out her phone and glanced at the screen.

"There's something important I need to tell you. You are in mortal danger. Call me immediately."

She sighed and shook her head, resolved to ignore her mother's one-sided text conversation. *Yeah, Mom,* she mused wryly, *I'm usually in danger these days, but at least I can spot it coming—unlike when you kidnapped me as a child and had your witch buddy give me magical amnesia. Oh, and how about the time before that when I was just a toddler, and you tried to sacrifice me to the gods so you could steal my Keeper heritage? Now, that was dangerous.*

Turning her phone off with an angry swipe, she headed back to the room to finish packing. She'd deal with her dangerously ambitious mother later. Much later. *Bitch.*

12

THE PRIESTESS NUN

The journey from the London Crossroads to the Grenoble Crossroads in France was uneventful. During the trip, most of the team remained subdued and quiet, all still exhausted from the trip and the late nights of the past few days.

Larry and Grenoble snickered and shared crude jokes between themselves throughout the journey. Alex suspected Larry was trying to distract Grenoble from the sad memories the exiled goblin must be feeling as he traveled back to his former homeland after more than a decade away. Thoughts of the family and kingdom he had lost to betrayal and war all those years ago must cut deep. Poor guy.

JUST BEFORE MIDDAY, Alex and her team stumbled wearily onto the platform at the Grenoble Crossroads, which was buried in a cave under an Abbey located deep in the French Alps. Disoriented, as always, by ley line travel, she blinked and wondered if she was seeing things. A group of tall penguins stood at attention against the solid rock wall across from the ley station's platform. Rough gray rock formed an imposing arch overhead. Torches dotted the cave walls at distant intervals, their flickering light barely penetrating the pervasive gloom.

The shortest penguin detached itself from the group, waddling toward Alex with a welcoming smile. Alex squinted at the scene until her eyes cleared and she realized the welcoming committee comprised a flock of nuns. *Not penguins*, Alex realized with a strange sense of relief.

The tiny nun standing before Alex wore floor-length black robes. A white headpiece, covered by a black headdress, flowed down over the woman's shoulders, hiding her hair and framing her wrinkled, kind face. A simple silver cross hung from a beaded chain at her waist, while a golden brooch glittered from its spot just under her left shoulder. Alex's eyes widened when she realized the brooch bore the same image as the pendant Hecate had lumbered her with the previous month. A towering mountain was the backdrop, while at its foot, an island rose from a lake. Atop the island sat the Temple of Hiereiai. A scattering of demi-goddess priestesses went about their business on the temple steps.

Alex realized the diminutive nun standing before her must be the Grenoble Keeper, as well as a fellow Priestess of Hiereiai. This ancient woman was Demeter's demi-goddess daughter.

Her blue eyes twinkling with merriment, the little nun held out her hand in greeting. "Welcome to the Grenoble Crossroads, Alex," she said in lightly accented English, shaking Alex's hand with a firm grip. "It is a pleasure to meet you, my dear. Your aunt has told me so much about you." The woman's French accent gave a lilting cadence to her words of welcome.

Alex shook the beaming woman's hand with a bemused smile. She strongly suspected who this woman was, but didn't want to embarrass herself if she was wrong. "Uh, it's good to meet you, as well..."

"Oh my, where are my manners?" The older woman gasped. She placed both hands over her heart and bowed formally. "Merry

Meet, Keeper Alex. My name is Olympe, Keeper of this Crossroads and Abbess of the Mère des Dieux Abbey that sits above us. You deeply honor us with your presence, and we are very grateful for your team's offer of assistance."

Alex bowed awkwardly, unsure of the proper protocol and slightly embarrassed by the effusive greeting. "Thank you for the welcome, Keeper Olympe. We're ... uh, happy to be here and glad to be of assistance." *Not really,* Alex reflected silently. She'd rather be home amongst her heart family, protecting her own Crossroads, and she certainly hadn't offered to help. Instead, she'd been coerced by a demanding goddess with a dilemma.

Olympe grinned, her deep blue eyes twinkling with delight. Wrinkles on the elderly nun's face fell into well-used smile lines. *This was a happy, wise—and extremely ancient priestess nun,* Alex mused. An unfamiliar voice inside her mind interrupted her thoughts.

"I understand that my mother, Demeter's, orders brought you and your team here, Alex, but I appreciate your presence nonetheless."

Alex's eyes widened when she realized Olympe had mind-spoken to her. Soooo, this centuries-old magical nun with a goddess for a mother and a human priest for a dad, could access her mind with no effort or magical connection to her. *Holy crap!*

Tentatively, Alex mind-spoke her reply. *"It wasn't* exactly *duress your mother used, Olympe, but ... well, let's just say Demeter can be very persuasive. Anyway, we're here now, so what do you need from us?"*

The diminutive nun grinned cheekily at her and replied out loud. "Oh, Alex, you are all grown up and just as delightful as your aunt Maia told me you were all those years ago."

Before Alex could make an embarrassed reply, a low grumble startled her. She glanced down to find Grenoble crouched at her side, his wide-eyed gaze fixed firmly on the nun. The little goblin wasn't much shorter than the elderly woman. When Grenoble bowed so deeply that his long green nose almost touched the ground, Alex's eyebrows rose.

"Keeper Olympe, it is good to see you again, my friend," Grenoble said as he rose from his bow. "I have come to aid you, as you aided me in my distress more than a decade ago." He flicked a glance at Alex and added, "While your good friend Maia cannot be here, she sends her greetings and asks that you accept the assistance of her niece, Alex. She is Hecate's oath-bound priestess and the current Keeper of the San Antonio Crossroads." The goblin sniffed, as if questioning the wisdom of the goddess's choice, but refrained from further comment.

The nun formally thanked the goblin, then watched with a soft smile as Grenoble loped back to Alex's team, who were all still hanging back near the ley line entrance, leaving Alex to handle the introductions.

Olympe turned her gaze back to Alex, leaned in, and whispered, "I don't know about you, dear, but I'm very glad the stuffy formalities are over." With a conspiratorial grin, she grabbed Alex's hand and pulled her toward the largest tunnel. "Let's not remain in this chilly cave one moment longer. Hurry now, my dear. It's a long trek up to the abbey."

GRACEFUL GRECIAN COLUMNS carved out of the cave's flinty, gray rock stood sentinel on each side of the tunnel, while a massive lintel overhead sported crisp carvings of ancient gods. As Alex passed underneath the lintel and into the tunnel, she glimpsed another opening on the left. Flickering torchlight revealed a large cave containing an altar similar to that of her own Crossroads temple. She spotted half a dozen women in neat, white togas kneeling before the altar, but Olympe drew her past the cave before she saw any more of what was obviously the Grenoble Crossroads temple.

"Let's head up to the Abbey for some refreshments, Alex," Olympe said. "Don't worry about your team's luggage. The porters will bring it to your rooms while we have an early lunch."

The tiny woman took off at a fast trot, Alex's hand still in her firm grip, so she had no choice but to keep pace with the spry senior. She called out to the rest of her team, who were still hesitating by the tunnel entrance, "Let's go, guys. Time to move. Leave the luggage and supplies. Porters will bring everything up to our rooms."

The group traveled swiftly along the tunnel's stone path for what seemed like forever. Finally, after half an hour or so—and a very steep hike—Alex noticed the walls changing and the light increasing. The rough-hewn rock walls and floor smoothed. Overhead, fluorescent lights took over from flickering torches. Shortly after that, the tunnel opened into a massive chamber fitted with elegant marble walls and floors. An elaborate barrel ceiling arched high overhead, covered with ethereal paintings, and gilded with gold. An enormous glittering crystal chandelier hung from a sturdy golden chain fastened to a massive wooden beam high overhead.

Realizing her mouth hung open in awe, Alex snapped it closed and lowered her amazed gaze to Olympe. "It's magnificent. I thought *my* Crossroads estate was beautiful, but this..."

"Yes, it does rather take one's breath away, doesn't it?" Olympe agreed with a merry nod. She grinned up at Alex, excitement dancing in her eyes. "Wait until you see the chapel, dear! It's even more magnificent," the little nun enthused. "I'll give you a tour of the abbey later. I don't know about you, but I'm famished." With that, she ushered Alex forward at a trot.

Nodding absently, Alex hustled after the energetic nun, her mind still grappling with the idea of a Crossroads Keeper—a supernatural pagan priestess—that was also a nun, and an abbess, at that. Damn, this capable woman wore many hats. Or wimples. *Whatever.*

Larry, who had been trotting along quietly at Alex's heels, had sped up at the mention of food. "I'm starving, Alex. Ley line travel always makes me hungry."

She grinned down at the small white poodle with bright pink ears and mind-spoke her reply. *"Literally everything makes you hungry, Larry. Why would ley line travel be any different?"*

Larry barked sharply in agreement, then broke into a trot, his goblin companion keeping pace. *"We're gonna check out the kitchen and see if we can get a pre-lunch snack. See ya later, alligator."*

Alex watched the duo speed off and gave Olympe a rueful smile. "My apologies, ma'am. My Familiar and his friend are eager to ... er, tour the abbey."

"Tour the kitchens, more like," the priestess nun replied with a snicker. She took Alex's arm and said, "Come this way, dear. Let's talk privately over lunch in my study. We have a lot to discuss. The staff will serve the rest of your team in the refectory." She steered Alex away from the rest of her team and ushered her along at a brisk pace.

13

THE PAGAN CONVENT

"Have another croissant, Larry. You must still be hungry from your travels," Olympe said as she held the heaping platter of fluffy pastries down so Larry could reach the tasty treats. "Grenoble, help yourself to more from the meat platter. I had everything specially roasted for you, my old friend."

Alex hid a grin behind her teacup as she watched Larry and Grenoble help themselves to seconds—or was it thirds? *"You're both going to be sick if you don't stop stuffing your faces soon. After all, this is your second lunch, as I'm darn sure you both scrounged up a meal when you visited the kitchens earlier."* She mind-spoke her warning to the two hungry little hippos as they munched and spread crumbs and worse all over the elegant oriental rug in Olympe's cozy sitting room.

She sipped tea from a delicate china cup, trying not to spill any on her chair's expensive-looking upholstery, and shook her head when Olympe offered her more buttery French croissants. "No thank you, Olympe, I'm stuffed. One was more than enough," she said, with regret. The rich, flaky pastry, smothered with bright yellow butter and slathered with jam, that she'd already eaten had probably maxed out her calorie count for the week, Alex reflected with a sigh.

The older woman placed the platter back on the table and fixed her eyes on Alex, determination filling her gaze. "You're probably wondering why I invited you to share a private meal in my office, rather than join the rest of your team in the refectory," Olympe stated.

"Well, um ... maybe," Alex hedged. She leaned forward and carefully placed her teacup on the table, relieved to have her hands off it before she broke the damned thing. "I figured you wanted to have a private chat. Maybe about our shared divine ancestry?" She hesitated and added, "I'm not sure how much the other nuns—uh, priestesses here know about your parentage and, um, other things."

Olympe burst into gales of laughter. "Oh, Alex, there's no need to beat around the bush, nor are there any secrets here. My priestess nuns know all," she said with a grin. "As you no doubt know, my mother is a goddess, as is your grandfather—who is a Titan, no less. Both of us have divine ancestry, and very similar duties as Crossroads Keepers. Of course, as Mother Superior and Abbess of this convent, I have a few other duties to attend to as well."

"Uh, okay, I understand ... I think," Alex stuttered.

The old woman's eyes twinkled gaily. "I'm sure you are just bursting with curiosity about this matter, dear, but it's really quite simple. The nearest town, Grenoble, is one of the supernatural cities that grew up next to Crossroads around the world after their creation, well before the advent of Christianity, of course."

Sobering, with a trace of sadness filling her gaze, the priestess nun explained, "When Christianity swept across Europe in the third and fourth centuries, our Crossroads had to go underground to survive. What better way to hide a temple full of priestesses than in a convent—even if the name of the deity on the door has changed?"

Olympe's knowing gaze met Alex's expectantly, a small smile playing on her lips. "I imagine you still have some questions, dear?"

Oh, I have just all the questions, Alex mused, enchanted by this smiling, wise, and downright joyful woman.

"Um, everything you said so far makes perfect sense, but how..." Alex stopped speaking and rolled her eyes. "Never mind. I can't expect you to give me a blow-by-blow account of how a temple-ful of Hecate's priestesses managed to 'convert' to Christianity, continue practicing their pagan ways, and keep a whole damn—er, darn Crossroads secret for almost two thousand years."

Olympe chuckled and replied, "With a whole lot of effort, Alex, along with some minor subterfuge, and perhaps a touch of blackmail. Oh, and magic, of course, dear. Lots and lots of magic." The tiny nun gave Alex a sly grin. "As you no doubt know, until the last fifty years or so, men oversaw most things in our world. And frankly, as I'm sure you'd agree, most of them aren't that observant." The diminutive nun sat back in her chair and daintily sipped her tea, her wise, old eyes gazing at Alex over the rim of her cup.

Speechless at the sheer audacity and bravery of a long line of women, much like the one sitting in front of her, who kept their allegiances to the old gods and their actions on behalf of them secret for almost two millennia, Alex merely nodded mutely.

Olympe's blue eyes sparkled with merriment, and she giggled like a young girl. "Here's an example, Alex. Our convent's name is Mère des Dieux Abbey, which means 'Mother of Gods.' Plural. Instead of the more Christian 'Mother of God'—singular." The ancient nun clapped her hands gleefully. "As you and I both know, dear, there are lots and lots of gods. Plural—to the max. Heavens! Why would anyone with any sense limit themselves to just one?"

Alex smiled tentatively at her new friend, then frowned in

confusion. "But didn't anyone ever notice the plural 'gods' instead of the singular 'god' in the abbey's name? I mean, in the last fifteen hundred plus years, surely *someone* must have noticed."

"Oh, of course they did, dear," Olympe said. "Even the most unobservant of men is bound to have a moment of clarity once every hundred years or so. Whenever one priest or government official or another mentioned the spelling 'error', the Abbess at the time would just look horrified and pretend we had made a mistake." Her lips curved in an almost evil grin. "After all, until recently, men—especially educated ones like priests and civic officials—didn't expect anyone of the supposedly ignorant and feeble-minded female sex to read and write properly, if at all. Any time a visiting dignitary noticed, we'd just apologize profusely and promise to fix the spelling mistake once we raised the money to have the 'correct' name re-carved into the stone above the abbey entrance."

The tiny nun shrugged and raised her hands, her wrinkled face the picture of innocence. "After a time, and with the judicious application of a little magic, anyone who mentioned the spelling mistake would simply forget, or die of old age, and the plural French 'x' remained in the abbey's name." She smiled brightly at Alex and sipped her cooling tea.

Alex only hoped she'd be as brave and wise, and even duplicitous as this wonderful old woman, when ... if she reached her senior years. "You guys, er, women, are absolutely brilliant. To think there's been so many generations of priestesses here, keeping the pagan faith and protecting the Crossroads, right under the nose of the Catholic Church. I'm thrilled you have shared your Crossroads' ... uh, Abbey's amazing story with me. It's been very illuminating."

Olympe smiled and finished her tea before placing her cup gently on the table. "Well, I've tried my best over the past few centuries to preserve our Crossroads' secrets, continue in Hecate's service, and train the next generation of priestesses," she replied demurely.

After a mutual moment of silent contemplation, Olympe leaned forward and tapped the table sharply. "Now, Alex dear, it's time to get down to business and discuss the attacks on my Crossroads. We must plan how you and your team can help us return safety to our community, and send the bloody assholes who are attacking it straight to the Underworld."

Alex's eyes widened at the nun's profane and bloodthirsty statement. "Uh, sure, Olympe, just let me know how we can help," she replied with quiet determination.

After all, Alex mused sadly, *Olympe's sentiment was accurate. Battles always brought blood and death.* Why would she think this one would be any different just because it was taking place in an Abbey and she and her team would fight side-by-side with a convent-full of nuns ... priestesses ... whatever?

BEFORE SERIOUS DISCUSSION COULD BEGIN, the door flew open, and a goddess swept into the room. Olympe jumped spryly to her feet and ran to the tall, elegant woman, who enveloped the tiny nun in a tight embrace. "Olympe, my child, it is so good to see you. Don't worry, I'm here now. We'll get this mess sorted out." Tears sparkled on Demeter's smooth cheeks as she hugged her daughter tightly.

After the emotional greeting, Demeter gently steered Olympe back to her chair. The goddess's normally reserved demeanor returned as she took a seat next to her daughter and across from Alex. "I didn't mention my plan to come here, Keeper, and delayed my arrival a bit to give you time to get to know my wise and kind daughter, so you can understand the importance of my dilemma." The goddess's lips curved in a wily grin. "I hope my ploy worked, since I have tasked you and your team with helping her defend this Crossroads and defeat its attackers."

Right down to business then, Alex mused. She could have objected to the wording of Demeter's comment, but didn't. She was sure the face—and very likely mind—reading goddess knew she had bristled at being 'tasked' with anything, especially since she had agreed to help Demeter out of the kindness of her—

"Keeper," Demeter growled, the warning in her voice clear. "Remember, Alex, I may not be the public face of the Crossroads system, as is Hecate. However, along with Hecate, Persephone and I make up the triune of goddesses who created the vast Crossroads system. After Hecate created the first Crossroads to rescue Persephone from the Underworld, we realized how useful these portals could be. After that, all three of us worked intricate magic together to join the ley lines in this and other realms, fully developing the Crossroads system still in place today. Each member of our triune has an equal right to call upon its Keepers when danger threatens *any* of these sacred ley line portals. Do you understand?" The goddess's stern gaze pinned Alex in place.

"Uh, yes, ma'am ... I mean, Demeter. I understand completely," she replied nervously. It didn't do to anger an ancient and powerful goddess. The goddess may have phrased her initial plea for help as a request, which Alex had readily, if reluctantly, agreed to. But she knew the goddess's request had actually been a demand. As Demeter gazed at her inquiringly, Alex felt the iron fist of raw divine power under the velvet glove of civility the goddess typically displayed.

Olympe's mild voice interrupted Alex's brooding thoughts. "Now, Mother, there's no need for threats or intimidation. Alex and I had a lovely chat just now, and we both agree that an attack on one Crossroads is an attack on all of them. She's happy to help."

Silently thanking Olympe for the verbal lifeline, Alex quickly agreed. "That's right, Demeter. My team and I are eager to defend Olympe's Crossroads against the immediate threat. Protecting this Crossroads will help protect mine, and all the others, of course."

"And hopefully, it'll help me even a score," Alex muttered under her breath. If Demeter was right, she and her team would battle Morpheus in the caves under the Abbey. The rebel god had been a conspirator in the attack on the San Antonio Crossroads several months ago. He had even stolen a piece of her aunt's soul and taken it to the Underworld. When she had traveled there to retrieve it, the god of nightmares had threatened Alex with death the next time they met. Yup, she had a score to settle with that divine asshole.

Two Crossroads Keepers and a goddess discussed the current situation and planned defense and battle strategies for the rest of the afternoon. Larry and Grenoble had gotten bored after the first hour. When it became obvious no more food would be forthcoming, the two friends left to explore the abbey grounds.

As the intense afternoon meeting wound down, Olympe offered to take Alex to the infirmary to meet those seriously wounded in the first two attacks. "You might come up with something to ask them I've failed to think of, my dear," the little nun said with a sigh.

Demeter yawned deeply, her lovely eyes shadowed with fatigue. "I must leave you now. I have arranged a clandestine meeting with Zeus to see if I can convince him to postpone his blasted dinner. If I explain the situation, perhaps he'll see the wisdom in the delay." The goddess rose languidly and added, almost as an afterthought, "Maybe he'll even agree not to have you killed for deciding not to attend, Alex."

Alex smoothed her face and bit back a sarcastic reply. Larry's smart mouth really was rubbing off on her. Instead, she calmly agreed. "That would be great if you can arrange it, Demeter." She couldn't help adding, "Especially the part about him not killing me."

After the goddess left, the air in the room seemed to settle back into place. Demeter's powerful presence certainly dominated a space. Alex took a deep breath and blew it out slowly, ending with a sigh.

Olympe patted Alex's hand and said, "I know that my mother can be a bit domineering, dear, but her heart is in the right place." The elderly nun's wise gaze met Alex's. "Remember, however, that Demeter is a deity, above all else. Divine beings do not have the same natures as their supernatural or human creations. While you and I both have a certain amount of divine blood, the parts of our souls that are not divine contain traits such as empathy, compassion, and understanding. Those words mean nothing to the gods. Their unique ethics—or lack thereof—are common to their species."

"They're a bunch of freaking psychopaths, you mean," Alex blurted. Once she realized the implied insult, she tried to backtrack. "I, uh, didn't mean your mother, of course."

Olympe just smiled knowingly at her. "Yes, you did, Alex, but that's okay. It's a mistake, though, to categorize behavior that doesn't fit human mores and ethics as evil or, in human terms, psychopathic. I know you're new to the supernatural world, but it's important for you to learn that there are as many shades of gray as there are supernatural species—or humans, for that matter—and each shade can just as easily be neutral, or even good, as evil, my dear."

Alex didn't fully agree with Olympe, but who was she to argue with an almost five-hundred-year-old priestess nun who was half divine, herself? "Yes, ma'am, I think I understand," she replied meekly.

"Have you never taken an action that most would consider a crime in the human world, Alex?" Olympe's shrewd eyes held Alex's gaze. "Can you say honestly that, since your heart family found and reintroduced you to the supernatural world, you've *never* had to take an action that humans would consider abhorrent? Even criminal?"

Disturbing images Alex had thought well-buried replayed in her mind. She swallowed in disgust at the memory of killing Chris, the Fae spy who'd betrayed her Crossroads and his close friend, Conor. Sure, she'd done it both to save Conor the grief of killing his friend and to protect the Crossroads. However, in the human world, she would have gone to jail for murder. Many other actions she had taken since being thrown into the supernatural world flew through her mind: killing dozens of Regenerants when they attacked her Crossroads, destroying her father's very soul when he tried to kill her ... Alex closed her eyes and mind against the bleak memories and shook her head in mute denial.

"Yes, dear, I think you do understand, after all," Olympe murmured softly.

Her new friend's kind words almost broke Alex, but she refused to shed tears over her past actions. They had been necessary to protect her Crossroads, her heart family, the wider supernatural community, as well as the humans who shared the earth with her kind. A lone tear tracked down Alex's cheek. *Olympe was right,* she admitted silently.

The diminutive nun jumped to her feet, yet again belying her great age. She placed a gentle hand on Alex's shoulder and squeezed. "That's enough of serious subjects for now, my dear. Let me give you a tour of the abbey, and then we'll visit the infirmary." She led a bemused Alex from the room. "Did I mention that Giotto himself painted the ceilings in the main chapel? And that we have several wonderful statues created by Da Vinci, the master sculptor? No? Well, let me show you..."

Alex let Olympe's torrent of words distract her mind from the moral dilemmas that had consumed it moments before. "I'd love to see the statues," she said, hurrying after the energetic little nun. *Boy, could this woman haul ass for someone so ancient,* she thought as she puffed along at Olympe's side. *And I thought I was in shape*, Alex lamented to herself. She committed to spending more time working out with Conor. She winced at the thought of how things had been left between them and pulled her mind resolutely back to the present.

Olympe gave Alex a wicked grin as they hustled through hallway after hallway in the massive abbey. "I like that expression! 'haul ass'. I think I'll start using it in conversation."

"Oh, did I say that out loud? I'm so sorry," Alex sputtered, horrified that she'd allowed her distraction to offend her new friend.

Olympe barked a delighted cackle. "No, dear, you didn't say it out loud." She gazed up at Alex, eyes twinkling with mischief. "But great longevity is not the only asset my divine mother's genes have given me."

Alex's eyes widened in shock. "You can read minds?"

"Yes, dear, I can," the little nun said as she ushered Alex down yet another marble-lined hallway. "I must admit, though, that it's really more of a curse than a blessing." She grimaced. "Believe me when I say that you really don't want to hear most people's thoughts."

"I can certainly understand that," Alex agreed. After all, half the time, she wished she couldn't read her own thoughts, let alone those of others.

A disturbing thought struck Alex. "Um, I suppose that means your mother can read minds, too," she asked Olympe, dreading the answer. When the wily goddess had told Alex she could read her face, that was bad enough ... but what if Demeter could actually root around in her mind?

Olympe gave Alex an impish grin. "She told you she was reading your face whenever she uncannily knew what you were thinking, correct?" The nun snickered and rolled her eyes. "My mother prefers to keep her mind-reading abilities on the down low, Alex. She says it leads to more revelations that way."

"I just bet it does," Alex muttered, disturbed by the duplicity that seemed endemic in the divine race.

Olympe merely nodded sympathetically and continued with the abbey tour.

Before long, they arrived at a set of massive, intricately carved wooden doors. Olympe grasped an ancient iron handle and heaved one side of the door open. "Come dear, let me show you our magnificent chapel. Just look at those statues..."

For the next several hours, Alex let herself enjoy Olympe's tour, oohing and ahhhing at the amazing sights and sounds of the massive, ancient abbey along with its extensive grounds. She listened as a group of nuns chanted in the main sacristy; the amazing acoustics of the enormous church amplified the choir's strong harmony. The paintings and carvings, along with the intricate stonework of the abbey's many massive buildings, left her breathless, while the beauty of the medieval walled gardens soothed her soul.

"Your abbey is amazing, Olympe. I can see why you love this place so much," Alex said at the end of their extensive tour. "My Crossroads estate is beautiful, too, but this place..."

The little nun's cheeks flushed with pleasure and she smiled up at Alex. "Thank you, my dear. Sometimes one becomes inured to the beauty that surrounds one, don't you think? It's such a pleasure to view my demesne anew, through your eyes."

And likely my thoughts, too, Alex mused wryly, very sure that Olympe had listened in to her amazed thoughts, as well as her delighted verbal praise.

Olympe's lips curved in a merry grin, and she nodded in affirmation as she led Alex through yet another of the abbey's extensive gardens.

Alex rolled her eyes and said, "I'm not gonna be able to keep any secrets from you, am I?"

"No, dear, but that's not such a bad thing," Olympe replied. She tucked her arm through Alex's and steered her down a hedge-lined path. "After all, now that we're connected, I'll know if you're in danger and can send help to your side."

"Connected?"

"Magically, my dear. Until we met in person today, our magical connection has always been tenuous." Olympe gazed earnestly up at Alex. "I sincerely apologize for that, dear. After all, I'm only half divine. But now, the magic of our familial divine connection has locked into place. I'll know if you're in danger, as you will, me."

"Familial connection?" Alex realized she was parroting the old nun's words, but she couldn't help herself. Anxious apprehension roiled her stomach. Another massive revelation was imminent; she could feel it.

"We're cousins, in case you haven't figured that out yet," Olympe replied, using their linked arms to urge Alex along the graveled garden path.

Alex stopped suddenly, realization crashing through her mind. Her sudden halt unbalanced the tiny woman still holding onto her. She quickly placed her arm around the elderly woman's shoulders, steadying her, and realizing as she did so that the top of Olympe's head didn't even reach her shoulder. A surge of protectiveness filled Alex, and she squeezed her newfound cousin gently in a sideways hug.

"I'm slow on the uptake today, Olympe," Alex apologized. She recalled Grenoble's curt words about her divine family tree before they left the San Antonio Crossroads. *'Alex, you're related to all of those divine idiots in one way or another...'*

"Um, exactly how are we related?" Alex asked, not even sure she wanted to know or would understand the complicated family connections, even if she did.

Her newfound cousin chuckled and said, "It's quite complicated, dear." The diminutive nun withdrew from Alex's embrace, but grabbed her hand and urged her forward before explaining. "Think of it this way, cousin. The demographics on Mount Olympus are just like those of any small, isolated human village, where everyone knows everyone and most are related, in one way or another ... and sometimes in more than one way.”

Alex heaved a sigh and let the tiny woman urge her forward. “So, you’re saying our divine ancestors all slept around. A lot.”

Olympe giggled and threw Alex a mischievous grin. “Yep, they sure did, dear. Still do, if my intel is correct.”

Alex suppressed an embarrassed groan and allowed her newfound semi-divine cousin to lead the way to their next destination.

14

APHRODITE'S POWER

Alex chewed on her thoughts as she followed her indefatigable little cousin along yet another graveled path. Lush hedges on either side filtered the waning sunlight, dappling the ground with moving circles of golden color, which glittered amidst the general gloom of the narrow path. After a while, the tall hedges gave way to a large courtyard. A geometric maze of precisely clipped low boxwood, all right angles and smooth patterns, spread out before them, with fragrant flowers filling garden beds scattered amongst the maze. A low stone building crouched just beyond the maze; the building's small, leaded windows glowed from within. The overall effect was welcoming, if slightly spooky in the growing dusk.

Olympe tugged Alex forward. "Come, dear, it's getting chilly out here and the Infirmière is waiting for us." She rolled her eyes and flicked an irritated glance at the building as they approached. "Sister Reine wants to talk with you before she agrees to let us interview her patients."

Alex realized the building they were heading toward was the infirmary. She assumed the Infirmière must be a doctor or nurse, especially if she controlled access to the patients. Alex wondered if

Olympe's obvious irritation was directed at the Infirmière or at herself for not preventing the attacks, which had caused such serious injuries to her people. Alex quickened her pace to keep up with her newest cousin. *I'll definitely lose a few extra pounds just keeping up with this tireless woman,* Alex mused wryly. She heard Olympe snicker quietly and knew the nun had heard her thoughts. *Oh, well.*

As they climbed the porch steps, the front door opened, warmth and light spilling out from within. A tall, thin nun, all angles and irritation, stood to one side, gesturing at them impatiently. "Come in, come in! You're letting all the heat out. My patients mustn't catch a chill."

The woman's plummy British accent surprised Alex. She had assumed all the nuns—priestesses—at the abbey were French.

Olympe's introduction interrupted Alex's musings. "Infirmière Reine, allow me to introduce Alexandria, Keeper of the San Antonio Crossroads, and my cousin through my mother's line."

The angular nun's eyebrows rose, and her annoyed expression eased slightly. "I didn't realize, Mother Olympe, that our guest Keeper was a relative of yours." The woman bowed her head to Alex, her show of respect at war with the mutiny in her eyes. "Keeper Alex, I'm pleased to meet you. Welcome to my infirmary." With a rustle of her heavily starched white robes, the Infirmière pointed to a door across the small foyer, and said, "Come, let us go into my study so I can update you both on the patients' conditions."

Olympe and Alex exchanged an amused glance, then hurried after the imperious nun's ramrod-straight back as she marched them to her inner sanctum.

Once seated in the impeccably tidy office, the Infirmière quickly dispensed with the niceties. "Coffee, tea? No? Let's get down to business, then." Folding her hands in her lap, the nun fixed both women with a narrow-eyed glare. Her angular jaw jutted, while her thin lips were pursed in disapproval. "I must

"Alex, please draw up a chair to make it easier for all of us to chat," instructed Olympe. The tiny nun smiled and said, "Keeper Alex, allow me to formally introduce Sister Zoé. She leads our supernatural posse and also serves as the Assistant Keeper of this Crossroads."

Alex nodded politely and settled into her chair before risking another glance at the lovely woman lying in the bed.

"Hello, cousin," Zoé murmured, giving Alex a warm smile. "Olympe has told me so much about you. It's a pleasure to finally meet you." She reached for Alex's hand and gave it a gentle squeeze. "Please forgive me for the rude display of my magical power earlier. I was aiming it at the dragon lady behind you. Sister Reine needs a little happiness in her life, don't you think?" The lovely woman grinned mischievously. "It might make her more pleasant to deal with, wouldn't you agree?"

Alex's jaw dropped open in shock, her earlier suspicions confirmed. "So, you *can* influence other people's emotions? How does that work? Which divine power is that?" Quickly realizing that her questions were highly inappropriate and not wanting to tax the injured woman more than necessary, she apologized. "I'm sorry, Cousin Zoe. Forgive me, please. It's really none of my business—"

Zoé's silvery laugh floated on the air and she squeezed Alex's hand again. "Don't worry, cousin. No offense taken. To answer your questions, yes, I can influence emotions, although it's easier to do with humans and normal supernaturals. *You* only felt a general happiness when I used my semi-divine power, but I actually sent overwhelming joy and well-being towards that miserable Infirmière. Your divine bloodline shielded you from the full effects of my magic."

Alex's newest cousin gave her a lopsided smile. "To answer your other questions, I'm not sure exactly how my magic works. It just does. I focus on what I want someone to feel and kind of 'point' my power at them. And where does my magic come from?"

The lovely woman grinned, her eyes twinkling with humor. "My grandmother, Aphrodite, of course. The only trait that made it into human myths about Aphrodite is her incredible beauty, but my grandmother's divine power is the ability to influence emotions. She can even influence those of the gods, which makes her quite popular ... or unpopular, amongst the divine inhabitants of Mount Olympus, depending on how she uses her magic."

Zoé chuckled wryly and shrugged one shoulder. "Luckily, I inherited a mere fraction of my divine grandmother's magical power. I can't make men or even gods go to war, or topple kingdoms with a glance, like Aphrodite can. And has."

Alex nodded numbly as she considered the possibilities such a divine power would grant. A slight tap on her hand brought Alex back to the present. She refocused her gaze on her newest cousin, whose lovely grin made her smile.

"I hear your divine magical inheritance is even greater than mine, Cousin Alex," Zoé said. "Is it true you have inherited a full dose of your Titan grandfather's Primordial power over death and time?"

Her cousin's bright, questioning gaze made Alex slightly nervous. She sat back, removing her hand from Zoe's loose grip, and shook her head. "Um, don't believe everything you hear."

Olympe interrupted, "Yes, it's true, Zoé, although Alex is still new to her Primordial powers and has yet to fully accept them, or her new station in life."

The wise nun's gaze met Alex's. "I know it's hard to accept, dear. Both death and time magic are frighteningly strong magics. It would be hard for anyone to embrace them, let alone someone so new to the supernatural world."

Zoé gasped and gave Alex a wide-eyed look of respect. "A full measure of not one, but *two* divine powers? Alex, that makes you at least a demi-goddess! Right?!" The lovely woman bounced excitedly on the bed, then lay back with a pained grimace. She gazed at Alex, her lovely eyes wide with wonder. "So, you're a kick-ass demi-goddess, then, cuz. Wow, I'm related to divine royalty! I just can't wait to see what you can do."

Embarrassed, Alex lowered her eyes and admitted, "Yeah, I'm a demi-goddess, I guess. But no, I'm not 'divine royalty.'" She rolled her eyes and huffed in frustration. "And you'll be waiting a long time to see what I can do because I don't plan to use my death magic ever again. It's way too dangerous. And the jury is still out as to whether I have time magic. I still think what happened that one time was a fluke—"

"But cuz," Zoé whined, giving Alex an engaging grin. "I have a list I need your magical demi-goddess help with."

Alex realized with a start that her cousin had suddenly gained a strong Southern drawl. She wondered if she had missed it when they met, or if the woman could change her accent at will, perhaps as part of her powers of emotional influence. *Interesting.*

Olympe clapped her hands sharply, startling both women. "Enough with the introductions and merriment, you two. It's time to get down to business. Now, Zoé, please tell us everything you can remember about the attack on you and the rest of the posse."

It took a long while for Zoé to recount what she knew, and she ended her report with an apology. "I'm sorry I didn't tell you about the nightmares and sleepwalking weeks ago, Olympe." The injured woman's eyes drooped and she smothered a yawn. "But you're just so busy all the time, and I'm the Assistant Keeper. I'm *supposed* to handle things for you. I tried..." She broke off her explanation, exhaustion shadowing her eyes, her pale face almost matching the starched white of the pillows that propped her up in the narrow hospital bed.

"I understand, Zoé," said Olympe, with a warning glint in her eyes. "However, your actions not only endangered yourself, but everyone who lives and works in our community. Once you realized the nightmares were causing you to sleepwalk, you should have told me." The older woman sighed and shook her head. "It seems certain that you opened the ley lines and allowed the attackers to enter through our Crossroads. Twice!"

"I'm so sorry," Zoé wailed. "I don't know how that man ... er, god convinced me to do that!"

"I do," blurted Alex bitterly. "My cousin Morpheus can convince anyone that black is white and up is down." The dark memory of Chris, a once-loyal Fae who had betrayed her Crossroads, slithered through her mind. She closed her eyes, fighting off the memory of killing him, so that his former best friend, Conor, didn't have to. Chris's mind had been warped beyond repair by the deceitful manipulation of Morpheus, the god of nightmares—and her cousin.

A sharp knock startled the trio of women. The door opened a crack, and a cheery nurse eased her way into the room. "Hello, everyone," she said. "I'm sorry to interrupt, but it's time for the patient's medication, and I need to check her vitals." The nurse bobbed a curtsey to Olympe, eyes down in respect. "I can come back—"

"No, stay, Sister Lisette," Olympe replied. "We will go now. It's time we visited some of the other patients, and Zoé needs to rest."

The tiny nun hopped off the chair and leaned in to embrace the woman in the bed, standing on her tiptoes to do so. She patted Zoé gently on the cheek and murmured, "You did what you thought was best, dear, so please don't beat yourself up over it." Olympe gently scolded, "In the future, Sister Zoé, please inform me of anything unusual, such as these nightmares you and others have been suffering. Remember, I've been around a very long time and have seen more things in my lifetime than you can imagine. This isn't the first time a rogue god or two has brought danger and divine mischief to these Crossroads, and it surely won't be the last." The Abbess's lips firmed as she gazed at her injured subordinate. "Just ... keep me informed when weird shit happens, okay? We're supposed to be a team."

Zoé slumped back on the bed, her cheeks flushed a pretty pink with embarrassment. She said in a small voice, "Yes, Abbess, uh, Keeper. I won't try to handle things I don't fully understand without consulting you again. I'm so sorry." The chastened woman's eyes closed, exhaustion pulling her into sleep.

Olympe sighed, shook her head, and turned away from the bed. The nurse, who had been hovering nervously by the door, moved towards her patient.

Grasping the nurse's sleeve in a firm grip, Olympe pulled her to a stop. "After you have made your patient comfortable, please inform the Infirmière that I will shortly send several of Alex's team to stand guard at the infirmary." She gave the frightened nurse a firm admonition. "Tell Sister Reine my orders are non-negotiable and she must not interfere with the guards in any way. If she has questions, she is to contact me directly. Do you understand?"

The nurse quailed at Olympe's stern commands, but nodded her head quickly, her starched white headdress flapping with the movement. "Yes, Mother Olympe. I'll tell her right away. Er, as soon as I've treated my patient."

"Very good. Thank you, Sister Lisette," Olympe replied, before drawing Alex from the room. "Come, dear, as I'm sure you have gathered from your own experience with our infernal cousin, Morpheus, this news is very distressing. We have much to do before anyone can safely sleep tonight."

15

NEWS & NIGHTMARES

The afternoon passed in a whirlwind of activity. Olympe pressed Larry, Grenoble, and even Crazy Sam into service as she issued instructions and integrated Alex's team with the Crossroads defenders.

The tireless nun called an emergency dinner meeting; Alex barely had time to shower off the grime of the day before trying to navigate the maze of unfamiliar hallways and find her way to the refectory. During an afternoon spent trotting along beside her busy cousin, Alex had visited so much of the abbey and met so many new people that she knew she'd never keep everything straight in her head.

Upon their return from the infirmary, Olympe had introduced Alex to Grigory, a Barghest Hellhound shifter and Guardian of the Grenoble Crossroads. The stocky, powerfully built man had a weathered face dominated by expressive amber eyes and shoulder-length silver hair tied back with a simple length of cord. Grigory had bowed respectfully and welcomed her to the community. His full lips had split into a sly grin as he eyed her. "Now I see what my friend Conor meant when he said his new Keeper is a beautiful and strong woman."

His flattery had flustered Alex, but Olympe had come to her rescue. "Grigory, you can flirt with my cousin later, my friend. We have much to do over the coming hours to ensure the safety of our people."

The Guardian had snapped to attention, gazing down at the tiny nun and giving her a respectful nod before replying, "Yes, ma'am. Sorry, Keeper. I'll send guards to protect the infirmary and instruct everyone else to meet us in the refectory for the strategy meeting." Grigory had then trotted off without a backward glance.

Alex had had a tough time keeping up with her centuries-old cousin during the rest of the busy afternoon. Everywhere they went, Olympe had barked orders and sent subordinates scuttling to obey. She only hoped she'd have a tenth of the authority her tiny Keeper cousin had when she was as old as ... oh, fuck. *Did she have centuries ahead of her? Alex wondered. Just how long a life would her demi-goddess status grant her? And did she even want to know?*

AFTER DRESSING FOR DINNER, and after another twenty minutes spent aimlessly wandering through the Abbey's many stone hallways, Alex finally found the refectory. She dashed into the room, hastily filled a plate from a long table groaning with heavenly-smelling food, and then searched for an empty spot on one of the long benches lining the tables in the massive dining hall. A sharp bark caught her attention and, Alex spotted Larry sitting with his goblin friend, Grenoble. Crazy Sam hovered over the bench next to Larry, hungrily eyeing Larry's heaping plate.

"Hurry up, Alex!" Larry mind-spoke his plea. *"Crazy Sam is holding your spot, but I don't know how much longer I can keep him from attacking my plate. As a ghost, he can't eat it, but he sure could make a royal mess of my dinner."*

Alex hurried over, hoping Crazy Sam would yield his seat to

her willingly. She had no desire to lower herself into the ghostly chill of his transparent body if he didn't. Fortunately, the ghost lost interest in Larry's plate and shot up from the bench toward the wooden rafters crisscrossing the room's soaring ceiling. He swung himself up onto a massive beam with a holler, then dug his spurs into the ancient wood and pretended to ride it. "Giddyap, horsey!!!"

Alex placed her tray on the table next to Larry and sat with a sigh. Embarrassed by the outrageous behavior of one of her team members, Alex lowered her red face and tucked into the delicious food, hoping no one would notice her—or the crazy ghost that hooted and hollered over everyone's heads.

"You gonna finish that?" Larry mind-spoke his query, which was a good thing, Alex mused, as her furry Familiar's muzzle currently bulged with food. The pink-eared poodle eyed her plate with interest. *"If not, can I have it?"*

Alex pushed her half-full plate towards her famished Familiar with a sigh. "Sure, bud. Help yourself," she muttered. She had no appetite but had forced herself to eat at least some of her dinner, still reeling from her visit to yet another cousin. Despite her hectic afternoon, dark memories had lingered at the edges of her mind after her visit to the infirmary. Her newfound cousin, Zoé, had mentioned powerful nightmares that had haunted her mind and controlled her actions before both attacks. Olympe was right to be concerned about the safety of her people. What if Morpheus wasn't the only Oneiroi brother involved in the attacks? Alex and her posse had previously fought only one of the trio of divine brothers—and the powerful god of nightmares had almost won. What if two, or even all three, of the brothers had turned to the dark side? She didn't know if even a Keeper as powerful as Olympe could hold her Crossroads against a triple divine threat, even with Alex and her team to help.

∾

"Is anyone sitting here?" A familiar male voice asked in lightly accented English, drawing Alex out of her dark musings. "Mind if I join you?" At Alex's nod, the lithe French police officer quickly settled onto the bench next to her. He had no tray, but then Regenerants didn't need to eat. Not food, anyway.

Alex wasn't positive, but she suspected her Regenerant friend sought sustenance somewhere, and she really didn't want to think about where. She knew that her Uncle Vinnie was helping Leonard to obtain his 'food' and suspected blood was on the menu for Regenerants, as well as vampires. *Ugh.*

Before Alex's thoughts could travel further down the crimson path of Regenerant sustenance, several echoing bangs brought the room to attention. She swung her gaze toward the raised platform at the front of the room, where Olympe stood behind a heavily carved wooden podium. Several women dressed in tactical gear guarded the short spiral steps leading to the tall platform on which the podium rested.

Somehow, Olympe towered over the podium. Alex realized her diminutive cousin must be standing on a stool. Her eyes widened at the change in her newfound cousin. In place of the merry little nun Alex met earlier that day stood a priestess warrior. Olympe wore a short black toga that ended well above her knees. Armored shin and shoulder guards glinted in the spotlight focused on the podium and its regal occupant. Forearms encircled by elaborate wristbands rested lightly on the podium's ancient wood.

The warrior nun struck the podium with a metal wristband, bringing the last of the conversations still shifting around the room to an abrupt end. Olympe's sharp gaze swept over the now riveted audience. The centuries-old woman's demure demeanor had been replaced with an alert forcefulness as she addressed her rapt audience. "Nuns, priestesses, guardians of this sacred place, we must end the attacks that threaten our Crossroads, our abbey, and our very lives." She nodded sharply at Alex. "Keeper Alex has brought reinforcements to help us fight the coming battle. Please welcome her and her posse and treat them as family. Together, we must defeat our enemies and drive them from this Crossroads. No more will they darken our dreams and threaten our community. No more will they wreak death and destruction on our beloved abbey or on the sacred Crossroads that lies beneath it. As we have in centuries past, we must band together and destroy the invaders!"

Alex marveled at the change in her formerly soft-spoken cousin. The compact woman had a boatload of charisma—and she sure as heck knew how to use it. Excited murmurs of support and agreement swept the room, while all eyes focused on the warrior priestess who ruled minds and motivated hearts with her fierce words.

"Let's get down to business," Olympe said more softly, now that she had everyone's rapt attention. Grigory joined her at the podium and she waved him forward. "Grigory has command of the abbey's supernatural posse for now, while our injured Sister Zoé recovers. He remains Guardian of this Crossroads as well. He will act as my right hand during the coming battle. His commands are my commands," the warrior nun thundered. "Do I make myself clear?"

All heads in the room, including Alex's, nodded in acquiescence to Olympe's stern orders. As Olympe's stocky Guardian stood impassively by her side, the warrior nun ended her speech with one last demand. "Before I hand the meeting over to Grigory, let me stress one last thing." Her hawklike gaze fixed on Alex, pinning her in place, eyes wide. "As most of you know, our guest, Alex, is not only a Crossroads Keeper; she is also my cousin through our shared divine ancestry." Olympe grinned down at Alex and added, "In fact, her divine lineage and power far outshine my own. Alex has command of her own posse, who will support us in the coming battle, and she *also* speaks with my voice. If she issues an order, I expect you all to obey. Do you hear me?"

Alex suppressed a shudder and kept her expression neutral as a roomful of interested eyes swung towards her. *What the hell was her cousin doing giving her a command role in the coming battle?* Sure, she'd had some success in defending her own Crossroads against wayward gods, but that was more because of luck and bluster—and the support of her experienced supernatural posse—than anything *she* did. *Right?*

Olympe's next words confirmed to Alex that the ancient, powerful woman on the podium had listened in on her panicked thoughts.

The warrior nun gave Alex a knowing wink. "Alex may be new to the supernatural world, but she has successfully defended her Crossroads several times over the past months. She and her team have battled those who now threaten our Crossroads and won. My intrepid cousin has even traveled to the Underworld to save the soul of one dear to her. While there, she battled gods, demons—and even her own father, a powerful necromantic mage—to end an incipient attack on this realm by the goddess behind all this ... Nyx. She now commands an army of Regenerants created by her rogue mage father. By her command, this army has re-imprisoned Nyx in her castle at the edge of the Underworld and guards her still."

Olympe's intense gaze swept the room. Her voice was heavy with portent when she stated, "However, we know Nyx has co-conspirators, even amongst the gods, who work on her behalf to bring her evil vision of chaos to this realm. They have recently been attacking Crossroads, including ours, in their attempts at gaining control." The warrior nun pointed a commanding finger at Alex, adding, "My cousin is a demi-goddess; she wields a divine level of both death and time magic. Her powers will help us defeat our foes and return peace and safety to our Crossroads — and this realm, once more."

Shocked gasps swept across the room at Olympe's revelations. Alex smoothed her expression and tried not to cringe as the questioning gazes of those in the room morphed into respect and even awe. *At least my scheming cousin has given me a powerful pedigree,* she reflected wryly. *Now all I have to do is live up to it.*

Larry's mind-spoken words interrupted Alex's worried musings. *"Well, the cat's really out of the bag now, Alex. We'll have to work hard to live up to your cousin's faith in our—er, your magical abilities. Good luck with that."*

"Yeah, I realize that, you numbskull," Alex mind-spoke her irritated reply. *"Thanks for the vote of confidence, bud."*

Larry snickered, but pressed himself to Alex's side in unspoken support.

A warm sense of comfort and assurance filled Alex as all those magically connected to her entered her consciousness.

"You are brave, and much stronger than you know." Conor's mind-spoken words of reassurance traveled effortlessly across the thousands of miles that separated them. *"I can feel your self-doubt and worry, Alex,"* he added. *"But you are one of the most capable Keepers I've ever met, and a hundred times more powerful than any other Keeper in existence."*

Tyre's rumbling agreement came next. The Indigo Fae echoed Conor's words. *"You are a worthy Keeper, Alex. You have great power and great courage. Your foes cannot help but bow before you in defeat."*

Others magically bound to Alex echoed similar words of support until a chorus of encouragement rang in her head. Her chosen heart family believed in her, so why did she still doubt herself? Alex suppressed a smile and silently thanked everyone, feeling their presence fade from her mind. With effort, she buried her doubts and brought her mind back to the present.

While Alex was occupied with her internal conversation, Olympe had ceded the podium to Grigory, who was now addressing the room. Olympe sat to one side, regally reclining on an ancient high-backed throne of a chair. The warrior nun gazed intently up at Grigory as the Guardian spoke, so Alex turned her attention to his speech.

"...and Grenoble will join the team at the Crossroads ley

station. His knowledge of the vast cave systems that branch out in all directions from our Crossroads will help when pursuing the enemy," the Guardian said. He tilted his head at Grenoble and addressed the little goblin directly. "Grenoble, when we break out into teams tonight, please share your knowledge with your assigned team."

Grenoble climbed onto a table so he could see over the heads of those gathered. The little goblin gave Grigory a sharp nod of agreement. "It will be as you say, Guardian. I ask permission to have Lieutenant Allard lead the second shift team, which will be on duty directly after mine. During his previous life, the lieutenant grew up in this area and is familiar with many of these tunnels as well. We have worked together to create maps—"

"Permission granted, my friend," Grigory interrupted, giving Grenoble a small smile. "I trust both your knowledge and your judgement."

Alex realized that Grigory and Grenoble must know each other well; their friendship had been forged when the little goblin had taken refuge at this Crossroads more than a decade earlier. There seemed to be mutual liking and respect between the two.

As the meeting continued, Grigory issued further instructions and commands, and Olympe added to them. Just before midnight, the meeting broke up and everyone scattered to join their individual teams and make their way out of the refectory to assume their battle preparation duties. There was no way to tell when the next attack would come, but they would be ready for it this time.

Stifling a yawn, she rose from the hard wooden bench that had become increasingly uncomfortable as the hours passed, absentmindedly rubbing her sore rear end.

Larry bounded easily off his perch next to Alex. He landed between her feet, almost tripping her. She stumbled but caught herself before falling onto the unforgiving flagstone floor. Growling in irritation, she snarled, "Watch out, you doofus! You almost killed me!"

"It's not me that wants you dead, Alex," Larry replied with a grin as he skittered away. "Not that there isn't a long line of those who do, mind you. But I'm not among them. Honest."

Alex rolled her tired eyes and shuffled toward the podium, where a small group had gathered. "Thanks for reminding me. Come on, fur-face. Grigory wants us to meet with the head honchos to go over 'command strategy', whatever that means."

ALEX FELL into bed in the wee hours of the morning, totally exhausted. She closed her burning eyes and heaved a sigh of relief. After the main meeting, Grigory had led the smaller group of leaders into a bland conference room, where the strategy meeting had dragged on for several more hours. Many of the technical aspects had gone straight over Alex's head. Curbing her frustration, she had nodded sagely in agreement at what she thought were appropriate times, but spoke little and understood less.

Larry, seated by her side, had assured Alex that he understood Grigory's plans and mind-spoke that he would help her be 'in the right place at the right time ... no worries.' His furry forehead had creased in a frown when he gave his assurance, so Alex hadn't felt reassured. Much.

"SCOOCH OVER. You're hogging the bed," Larry growled as he finagled for more space on the narrow mattress. "We both need to get some serious shut-eye. Don't forget, we gotta relieve the first watch shift in a few hours."

"Don't remind me," Alex muttered tiredly, flicking a glance into the room's corner, where a comforting shadow lurked. Much as she hated to admit it, Grigory had been right to assign posse members to watch over everyone who would sleep during the rest of the night. From bitter experience, Alex knew Morpheus could use his divine magic to infiltrate the unconscious, causing nightmares that could harm or kill. Her cousin's vast powers could lead good people into evil actions and even twist a person's very soul.

It was critical that each sleeper had someone awake watching over them. Unfortunately, that had lowered the numbers available to guard the Crossroads, spreading their forces thinner than anyone would have liked. As the worries and cares of the long day tumbled through her tired mind, Alex felt herself slipping into sleep until a spurt of primal fear startled her awake. She knew how insidious her damnable cousin's powers over the unconscious were. Had he just attempted to access her mind? Again. *Damn it. Now I'm wide awake,* she brooded.

A soft voice spoke from the shadows in the room. "Sleep now, Alex. I'm keeping watch. I'll wake you at the first sign something is wrong."

She allowed her eyes to close again. Just before sleep finally pulled her under, she mumbled a thanks to the vigilant Regenerant whose watchful police officer's gaze guarded her through the night.

16

AN OLD ENEMY RETURNS

As the sky lightened toward dawn, a malign presence slithered into Alex's sleeping mind; an insidious voice whispered evil things and encouraged even worse. She tried to close her ears to the insistent, sibilant whispering, struggling to wake from a very familiar nightmare, having experienced it ... him for weeks during the prolonged attack on the Crossroads several months earlier. Back then, Alex had resisted Morpheus's sibilant evil, fighting him in her dreams until she faced him in real life while standing over the body of one of her team members during their rescue mission in the Underworld. She had won that battle, successfully freeing the piece of her aunt's soul Morpheus had stolen, but the personal cost had been high, and the rogue god's parting words still haunted her. "Next time we meet, Alex, I'm going to kill you."

"Not if I kill you first," she had snarled at the powerful god. Thankfully, the memory of her earlier defiance helped Alex fight off the current nightmare. Forcing her eyes open, she shot upright, chest heaving with the effort. Her gaze swung wildly around the small bedroom as the last wisps of nightmare clung to her thoughts. A dark figure crouched beside the bed, holding Alex's arm tightly. Panicked, she twisted out of the intruder's grasp, lashing out with her fists.

"Ouch! You've got a great right hook, Alex. Conor has taught you well." Lieutenant Allard's wiry form lay sprawled on the rug beside the bed. He rubbed his jaw, eyeing Alex ruefully. "That really hurt."

Alex gazed down at her injured friend in horror. "Oh, I'm so sorry, Leo. I didn't mean to do that." She fought her way free of the tangled covers and slid off the bed to kneel by her friend's side. Touching his cheek gently, she whispered, "Your lip is bleeding."

The former French police officer and current Regenerant smiled and patted her shoulder. "Only a little. But you're awake, and that's the important thing, my friend. I've been trying to wake you up for a while now," the Regenerant stated wryly. His kind smile ended with a pained grimace as he gingerly dabbed at his bleeding lip with a starched linen handkerchief. "I really need to take better care of this new body, since I'm only borrowing it," he muttered.

Alex rolled her eyes and helped the injured man to his feet. "I've told you, Leo. Possession is nine-tenths of the law. Your body's former occupant is dead. He has no need of this body anymore."

"And so was I ... dead, I mean," murmured the man at her side absently. "Until I allowed your father to insert my soul into this body and work his dark necromantic magic—"

"Oh, just stop," Alex protested, giving her morose friend a heavy dose of side-eye. "We've been over this before, bud. Your intentions were good. You knew my late father was up to something evil down there in the Underworld. The only way to discover his plan was to volunteer for his necromantic experiments, so you did." She fought to contain her frustration, having had this same conversation with her undead friend many times. Intellectually, Leonard knew his actions had helped subvert her father's evil scheming, but Alex knew he still sometimes grappled with his newfound undead status.

To create his army of Regenerants, Alex's father had bound the souls of criminals who had passed to recently dead corpses. Once the dark magic was complete, he had reanimated the corpses and pledged them to his lover, Nyx's service. Alex snorted in disgust at the memory. Her evil mage father had created an army of murderers to help aid Nyx in her plans to bring chaos to all the realms, starting with Earth ... with his own daughter's Crossroads. *The bastard.*

"I know, I know. You're right," Leonard agreed, shaking his head to dispel his dark mood. "I'm happy to have a second chance at life, Alex. But sometimes it's hard—"

"Sometimes life's hard the first time around, too, Leo," Alex replied with a wry grin. She gently patted her friend's shoulder. "I imagine it's not any easier the second time around."

Leonard grinned back at Alex. His lip had already stopped bleeding, and the wound was rapidly healing, which was a perk of his Regenerant status. "That's why I like you so much, Alex. You always help me put things in perspective." He glanced around the room with a frown. "Where's Larry?"

Alex's gaze followed Leonard's, and she couldn't see the little poodle anywhere. Heart pounding in fear, she tried to think clearly. Where *was* her canine Familiar? The last time she had seen him, he'd been curled up at her side as they both drifted off to sleep. *Crap.*

Throwing on her clothes, Alex raced from the room with Leonard on her heels. Frantically, she reached out with her mind for Larry's presence, but she couldn't sense him at all. Usually, she could pinpoint her Familiar's location with a thought. Not this time.

"Maybe we should head to the abbey kitchen," Leonard whispered as he ran down the stone corridor at her side. "Food is never far from Larry's mind—or stomach."

Alex jerked to a stop at a T-junction and bent forward, panting. *I need to spend more time jogging*, she brooded. Conor usually asked her to run with him in the mornings, but she had been coming up with excuses to avoid it for weeks. *Dammit.*

"The kitchen's gotta be near the refectory," Alex reasoned. "The food was still hot when they served it last night."

After a few false starts and dead ends—the ancient abbey was a maze of echoing stone corridors—they finally found the kitchen. Delicious scents and bubbling pots greeted them as they hurried into the massive room. Henri, the French chef who had accompanied Alex and her team on their journey, was busy stirring one steaming pot after another on the huge cast-iron stove.

"Henri! Have you seen Larry?" Alex asked abruptly.

The rotund chef swung around to face Alex so fast his tall chef's hat deflated and flopped over one ear. "Mon Dieu, you startled me." Henri gazed at Alex, eyes filled with growing concern. "I haven't seen Larry since just after dinner last night, when he and Grenoble came begging for leftovers, the little scamps."

What little hope Alex had held onto in her race to find the kitchen deserted her. She admitted to herself that she had known she wouldn't find her Familiar in the kitchen. In fact, she couldn't sense him anywhere on the abbey grounds.

"He can't be missing, mon chère," Henri protested. "Grenoble knows this place like the back of his hand, and those two are always together."

Alex crossed her arms and shook her head mutely, her mind racing with possibilities-most of them unthinkable.

At her side, Leonard swiped a harried hand through his hair. "Grenoble took first shift tonight, remember. He's down at the Crossroads helping protect the tunnels. Larry was asleep next to

Alex the last time I saw him. I had first sleep-watcher shift and I never took my eyes off the bed—"

A massive pot on the stove hissed and bubbled over. Henri deftly removed the lid and stirred until the boiling liquid calmed. "Breakfast is in a few hours. I'm sure Larry won't miss that. He never does."

Determination firmed the chef's features, and he leaned on the rules of hospitality and hope. "Would either of you like a cup of coffee while you wait for Larry to appear?"

Alex shook her head and began pacing the length of the vast room. "Something's happened. I just know it," she muttered, voice rough with concern. "I really need to talk to my cousin. Olympe will know what we should do."

"What *you* should do is calm down, child." Olympe's firm words startled everyone, and Henri dropped his spoon with a clatter. As the chef muttered imprecations and cleaned up the mess, Olympe sailed into the room, her voluminous white nightgown flowing around her thin legs. She wore a matching sleeping cap on her head; with her pale face and all-white attire, the diminutive Keeper resembled a ghost.

Gazing up at Alex with a kind, if slightly harried, smile, Olympe assured Alex, "Larry is fine, dear. At least he was the last time I saw him an hour ago."

"What do you mean 'the last time you saw him?'" Alex queried sharply. "The last time *I* saw him, he was asleep on my bed. Leonard was watching over both of us."

"Leonard was watching over *you*, Alex, not Larry," Olympe stated calmly. "Larry is an extremely old and powerful Familiar. Morpheus would think twice before tangling with him, even in the dream world." She switched her gaze to Leonard and grinned up at him. "Larry told me your eyes never left Alex's sleeping form. You did your job well, Lieutenant."

"But how did Larry get past Leonard—" Alex sputtered.

"As I said, dear, Larry is a powerful Familiar," Olympe replied, her eyes twinkling with mischief. "That diva of a poodle has more magical tricks up his sleeve than you might imagine."

Leonard verbalized the question looming over Alex like a dark cloud. "But where did he go? Where is he, Olympe?"

The little nun sobered, a hint of concern gleaming in her gaze. "He's currently tracking the attackers who kidnapped Grenoble just over an hour ago."

17

KIDNAPPED!

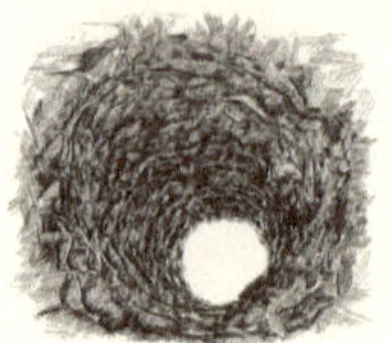

Larry raced down the dark tunnel, his paws raising tiny puffs of dust as he ran. His almond-shaped eyes glowed amber, providing faint illumination in the absolute darkness of the cave system. *Good thing I can see in the dark,* he mused, before returning his mind to the tiny problem at hand. Okay, it was more than a tiny problem. It was a huge, honking disaster of a problem.

Just over an hour ago, while Grenoble and his team were guarding the tunnel entrances, a flash attack had distracted the protectors. They had easily fought off the attackers. However, once they had regrouped, Grenoble was missing.

A plaintive cry for help from his goblin friend had woken Larry from a sound sleep. The unusual magical mind connection Larry shared with Grenoble had started soon after they first met and had only strengthened over the following months as the pair protected their Crossroads and got up to shenanigans best left unmentioned. They could now communicate across long distances. *Good thing, too,* Larry reflected.

He scrambled to a halt upon reaching an intersection. Five pitch-black tunnels branched off in different directions, each heading deeper under the mountain that housed the Crossroads and supported the abbey above. *Which way?*

"Stop following me. It's a trap!" Grenoble's harsh words reverberated in Larry's panicked mind.

Larry shook his head, sending his pink ears flapping. *"No! I'm coming to get you whether you like it or not."* He'd been giving his goblin friend the same reply for the past hour. He would be damned if he let Grenoble's former nest mates hurt him—or worse.

Grenoble's angry shout echoed in Larry's skull. *"Listen, you foolish Familiar, this matter has nothing to do with you. My former goblin family wants a word with me. That's all. You need to head back and protect the Crossroads from the real danger, you idiot. I should be back shortly."*

It was the 'should' in Grenoble's admonition that had Larry worried. The bravado in his friend's words didn't reassure him in the least. After all, the last time Grenoble had tangled with his family, they had beaten him severely and then thrown him in the cave river, leaving him for dead. It was merely chance and Olympe's kindness that had saved the wounded goblin when his battered body had washed up on an underground beach near the Crossroads.

Larry dithered. *Which is the right tunnel? Or should I listen to Grenoble and head back?* He knew his primary duty was to protect his magical partner, Alex, but the pull was strong to rescue his friend. But what chance did he really have? He may be the world's most powerful Familiar, but he was only one small, pink-eared poodle in this incarnation. He would need reinforcements before entering the massive goblin nest.

Reluctantly, Larry turned around and forced himself down the tunnel leading back to the Crossroads. *Damn it.*

"Hang on, Grenoble. I'll come for you as soon as I can."

"No, you'll protect the Crossroads and let me deal with my own mess, you idiot. Go! Alex needs you! Ooof! You hit me like that again,

Methol, and I'll..." Grenoble's pained words broke off as he slammed the magical mind connection he shared with Larry closed.

Larry picked up his pace and raced through the maze of tunnels. He better get to work sorting out the danger at the Crossroads so he could rescue his friend before ... before what, he didn't know, but goblin society was not kind to outcasts. Fur raised along Larry's spine, and he howled in fury. Those goblin assholes who had kidnapped his friend wouldn't know what hit them when Larry and his team descended. He'd get his friend back or avenge his death. *It damn well better be the first option,* Larry brooded as he skidded headlong into the Crossroads cave.

18

FAMILY UNFRIENDLY TIES

Grenoble forcibly cut the magical mind connection between himself and Larry. That furry fool needed to concentrate on his primary job—working with Alex to protect the Crossroads. *I love that idiot like a brother*, he mused wryly, then reconsidered his phrasing when another forceful blow caused him to double over, gasping in pain and spitting blood. Since his *actual* brother was presently beating the shit out of him, maybe that comparison wasn't the best.

Methol's gravelly voice interrupted Grenoble's pained musings. "I'm going to ask you one more time. Why did you return to our nest, brother? When I tossed you in the river all those years ago, I never expected to see you again."

"You never expected me to live, you mean," Grenoble retorted, working hard to keep the pain out of his voice. He'd be damned if he let his asshole of a brother know how much pain he was in. Methol had always had a mean right hook.

"Well, to be fair, goblin society requires traitors to be executed," Methol replied dryly. "You were supposed to die back then, brother." The hulking goblin gazed down at Grenoble with a frustrated frown. "Why didn't you die?"

Grenoble gave a bitter laugh. "Sorry to disappoint you, asshole."

An irritated female voice interrupted the brothers' argument. "Grenoble, you've been disappointing me since you were a mere child. You are certainly disappointing me now by returning from the dead."

Grenoble swung his head toward the speaker, his blurry gaze picking out a squat female goblin standing near the cave's rough-hewn wall. "Hi, Mom," he muttered. "Long time, no see."

The female goblin strode forward, stopping a few feet short of the bloody dirt where Grenoble sprawled. With her thick lips pursed in distaste, she retreated a step before studying her satin slippers carefully.

Grenoble snorted in disgust. "Yeah, step back, Mother. Wouldn't want to get the blood of your firstborn on your fancy shoes. Step back, as you have always done in the past, thus enabling my younger half-brother to unlawfully rule our kingdom, as he always did our home."

"Oh, stop whining, you fool," the female goblin snapped. "Your brother has always been more suited to rule than you, and you know it." She sneered at Grenoble, then gave her younger son an approving smile. "Methol is tough, where you have always been weak. He knows how to dominate, which is what goblin society expects of its ruler."

"You mean he's killed all his opposition, so those remaining alive cower in fear?" Grenoble challenged, shaking his head in disgust. "Mother ... Yima, you always were a piece of work. I really don't know what my father ever saw in you."

Yima gave her eldest son a narrow-eyed glare. "You know very well your father married me because he needed the vast wealth I brought to his poverty-stricken kingdom. Love had nothing to do with it," she growled, her lips curled in distaste. "Love is weak. It's certainly nothing to base a meaningful relationship on."

Grenoble ran a weary hand over his bruised face and sighed. "I will not rehash old history with you, Mother. My father married you because he had no other choice to save his kingdom and feed his people. But little did he know the viper he brought into the nest."

The injured goblin climbed slowly to his feet, careful to keep the pain off his face. "You achieved your end goal, Mother. Your firstborn, the legitimate heir," Grenoble said, pointing to himself, "disinherited and cast out in favor of your bastard son sired by a nameless soldier." He spat blood and gave his mother a nasty grin. "But we all know who truly rules this kingdom, don't we, Yima? You've got your hand so far up Methol's ass—"

A vicious blow from his brother knocked Grenoble back to the ground. He grunted in pain but kept his face blank, glaring wordlessly up at the woman who gave him life and the half-brother who had attempted to take it away more than a decade ago ... and who might just succeed this time. "Before my father died, he named me his heir and asked me to finish his work. He wanted peace and prosperity for our people, but not at the expense of our moral code. That's why he repeatedly refused to join Nyx's Chaos Council, even under threat of war." Grenoble growled, lips curling in disgust as he studied the two dark-hearted goblins before him. "I'm assuming our nest is firmly in league with the Chaos Council now. Have you two no honor?" He shook his head, eyes filled with sorrow as he gazed at his traitorous family members. "You both bring shame to the goblin race."

A fraught silence followed Grenoble's accusations. The guards bearing witness to the confrontation gasped in horror at his bold insults.

Methol growled and lunged, but his mother held him back with a gesture. "No, son, let the traitor speak. He condemns himself with his words," Yima said. She waved the guards forward. "Take the prisoner to the dungeon and have the interrogator question him in the morning. We need to know everything he knows about the Grenoble Crossroads."

"You mean, have me tortured so you can gain information about the Crossroads and its protective measures so you can share it with your overlords on the Chaos Council," Grenoble retorted. He spat at his mother's feet. "You disgust me."

Yima's eyes narrowed and she gave her firstborn a thin smile. "The disgust is mutual, Nitus." She cackled cruelly. "Yes, I'm using your birth name, *son*. I hear you took the name Grenoble after your first 'death'. I promise you'll die properly this time—and it will be under the name your father and I gave you at birth—Nitus."

"My birth name died when your evil coup succeeded, you bitch," Grenoble ground out. "My new life deserved a new name, which I chose to honor the woman who saved me. I will protect Olympe and the Grenoble Crossroads with my life."

"Then we agree on one thing," Yima replied with a sly grin, her dark eyes glittering with malice. "Your life is forfeit."

19

RESPECT

Larry raced out of the tunnel and skidded to a stop in front of Grigory, who cursed and pulled his rifle barrel up toward the cave's ceiling. "I could have shot you, you fool," he shouted. "Next time, bark a warning so we know it's you and not the attackers coming back."

Larry gave the exasperated Crossroads Guardian an apologetic grimace. "Sorry," he panted, still out of breath from his headlong race through the tunnels. "Just ... gimme a minute and I'll give you my report."

Grigory's irritated frown dissolved and he grinned down at Larry. "Too much good food at your own Crossroads, eh? You need to get more exercise, little one."

"You've tasted Henri's cooking," Larry retorted. "It's impossible to resist. You and Olympe will have to visit us sometime. And I've got a vampire pal who makes the *best* pizza..." Larry shook his head and returned to the matter at hand. Food was a huge part of the little Familiar's life, but he knew his primary purpose was assisting his magical partner, Alex, in her magical endeavors. Right now, that meant helping her protect the Grenoble Crossroads and all those who inhabited the community it supported.

Once Larry's breathing returned to normal, he sat at attention and prepared to give his report. Although hating to admit it, Larry knew Grigory was right. He really needed to cut down on his food intake and get back to his daily morning runs. Well, the running, definitely. He'd consider moderating his food intake at a later date. Much later.

Shaking off his musings, Larry gazed alertly up at Grigory. "Sorry, sir. Larry the Kibble Guy reporting back from his reconnaissance mission. Sir."

The Crossroads Guardian's eyebrows rose and he burst out laughing. "Stop 'sirring' me, you impudent hound. You know as well as I do you went haring off after Grenoble without a thought to reconnaissance." Grigori narrowed his eyes at Larry. "You meant to rescue him single-handedly, right? What made you change your mind?"

Larry sniffed and shuffled his paws, embarrassed. "Um, I realized that I may have been a bit hasty and maybe even just slightly overconfident in thinking I could tackle a goblin nest on my own," he admitted. Looking away, he shook his head, his bright pink ears flapping. "But what would you have done? I was asleep when I heard Grenoble's cry for help—"

Grigory's gaze sharpened. "You share a mind connection with the goblin?"

"Uh, yes. It started a while ago when we stole .... um, well, that's not important right now," Larry muttered, grinning nervously. "But yeah, we can mind-talk."

"Hmmm. That's unusual. Most goblins cannot mind-talk. I've heard only senior members of their royal families have that ability," Grigory said, eyeing Larry with a confused frown. "Maybe your magical strength as one of the most powerful Familiars in existence makes it possible..." he trailed off in thought.

Larry realized with a sinking heart that he would have to reveal Grenoble's deepest secret—one he had taken an oath to protect. But he'd gladly break the oath to save his friend's life.

"Grenoble is of royal blood," he murmured softly. "In fact, he's ... well, he's the rightful heir to the Grenoble nest's throne."

Grigory's eyes widened in shock. "No shit!" He raked a hand through his thick silver hair and glared down at Larry. "When Olympe rescued him, she merely said Grenoble was an outcast from the nest. She never mentioned his royal lineage. Does she even know?"

Larry snorted and challenged his newest compatriot. "What? So, you wouldn't have helped Olympe rescue Grenoble back then if you'd known who he really was?" He curled his lip, adding, "I'm assuming you'd have been too worried about retaliation from the goblin nest to save an outcast king, right?"

"Damn straight," Grigory snapped. "The whole nest could have attacked us if they discovered Grenoble lived. Now you tell me he's their deposed *king*?" The Guardian scrubbed a hand over his mouth and blew out a frustrated breath. "This whole thing sounds like a leadership dispute. We can't help Grenoble—"

"What, afraid you can't defeat a few hundred little green men?" Larry growled. Maybe Grigori wasn't friend material after all.

"There will be no more discussion about this," snapped a sharp female voice. "We help our friends. Always."

Both Guardian and Familiar whirled toward the newcomer and bowed at the Crossroads Keeper.

"Yes, ma'am."

"Sorry, Keeper."

Olympe regarded the two before her with sharp eyes and thinned lips. She let them remain in their deep bows for several moments longer than was strictly necessary, then bade them rise.

The priestess nun, who was dressed again in her warrior gear, gave Grigory a thin smile. "I didn't tell you about Grenoble's royal heritage when I rescued him because he begged me to keep it a secret. I saw no sense in bringing the matter up with you, as we would have helped him, regardless. Correct?" She gave her Guardian a fierce glare. "Or are you telling me we would have refused a badly injured refugee based on fears for our own personal safety? That we would have compromised the oaths we both took to guard the Crossroads *and* protect all who seek refuge here?"

After a fraught moment, Grigory shook his head and heaved a sigh. "Of course not, ma'am, but—"

Olympe, arms crossed, glared up at the frustrated man standing before her. "But what, Grigory? Remember, Guardian, Hecate created your race—Barghest Hellhounds—to protect her other creation ... the Crossroads system. Your very soul is bound to this Crossroads and to protecting those who live, work, and seek shelter here."

Grigory bowed his head, face flushed with shame. "You are right, Keeper Olympe. As usual," the large man muttered. He sighed deeply, shoulders hunched. "Sometimes I lose sight of the bigger picture in my desire to protect you—"

Olympe stamped her small foot and growled, "When are you going to get it through your thick head that I don't need protecting, Grigory? I'm a Crossroads Keeper, for the gods' sake! I have more magic in my little finger—"

Alex, who had arrived at the Crossroads platform a while ago and had been listening to the confrontation in growing amazement, snickered as she watched her tiny cousin have the same argument that she'd been having with her own Crossroads Guardian, Conor, for months.

Both verbal combatants whirled to face Alex, anger still bright in their eyes. She held up a soothing hand and patted the air. "Whoa, you two. Sorry to interrupt your, er, discussion. But shouldn't we be concentrating on how to rescue Grenoble and protect the Crossroads against our enemies?" She threw Olympe a conspiratorial grin. "Your Guardian gives you the same disrespect as mine, I see, cousin. Must be a guy thing."

The diminutive nun's angry frown dissolved and she gave a reluctant chuckle. She snorted a laugh as she gazed up at her Crossroads Guardian and oldest friend. "I'm sorry, Grigory. I know you have only the best intentions, but you really *do* need to let me fight my own battles." She hesitated and added, "Well, at least let me fight them at your side, not from behind you, my friend. After all, divine blood flows through my veins, just as it does Alex's. Even if my divine magic is just a shadow of hers, it has been strong enough to successfully hold this Crossroads for the last half millennium."

Grigory gazed down at his Keeper and friend with a rueful grin. "Yes, ma'am. You are absolutely right. Sometimes my instinct to protect the wea—um..." he trailed off, eyes widening in comic horror as he realized the verbal cesspit he'd just blundered into.

"Weaker sex?" Olympe growled, her eyes flashing with anger. "You were going to say weaker sex, weren't you, Guardian?" She huffed an offended breath and studied Grigori through narrowed eyes. "Have you forgotten our history? Millenia ago, a trio of divine women created this Crossroads and the hundreds like it around the world. These same *women* chose other *women* to manage and protect the Crossroads system. Women like me."

The furious warrior nun gestured at Alex. "Women like her." Olympe grinned triumphantly at her now very contrite friend. "As I'm sure you remember, Guardian, after these three *goddesses* created the Crossroads, Hecate—she may be a goddess, but she's also a woman—blackmailed Hades ... a male, mind you, even if he is a god, into giving her his finest pack of prized battle Hellhounds to *help*, yes, *help*, the Keepers protect the Crossroads. This divine *goddess* then infused the original Hellhounds with her magic, gave them a second name—Barghest—and bound these magically enhanced creatures and their progeny to serve her Crossroads as

Guardians. These Barghests serve the Crossroads Keepers. These *women*—"

Alex interrupted Olympe's rant. Much as she agreed with her cousin's angry diatribe, now wasn't the time. She waved her hand between the two verbal combatants to get their attention. "Uh, guys? I think we've gotten a bit off-topic here. Don't we all have the same goal right now? To protect the Crossroads from those who wish it harm. Perhaps we can put off the 'misogyny is bad' discussion for another time?"

Silence reigned for a beat, then smothered laughter echoed from the cave's high ceiling. Soon, everyone was hooting with laughter, even Olympe and Grigory, who eyed each other sheepishly.

"My deepest apologies, Keeper Olympe," Grigory offered with a deep bow. "I do know better than to denigrate women. I won't argue that I'm a product of my time, having been born half a millennium ago, as that would be disingenuous," he added, before sighing deeply and rubbing his hands over his still-flushed face. "I know better. I really do."

Alex snickered and wondered if Grigory had a story similar to Conor's. Conor had shared with her a tale about how he had lost his misogyny a few centuries before—and gained a new respect for his Keeper—when the woman had ridden to his rescue, single-handedly saving him from a coven of black witches who were preparing to sacrifice him to their dark gods.

Larry interjected, gazing around with an affable grin. "How about we all agree that everyone is equal and deserves the same amount of respect?" He sobered, cut a glance at Grigory, and said, "And that includes goblins. Now, what are we *all* going to do about saving our friend, Grenoble?"

20

SISTERS ROCK

"*N*itus? *Can you hear me? Nitus!*"

The faint, nagging voice grew louder until it finally broke through the swirling gray fog in Grenoble's pained, exhausted mind. *Who is this Nitus?* He wondered dully. The name the voice kept calling out sounded familiar, but not in a good way.

"*Nitus, wake up this instant, you goober! It's your sister talking,*" the voice said. Despite the urgency of the command, the words contained an equal measure of desperation. "*It's Modi ... Modi, your sister, remember me? Please wake up, Nitus. Please.*"

Grenoble's eyes popped open and he returned to full consciousness. Hesitantly, he mind-spoke, "*Modi? Is that really you, sister?*"

A disbelieving snort came before the answer. "*Of course it's me, you lumbering idiot. How many sisters do you have? Just the one, last time I checked.*" Modi's voice gained a note of urgency. "*I have sooo many questions, brother, but we don't have much time. The guards will return to check on you soon, so listen up, buttercup.*"

Grenoble listened.

Just over an hour later, when the guards stomped toward his cell for the midnight prisoner check, Grenoble was ready for them. He crouched with his back to the wall beside the cell door, a sharpened piece of metal he'd wrenched from the bed clutched in his fist.

Just as the cell door cracked open, a loud, feminine scream echoed down the cave's narrow stone hallway. "Help! Help me, please! I'm being attacked!"

Several guards peeled off and raced toward the urgent plea. *Good. Less of them to kill,* Grenoble mused with a bloodthirsty grin. His sister was a strategic genius.

As the two remaining guards entered the cell, Grenoble leapt. The fight was over in seconds. Both guards lay bleeding on the cell's filthy floor, their dark blood pooling in the crevices between the worn stones. Grenoble frisked the dying guards for keys and weapons, plucking all he could find from their bodies and arming himself with his bounty.

A sharp crack and several pained grunts echoed down the hallway, alerting Grenoble to further danger. He peered tentatively around the cell's sturdy iron door, eyes wide in the gloom. A razor-sharp short sword was now balanced in his grip, while another hung in a scabbard at his hip. The goblin's thick lips split into a delighted grin when he spotted his sister finishing off the last of the guards who had thundered to her 'rescue'.

Blood and gore covered the female goblin's rich silken robes, although none of it appeared to belong to her. She pulled her short sword out of the last guard's body, wiped it on her cape, and grinned fiercely at her long-lost sibling.

"Nitus. Long time no see, brother."

"Modi! Still kicking ass and taking names, I see," Grenoble observed wryly.

A pained shadow flickered across Modi's face so fast Grenoble almost missed it. He imagined life under the iron fist of their half-brother and mother had not been easy for her. His heart sang with joy to see his sister still alive, her spirit unbroken.

Modi cocked her head, listening intently. "We need to get out of here before the rest of the guards in the break-room wonder where this lot have gotten to."

Grenoble snickered. "They've gotten to the River Styx by now is my guess, sister, with no small thanks to you."

"Or you, brother," Modi murmured as she impatiently waved her brother forward. "Come, we must get you out of here."

"Are you coming with me, Modi?" Grenoble whispered hesitantly. "Life must be hard for you here, and it's likely to get worse. Methol will realize you're the one who helped me escape. He's a moron, but he's not stupid."

Modi's lips thinned and she didn't reply. Instead, she turned away and loped off up the hallway at a fast pace. Grenoble shrugged and followed her. They slipped from shadow to shadow for some time, each turn of the tunnel taking them closer to the river cave that led to freedom.

As they approached their destination, Grenoble touched his sister's arm lightly, his silent plea insistent. "Please, sister, come with me," he murmured.

"I can't, Nitus," Modi replied softly. She paused and sighed, studying her brother's face with wise, sad eyes. "Our people need me here, brother. Sometimes, I'm able to blunt the cruel edge of our family's despotic rule." A sly smile curved her lips. "And I have used your decade of absence wisely. I've built a network of like-minded friends and supporters."

"My escape tonight will surely put your life in even more danger!" Grenoble protested.

Modi nodded slowly, grief lurking in her gaze. "My life has been in danger every day since our father died and our two dark-hearted brethren staged their successful coup against your ascent to the throne." The little goblin gave her brother a pained grimace. "I've been dancing on knife points ever since, brother. I will dance a while longer if it means I can save even a few of our people from pain and deprivation and keep hope alive for a future free of our half-brother's tyrannical rule."

Grenoble cursed foully, if quietly. "Sounds like he's been beating and starving everyone in the kingdom into submission. And our mother has been supporting him in every evil deed, I presume?"

Modi nodded her head but didn't reply. She drew Grenoble to a stop just before the next turn; the rushing river ahead echoed in the narrow tunnel. Peering hesitantly around the corner, she breathed a sigh of relief, her gaze tinged with sadness. "The river guards are ... asleep," Modi whispered. "We can get you safely to the dock and away from the nest while they present no threat."

"Come, brother. Quickly, now," Modi urged. She crept toward the river cave and waved Grenoble forward.

Grenoble hesitated. Something in his sister's voice worried him deeply. "What do you mean, the guards are asleep? Are they alive? I thought we'd have to fight our way out onto the dock."

Modi gazed at her brother, her enormous eyes pools of pain. "I couldn't take a chance that we'd be thwarted at the last hurdle, Nitus. The river guards on duty tonight are loyal to me. Earlier, they ate food I gave them that contained a sleep potion." With a heavy sigh, she added, "I'm trying to keep the guards safe by placing the blame for your escape solely on me, but it may not be enough to save them. Methol will punish them harshly for allowing your escape, even if seemingly unwittingly."

The smaller goblin shrugged wearily. "These guards know the risk, but they take it in hopes of a future of freedom for our people." She grinned wryly. "And it won't be the first time I've spent time in our brother's dungeons, or the last, I'm sure. Methol only hesitates to kill me because he knows our people love me deeply—even the ones that fear him. Killing me would weaken his authority."

Modi dashed away angry tears. "Doesn't mean he won't come close, though ... dancing on knife points, remember?"

Grenoble gazed at his sister in horror. "I'm so sorry, Modi! I had no idea. I thought that staying away and keeping my survival a secret would be enough to keep you safe." He stroked his sister's cheek gently. "I had hoped that taking the throne from me would quench Methol's thirst for power. I hoped he'd rule, if not justly, at least competently. If I'd known—"

Modi placed a gentle hand on Grenoble's bruised face. "Brother, if you had returned immediately after the coup, Methol would have killed you. By staying safe and away from the nest for the past decade, you have given me time to build support for our cause and given yourself time to heal, both physically and mentally."

A conspiratorial smile tilted her lips. "My sources tell me you now have powerful friends in high places, Nitus. And that your friends wish to defeat Nyx and her Chaos Council by destroying their centers of support." Modi cast her gaze down and shook her head. "Sadly, our nest is one such support center. Your ... our enemies include those who rule our nest and their Chaos Council cronies."

Grenoble pulled his sister into a fierce hug. "You are amazing, Modi. You should have been born first, then you could have ruled instead of me. Things might have been different if..."

Modi reluctantly withdrew from her brother's embrace. Gazing deeply into his eyes, she mind-spoke a firm reply. *"Make no mistake, Nitus, things will be different in the future. With your help, and that of your powerful allies, we will root out the evil in our midst and install a new, enlightened ruler on the throne."* She grinned slyly.

Grenoble's eyes widened as understanding dawned. He bowed deeply and mind-spoke his oath. *"My queen. Allow me to undertake this quest for you. I will gather support and help you free your kingdom from tyranny."*

Modi giggled and pulled her brother to his feet. "Just get on with you, you great lug." Then she sobered and added, "When the battle for our nest comes, I and my supporters will be ready to fight alongside you and yours."

"Any good ruler would fight for their people," Grenoble affirmed. He was so proud of his wise and patient sister.

Silently, they rounded the corner into the river cave. Rush torches in metal brackets fastened to the moss-covered stone walls flickered and smoked dimly, providing just enough light to spot the rough wooden dock, where a small watercraft bobbed and weaved on its rope-tie. Several guards lay sprawled on the ground near the far wall, unconscious.

"You must go, Nitus," Modi urged, giving her brother a push and a hopeful smile. "Next time I see you, it will be in battle—a successful one, I pray to all the gods."

"The battle will be successful," Grenoble growled. "I'm only sorry it's taken this long." He hugged his sister one last time. Sheepishly, he murmured, "Oh, and I've changed my name to Grenoble, sis. After I ... left the nest, I took a new name to remind me of my roots, my home, and my oath to protect them both, no matter how far away my travels took me or how long it took."

"Hmm. Grenoble. I like it. It suits you," Modi said. She eyed her brother approvingly and then shoved him toward the dock. "Go on then, Grenoble. Get going, so you can return with your allies and free our nest of Methol and the Chaos Council's unbearable yoke."

Grenoble, still weakened from the beatings he had received earlier from his brother and the guards, stumbled toward the rushing river, but caught himself just before falling in.

Modi snickered and smothered a laugh. "I suggest the watercraft as your method of departure this time, brother. Falling into the river and floating downstream to the Crossroads is almost as bad as being thrown in half-dead, as happened last time you so unceremoniously departed our nest."

Grenoble scrambled onto the dock, then gingerly lowered

himself into the little boat. He fumbled with the rope holding the watercraft to the dock. Once the little boat came loose, he pushed off with one oar and threw a grin at his irrepressible sibling. "I'll take your wise suggestion, sister. Don't I always?" The vessel caught the current and moved rapidly downstream. He waved but wasn't sure his brave-hearted sister witnessed his farewell in the cave's gloom.

21

HEART BROTHERS

And so that's the current situation in my former nest, Keeper Olympe," Grenoble said, voice thick with fatigue. He stood wearily, shoulders hunched in pain, in the flickering torchlight of the Crossroads platform.

His anxious gaze bounced between the three people and one small poodle facing him. "Olympe, Grigory, Alex, Larry ... my friends, I'm sorry to say that Nyx's evil has infiltrated my former nest. My half-brother, King Methol, has taken my people down a dark path and is giving shelter and support to the Chaos Council villains who keep attacking this Crossroads. Our only choice—"

"Our only choice is to take the battle to them," interrupted Olympe. Eyeing Grenoble with compassion, she murmured, "Many of your kind will die, my old friend."

Grenoble's thick lips quivered, his eyes full of hopeful despair. "As you have wisely counseled me in the past, Olympe, sometimes, it's the cure that can kill you," he growled softly.

Larry padded over to the goblin and leaned into his side. "We'll win the battle to free your nest together, bud. Sounds like it'll solve the Crossroads problem we came here to help with, anyway. Nothing like killing two birds with one stone." The little poodle cringed inwardly at his poor analogy; probably would have been more diplomatic not to mention killing when many of those who would fall in the coming fight would be Grenoble's kinsmen. He flicked a glance at his friend. "Um, yeah … what I meant was…"

Grenoble snickered and patted his furry friend on the back. Larry staggered a little under the goblin's heavy hand, but kept his footing. "I know what you meant, you airhead," he said with a grin. "Thank you for the words of support, brother. I'm honored to have you fight at my side."

Larry fought to keep the pride he felt at Grenoble's words to himself, but doubted he succeeded, especially when he heard Alex snicker and saw Olympe's smile.

"Same here, brother," he replied. "Same here."

MORNING CAME ALL TOO SWIFTLY. No one had gotten any more sleep after Grenoble's miraculous escape and homecoming. Instead, Alex and her team, along with Olympe's lieutenants, spent the morning huddled in the war room planning their attack on the goblin nest. Everyone agreed it was likely the attackers were using the nest as their base of operations from which to attack the Grenoble Crossroads.

Grigory maintained that the Chaos Council members embedded in the goblin nest must have used a Crossroads further afield, before traveling overland and using one of the cave entrances scattered over the mountain to enter the nest. Olympe agreed with him; the little priestess nun was adamant that the traitors had not used her Crossroads for their nefarious purpose.

Alex recalled her Cousin Zoé's confession the day before. In both recent attacks, Morpheus had influenced the assistant Keeper to open the Grenoble Crossroads for the attackers. How could Olympe be sure those were the only occasions one of her people had fallen under the rogue god's sway?

Olympe glared at Alex and mind-spoke an angry retort. *"Because I'm sure, Alex. My word should be good enough for you, cousin."*

Alex raised her hands in mock surrender and grimaced a silent apology. Better to leave that one alone, she mused. Instead, she asked out loud, "You say another Crossroads is being used to transport the conspirators. Don't the other Keepers know about the danger Morpheus and his Chaos Council cronies present? Aren't they aware of the earlier attacks on *my* Crossroads? Why would they allow him ... them—"

Olympe, who had been studying the map of the cave system, put the map down with a snap and then flicked a meaningful glance at Alex. "Can we discuss this another time, dear? Now is the time to deal with our current situation, not wonder how it came to be."

Chastened, Alex agreed. "Of ... of course, Olympe. I meant no disrespect."

"I know you didn't, dear, but there are some secrets that must remain hidden, for now."

Her new cousin's mind-spoken words eased Alex's nerves. She mind-spoke her assurance. *"Okay, I understand."*

Olympe shook her head and replied, *"You don't understand yet, Alex, but you will. The short answer is that there are several Crossroads Keepers whose loyalty Hecate—and I, doubt. We suspect Nyx's supporters are using these particular Crossroads to access the earthly realm and travel around it surreptitiously."*

The warrior nun heaved a sigh. *"But that's a problem for another time."* She gave Alex a knowing smile. *"One we'll need your help with, of course, dear. Your unique powers will aid us in the coming battles against the forces of chaos."*

"Of course they will," Alex muttered quietly, but she nodded her understanding and acceptance. Looked like she wasn't as done with her divine death magic as she wished to be. She didn't even want to think about the other 'gift' she *may* have inherited from her Titan grandfather ... time magic. *Nah. Not possible. Damn it.*

22

KELPIES & KILLING

Alex stared in wide-eyed wonder at the herd of sleek sea creatures bobbing in the cave's rushing river. Powerful rear fins swished rhythmically, allowing the massive horse-like creatures to hold their places in the swift current. Foaming water gushed past their stationary bodies as if the creatures were boulders instead of ... whatever they were.

Olympe's silent laughter echoed in Alex's mind. *"These creatures are kelpies, my dear, in their aquatic form. That's why they have tails on the back end instead of legs."*

"Sooo, they're half horse and half ... uh, fish?" Alex murmured, nervously studying the majestic creatures.

The largest kelpie turned its massive head toward Alex. It rolled its eyes and snorted, as if insulted by Alex's assessment. With one powerful sweep of its tail, the creature reached the edge of the river, then climbed onto the riverbank, its enormous front hooves gouging deep divots in the sandy gravel. The kelpie's back end emerged from the water, hunching and flattening, like a seal's body.

Alex gulped, but stood her ground, her face carefully blank. Her recent reintroduction to the supernatural world had quickly taught her never to show fear. Otherwise, whatever not-so-mytho-logical creature you faced would sense it and run right over you. Often literally.

The kelpie studied Alex, its large, fiery red eyes narrowed in annoyance. "We are shifters, Keeper Alex, just like your Hell-hound lover, Conor." The creature's booming voice echoed off the cave's stone walls, causing reverberations that quivered in the gut, as if a massive drum had sounded. Crimson highlights in the kelpie's short, midnight-black coat glinted in the flickering torch-light. The kelpie smiled, displaying several rows of razor-sharp teeth.

Alex bit back a scream when Larry raced forward and launched himself onto the kelpie's muscled shoulders. Before she could rescue her brave, if foolhardy, Familiar, Larry wagged his tail and planted himself on the kelpie's broad back.

Larry grinned and said, "Hi Lir. Long time no see. Oh, and stop trying to frighten my newbie Keeper, bud." He scampered up the kelpie's neck, grabbed a mouthful of the creature's long, seaweed-like mane and tugged gently. "She's not gonna fall for your 'I'm a terrifying supernatural creature' shit, dude. I've taught her to know better than that."

The kelpie rolled its glowing eyes, then twisted its long neck around to gaze directly at the small poodle perched calmly on its back. "Ahhh, stop spoiling me' fun, boyo. It's not often I get to terrify a wee raw newbie lass."

The creature's thick Irish accent gave Alex some trouble, but the friendship between Larry and the kelpie was obvious. She'd have to grill her Familiar later about what other amazing, dangerous—and supposedly mythological creatures were really out there ... and just how many he had made friends with.

Olympe hustled past Alex, hopping spryly onto the gravel beach and striding toward the kelpie. The enormous creature dwarfed the tiny woman. When the warrior nun placed both hands over her heart and bowed her head, Alex's eyes widened.

"Lir, it's a pleasure to see you again, my old friend," Olympe said. She gestured toward the other kelpies in the river, all still holding their positions against the rushing waters with lazy sweeps of their massive tails. "I'm happy to see your herd is still together and doing well. Thank you for heeding my call—"

The kelpie interrupted Olympe's thanks with a shake of its mighty head. "No need to thank me, Keeper Olympe," he replied. "You know well that you once saved me' sister's life when a pack of water demons invaded our aquatic pasturelands. It was your powerful magic that helped us banish the damn things back to the Underworld, where they belong." Lir placed one massive hoof forward and bowed. "I promised you then my herd would fight by your side whenever needed. I gladly honor that oath, my friend."

Olympe stepped forward and patted Lir's heavily muscled shoulder, smiling up at the enormous creature. "Your herd's help is both appreciated and needed, Lir. Nyx's dark shadows are approaching and we must banish her accomplices from my Crossroads."

Lir gently nuzzled the diminutive woman's shoulder, then whinnied, his eyes glowing crimson in the cave's dim light. "Always a pleasure, my friend. You know how we kelpies love a good fight."

Alex could swear she heard gleeful anticipation in Lir's words. She rolled her eyes and sighed. *Here's yet another blood-thirsty supernatural creature to add to my growing list,* she mused wryly. The memory of an earlier battle surfaced; she had once witnessed fearsome unicorns happily rampaging through hordes of undead Regenerants during the battle at her aunt's funeral. The unicorns' pure white coats had become stained with blood as they enthusiastically ripped apart their enemies with their sharp teeth and hooves. Thoughtfully considering the half-horse kelpie before her, Alex wondered if blood-thirsty behavior was a supernatural equine thing. *Who knew?*

"It's a supernatural thing, Alex, not just an equine one." Olympe

mind-spoke her reply to Alex's curious thoughts. *"The supernatural world has been in a battle for survival against Nyx's forces of chaos for millennia."* The warrior nun shrugged and gave Alex a small grin. *"It's a good thing we all enjoy the fight."*

Eyes widening at the anticipatory gleam in her cousin's deep blue eyes, Alex merely gave a resigned shrug. "Okay. I got it. It's just that, after two major battles in the past several months, I *was* hoping for a little less war and a little more peace at my Crossroads, at least for a while."

"Aren't we all?" Olympe replied simply. The small woman smiled as a pair of muscular arms covered in Celtic tattoos snaked around her shoulders, pulling her into a fierce hug.

"But now is the time for war, my love," purred the handsome man currently enveloping Olympe in his arms. Raven-black hair curled damply around the man's massive shoulders, while tanned, tattoo-covered skin rippled over a well-muscled, shirtless torso. The man's luminous brown eyes, gazed fondly down at the tiny woman in his arms. He dropped an affectionate kiss on Olympe's head, then dove smoothly into the rushing river.

Alex stared in amazement when a massive horse's head rose from the river's depths—exactly where the man had dived in moments ago. *Damn. Kelpies really are shifters,* she mused. She glanced over at Olympe, whose warm gaze remained fixed on the man-turned-kelpie, and wondered.

But nah, her cousin was a nun, for the gods' sake. Kind of. Wasn't she?

"I'm no more a nun than you are, Alex," Olympe murmured, her lips curved in a cat-like grin. She threw one last lingering glance at her kelpie friend and turned to face Alex. "I'm a priestess of Hecate and an oath-bound Keeper of this Crossroads—just as you are of yours, dear." The small woman's eyes twinkled up at Alex. "And it's a good thing Hecate doesn't require celibacy of her priestesses, or our family line would have died out years ago and we would have missed out on all the fun."

"But I thought you, um, were ... are a nun, as well?" Alex stammered. "After all, you wear a habit most of the time. And you *are* the Abbess of the honking great big abbey over our heads, right?"

"I am not and never was a nun," Olympe replied with a chuckle. "However, my fellow priestesses and I have had to disguise ourselves as nuns for so long that 'coming out' as pagan priestesses now that it wouldn't cause a death sentence seems rather passé, don't you think?" She smiled, her blue eyes dancing with merriment. "Besides, it's hard to break a centuries-old habit, my dear."

Alex burst out laughing at Olympe's clever play on words. She'd only known her newfound cousin for a few days, but she knew this wise and very brave woman had already joined her heart family. She silently vowed to do whatever it took to protect this tiny not-nun and help her save her Crossroads from Nyx's chaos-bringers.

LATER THAT DAY, the team put their battle plans into action. The herd of kelpies swam effortlessly upstream, making quick progress against the river cave's strong current. Their long, sinuous bodies carried over a hundred fighters between them. Alex still couldn't get over the image of the kelpie herd's already massive bodies elongating until the creatures resembled monstrous snakes. Each of the kelpies carried at least ten fighters on its back with ease. *Freaking amazing.*

"Not amazing, just reality," Larry snarked. "I thought you studied ancient history in college?" Larry eyed Alex doubtfully from his forward position, crouched between Lir's massive shoulders. "Kelpies can stretch their bodies to accommodate as many warriors as needed when heading into battle. It's one of their supernatural 'things'".

Alex rolled her eyes at her sarcastic Familiar. "I studied ancient *human* history, you dork." She patted Lir's slick side. "Not *supernatural* history, so there were no kelpies or unicorns, vampires or trolls—or talking dogs, for that matter—in any of my college history courses." She tilted her head in consideration. "Although I have to say, the classes would have been a whole lot more interesting if they *had* included those things."

Larry snickered at her answer, then started in surprise when Crazy Sam poked his head through a solid stone wall to their right.

"You're almost to the nest, you buncha' yahoos," the ghost whispered, his leathery face crinkled with worry. "And the goblins are expecting ya'll. Lotsa angry little green men with pointy weapons in the cave up ahead."

Well, shit. They must have a leak, Alex brooded. This was supposed to be a surprise attack; someone at the Crossroads had warned the goblins they were coming. They'd have to deal with the traitor later, though. She shook her head to clear her mind, then faced forward, gaze intent and body tensed for action. "Showtime," she muttered softly.

Shouts rose ahead as the kelpies rounded the last corner. Alex's heart sank when she spotted the heaving mass of battle-ready goblins awaiting their arrival. Someone had definitely spilled the beans. *Crap.*

Alex called her Keeper staff with barely a thought. There was no turning back now. Lir, who only had Alex and Larry on his back, hung back, letting the other kelpies and their riders charge into the fray. Fire-tipped arrows filled the air around the kelpies. Neighs and screams of pain echoed in the tunnel, but the kelpies swam onward, straight toward the goblin swarm. Alex narrowed her eyes and studied the crowd, soon spotting adult-sized attackers sprinkled amongst the child-sized goblins.

Larry muttered, *"Looks like Grenoble's sister was right. Nyx's Chaos Council cronies have partnered with the goblin nest."*

Alex nodded mutely, watching the battle with growing horror. There was no more time to think. Just fight. The massive kelpies shook off most of the arrows; the armored scales covering their undulating bodies gave them protection. However, several kelpies had taken arrows to their horse-like necks. Blood streamed from their wounds, but the injuries seemed merely to enrage the enormous creatures. After dropping their riders onto the floating wooden docks jutting out into the river, the kelpies brayed their rage, eyes flaring crimson in the flickering torchlight. Their massive tails raked across the stone wharf, hurling dozens of goblins into the frothing river, where sharp kelpie teeth and hooves ripped the drowning creatures apart.

Olympe's war cry reached Alex's battered ears. She spotted the warrior nun jumping nimbly onto the wharf. The tiny woman moved like lightning, leaping over swinging kelpie tails, and stabbing any goblins the kelpies missed.

Alex rose carefully to her feet on Lir's massive back. As per their plan, the chief kelpie trod water just out of reach of the goblins' arrows. She felt a strong surge of magical power and looked down to see Larry pressed tightly against her legs, his body surrounded by a golden haze. "Thanks, bud," she murmured. Raising her own power, she channeled it through her Keeper staff.

Crackling bolts of blue Keeper magic, entwined with her red necromantic magic, shot from the large crystal at the tip of Alex's staff. She took careful aim over the heads of the goblins and shot lightning at the closest Chaos Council fighter. The man screamed and fell; his blackened body was soon trampled under the heavy boots of goblins still streaming out of the tunnels toward the battle.

Taking aim at another Chaos Council fighter, she took that one down as well. Alex admitted Olympe had had the right idea when she'd convinced her to remain at a distance and target the taller, and much more magically dangerous, Chaos Council fighters. Alex knew her magical talents worked best at a distance. Plus, she had little hand-to-hand combat experience. Yet. *Sigh.*

"There you are, Keeper." A familiar oily voice slithered into Alex's mind. *"You and I have unfinished business to settle, cousin."*

Raking her gaze across the heaving battle scene, Alex searched for the god who had promised to kill her the next time they met. Finally, she spotted Morpheus tucked into a shallow nook in the cave's wall across the river from the ongoing fight. Morpheus's grim smile promised vengeance.

Before Alex could aim her staff, a massive onslaught of nightmares tore through her mind. *Her heart family screaming, falling, dying ... being ripped apart by the massive jaws of nightmare creatures. Larry's body, still and bloody, stretched out on a cold stone floor.* Her eyes squeezed shut against the visions, and she fought to regain control, knowing in her heart that most of what she 'saw' in her mind was false. Hopefully, tearfully, all of it.

A faint but persistent bark penetrated her horrifying visions. *Larry.* He was still alive! If that nightmare was false, so were the others, she desperately assured herself. Digging deep into her core, Alex willed the nightmares to cease.

Morpheus's vile laughter filled her head. *"Not a chance, Keeper. I've got you in my nightmare realm now. You'll die first, but I promise your family will follow,"* the god of nightmares snarled.

"No, they damn well won't, you bastard!" Alex screamed. She forced her eyes open and focused her defiant gaze on the rogue god. With a supreme effort of will and not a little magic, she threw the divine asshole forcefully out of her mind.

Aiming her staff at Morpheus, Alex pulled magic from the depths of her soul and poured all of it into the staff's smooth wood. She gasped when a dozen massive bolts of blue, red, and even black lightning shot from the crystal at the staff's tip and arrowed toward the crevice where the rogue god sheltered.

Morpheus's eyes widened as the multicolored bolts of lightning surged toward him, fear glinting in his gaze.

With an ear-splitting boom, the nook sheltering Morpheus exploded. Dust rose as chunks of rock flew everywhere, some splashing into the water around the kelpie Alex rode. She coughed and searched the now-destroyed crevice where the god of nightmares had stood, but nothing remained. As the air cleared, Alex's jaw dropped when she spotted the massive hole in the rock wall ... all that was left of Morpheus's hiding place. Icy fear slithered down her spine. *Have I killed a god?* She wondered. *Holy freaking shit!*

"I don't think he's dead, but you sure gave that jerk a scare," Larry muttered as he eyed the massive hole. "Unlike most gods, Morpheus and his Oneiroi brothers can apparate, which means—"

"I know what it means, you dingleberry," Alex interrupted, her eyes still searching the smoking hole for any sign of a body. "But maybe he didn't disappear quickly enough."

"We can only hope," Larry replied, but his worried gaze belied his words. "If you've badly injured or killed a god—even one on Nyx's side—there just might be hell to pay, Alex. Gods don't like it when 'lesser beings' injure or kill one of their own."

"Been there, done that," Alex replied with an evil grin as she recalled her journey to the Underworld to battle her mage father and his lover, Nyx. "Even bought the t-shirt."

23

LONG LIVE THE GOBLIN QUEEN

A lex remained on Lir's back as the battle for control of the goblin nest raged on. She identified Chaos Council fighters by their height, since they stood several feet taller than the child-sized goblins. Her new superpowered lightning bolts allowed her to take out many of the Chaos Council fighters quickly. Soon, weariness threatened to overwhelm her, and blackness wavered at the edge of her vision. She didn't know how much longer she could continue pouring magical energy into her Keeper staff. Larry slumped at her feet. Alex could still feel a trickle of his golden energy flowing into her, but her magical Familiar had little more to give, either.

Just when Alex despaired of success, a roar went up among the goblins. She shifted her gaze to the wharf and saw that most of the goblins had stopped fighting and were crowded around a barren circle, which had been cleared of live fighters and dead bodies. Squinting in the dim light, she gasped when she recognized a familiar figure. "Holy crap! Grenoble's in that ring!"

Larry's excited yelp told Alex he had spotted his friend, as well. The brave goblin stood in the center of a makeshift arena. Grenoble's chest heaved and black blood flowed sluggishly from several wounds. His face was blank, but his huge emerald-green eyes blazed with fury. Two other goblins shared the arena with Grenoble, each also sporting injuries, but they remained upright and deadly.

Anticipatory murmurs swept through the goblin crowd when Grenoble strode toward the smaller, female goblin in the ring, then placed himself protectively by her side. She flicked him a quick grin, but didn't lower her weapon.

Larry cocked his head as he studied the makeshift arena. "That goblin next to Grenoble must be his sister, Princess Modi," Larry whispered to Alex. "The bigger one is Methol, their dick of a half-brother and the current goblin king." He snickered, his avid gaze fixed on the grim tableau. "Looks like a change of leadership is about to take place," he murmured.

Alex considered the larger goblin. King Methol. She knew the traitorous bastard had staged a coup and stolen the throne from Grenoble over a decade ago. After his successful coup, Methol had beaten his brother severely, then flung his bloodied body into the cave's fast-flowing river, thinking him dead. Methol was both taller and bulkier than his siblings. He glared hatefully at Grenoble and Modi and spat in the dirt at their feet. Blood and several teeth came out with the spittle. Methol strode confidently forward, but couldn't prevent a grimace of pain as he did so.

"He's badly wounded, Alex," Larry whispered. "But he's still the most dangerous creature in that circle. Unfortunately."

Alex merely nodded, watching the drama unfold with wide, anxious eyes. By this point, the fighting had ceased. All eyes were on the makeshift arena where the current and former goblin kings faced off. Alex raked her gaze over the crowd, noting with grim satisfaction that no Chaos Council members remained. The ones she and her team hadn't killed must have escaped into the tunnels. Larry poked Alex with his nose, turning her attention back to the leadership challenge about to take place.

"YOU KEEP TURNING up like a bad penny, brother," Methol growled. "Must I kill you—yet again—to prove my right to the throne?"

"You can try, Methol," Grenoble replied with a bloody grin. "But I'm afraid we'll have to save our rematch for later ... if you live through the next few minutes, that is. There's another who wishes to challenge you for the throne first."

Methol glanced between his two siblings, his ugly face wrinkled with confusion. "What are you talking about, brother? Who must I fight before you?"

The smaller female goblin strolled casually forward and smiled at her furious half-brother. "Me, Methol. You must fight me." Modi raised her sword and shouted, "I hereby challenge you for the throne, brother!"

Immediately, waves of sound echoed off the cave's rock walls as the assembled goblins either cheered or booed. The crowd jostled closer to the makeshift arena, each goblin eager to watch the leadership battle.

Alex grinned when she realized there were far more cheers than boos. Most of the crowd had their hopeful gaze on Modi. His subjects obviously hated Methol. Alex was worried, though. Modi may be brave, but she was wounded and much smaller than her massive half-brother.

"Make way, make way!" A heavily-muscled goblin guard shoved a narrow path through the crowd, with a smaller goblin trailing along in his wake. Once the guard had cleared a path to the arena, the smaller goblin squeezed past his bulk and stalked into the ring.

"Uh oh," Larry breathed. "That's Yima, Grenoble's mother— and mother of the other two goblins in the arena, as well." He snorted in disgust. "She's pure evil."

"Yeah, I kinda figured that," Alex replied, her eyes fixed on the dramatic scene unfolding before them. "What kind of mother would pit one sibling against another in a bid for more power?"

"That one, that's who," Larry muttered in disgust.

"Shhhh," Alex whispered, placing a restraining hand on her canine Familiar. "Yima is saying something."

"Nitus, Modi ... I'm horrified that either of you would challenge your brother, the rightful ruler of this kingdom, in this vulgar way," Yima growled, glaring at her children and gesturing angrily. "You two traitors have brought danger and bloodshed to our nest. You both deserve to die—"

"No, you deserve to die, mother," Modi spat. "*You* are the one who whispered poison into Methol's ears for years until he finally agreed to betray and kill his half-brother and steal his throne. *You* are the one who has forced our nest to bow to the Chaos Council—who, by the way, has been using our nest as a base from which to attack our neighbors and friends at the Grenoble Crossroads. For generations, we lived in peace with the Crossroads community, until you and your bastard son welcomed Nyx's co-conspirators in, thus tainting our nest with their evil."

Yima's expression remained defiant as her daughter flung accusations at her. The goblins surrounding the makeshift arena shifted nervously, muttering their displeasure, most eyeing Yima with open hatred.

"Enough!" Grenoble's shouted command restored silence. "Everyone here knows the dark turn our nest took under Yima's malign influence. Our late king—my father—did all he could to obstruct her nefarious ambitions for decades until his untimely death." The goblin bowed his head in sorrow. "I only wish I had paid closer attention to my father's many dire warnings. If I had, I would have been ready for Methol's challenge."

Grenoble cast a sorrow-filled gaze over the goblins crowded around the arena. "I give you all my deepest apologies. My inattention forced you to spend the past decade burdened under the power-hungry yoke of my tyrannical half-brother and my black-hearted mother."

"Neatly done," Larry murmured, gazing proudly at his goblin friend. "Grenoble just reminded everyone that Yima became queen by marriage only, and that her youngest son, Methol, was born on the wrong side of the blanket, so to speak. Not a drop of royal blood flows through that asshole's veins."

The sound started softly but soon built to a deafening roar. Hundreds of boots and spears pounded on the wharf's flagstone floor, reaching a rapid-fire crescendo before breaking off suddenly. Silence enveloped the crowd, the air fraught with tension and hope.

The silence was broken when a muscle-bound goblin guard pushed his way into the arena. He strode forward and stopped mere feet from Modi and Grenoble. He nodded respectfully to Grenoble, then bowed deeply before Modi, his long nose almost touching the ground. Upon rising, the guard flicked a furious glare at Yima and Methol, then returned his gaze to Modi and bowed his head respectfully. "Queen Modi, I am General Garrus, commander of the royal guard. My troops stand ready to remove these traitors to the dungeons, Your Highness."

Yima snarled, "How dare you, Garrus?!" Her enraged gaze raked over the goblin general. "You dare to defy Methol, your rightful ruler, in favor of my traitorous daughter? Everyone knows my son won the throne fairly—"

"Oh no, he didn't, Mother—and you know it," Modi purred, her thick lips curved in a smug smile. "Our ancient laws state that, in order for a coup to be successful, the current ruler must die at the challenger's hands." She pointed a finger at Grenoble. "Yet here my brother stands, very much alive."

Snickers and nods of agreement spread through the goblin crowd. Modi pulled a reluctant Grenoble to the center of the makeshift arena and raised his arm in the air. "Here stands your rightful king, brethren."

The crowd roared their approval while Grenoble shook his head, horror dawning on his face. "But I don't ... I can't—"

"Never fear, brother," Modi said, her voice raised to carry to their rapt audience. "Over the past terrible decade, I have spent much time studying the ancient texts and laws of our people." She patted her bemused brother's shoulder reassuringly and gave him a sly grin. "There is one other legitimate way for the throne to change hands. The current king can abdicate and appoint a new ruler. However, this route requires the ruler to choose a replacement from among his or her *full-blooded* family members."

Understanding dawned, and Grenoble gazed at his brilliant sister in wonder. Quickly, he grabbed Modi's hand, raised it in the air, and shouted, "Hear me, my people! By my royal oath, I hereby abdicate my throne and appoint my full-blood sister, Modi, to rule in my stead."

Grenoble stepped back and bowed low to his sister. "The king has abdicated. Long live the Queen!"

Hearing his rousing words, the crowd went wild with applause. Hooting, hollering, and stamping their feet, the goblins chorused, "Long live Queen Modi!"

"No! Stop that right now!" An urgent shout cut through the crowd's merriment. A gunshot immediately followed it, deafening in the cave's close confines. A muttering quiet descended immediately, everyone craning their necks to identify the shooter. Methol stood to one side of the arena, arm raised, a still-smoking pistol in his grip. He smiled confidently, but the hand holding the pistol shook slightly.

Methol had one last chance to gain back control—and keep his kingdom—and he knew it. "I've been your king for the last decade," he started, but loud jeers drowned him out. He tried again, voice pitched to override the jeers of his people. "My sister and brother are liars and traitors to the throne ... my throne."

"It's not your throne, asshole," shouted a voice from the crowd.

"It never was," screamed another.

"Methol is our rightful king," responded a very brave soul who obviously hadn't read the crowd at all. That foolish goblin quickly became the recipient of jeers and painful punches from his fellow nestlings.

Modi shouted over the jeering crowd, "Calm down, everyone! Calm down!" Once the crowd had quieted, she straightened and gave a regal nod. "I will prove my right to rule. Even though, by our ancient laws, I have the right to it now, I'm willing to fight for my throne. I call on the laws of karma to prove my right to rule!"

Approaching her sneering half-brother, Modi drew off a leather glove and tossed it on the ground in front of him. She gazed resolutely up into his furious face and said, "I challenge you for the throne, Methol. May the Fates determine the winner."

The crowd roared with excitement. They would get their fight to the death, after all.

Larry muttered, "Bloodthirsty lot, these goblins."

Alex nodded in silent agreement, her eyes glued to the dramatic scene in the makeshift arena.

TWENTY BLOODY, violent minutes later, Modi placed her boot on the prone form of her half-brother and pulled her sword from his bloody chest. She wiped sweat and blood from her brow, peering down blank-faced as Methol heaved a final, gasping breath.

Tears mixed with the smeared blood on Modi's cheeks as she gazed down at her dead half-brother. *What a waste of a life. Of many lives.* "It is done," she murmured. She sighed and shook her head, then paced to the center of the arena and raised a triumphant fist to the cheering goblins. "By the laws of our people *and* by the laws of karma, I declare the throne mine."

The goblin crowd went wild, screaming their approval. "Hurrah! Long live Queen Modi!"

The new goblin queen smiled at her subjects, then spotted her mother, who was weaving her way unobtrusively through the crowd toward an exit tunnel. She raised her arm and pointed at Yima's retreating form. "Guards, seize her!"

General Garrus and his royal guards pushed their way through the rowdy crowd toward the retreating goblin. Before they could reach her, Yima cried out in pain and fell, her squat body disappearing from view. After a confused moment, the jostling crowd around her parted, revealing Yima's prone form, which was surrounded by a growing pool of blood. A short sword protruded from her back.

No one owned up to making the killing blow, but Modi had cultivated many supporters among her people over the past decade. One of them had obviously saved their new queen the trouble of a trial and execution.

Her worries about the outcome of the fight for the throne over, Alex grinned fiercely. "Yay," she whispered. "Go, good guys."

"Good for them," Larry replied, snorting in agreement. "That saves a whole heap of trouble. Modi's gonna have enough problems rooting out her late brother's supporters and freeing the nest from the Chaos Council's clutches. She doesn't need a deposed half-brother or martyred mother locked up in the dungeon and whispering treason to anyone they can."

SEVERAL HOURS LATER, Alex smothered a sigh and sipped her wine. She and Larry were seated at the head table in the goblin nest's massive dining cave. Long silken banners containing scenes of battles past cascaded down the rocky walls, while massive iron chandeliers hung from the high ceiling, each flickering with light from hundreds of fat white candles.

Alex winced as Crazy Sam flitted between the chandeliers, hooting in glee. She hoped the ghost didn't mount one of the damn things and try to ride it. She wasn't sure if ghosts could feel flames, but didn't want to find out now. A crazy cowboy ghost with his ass literally on fire flitting around in a cave full of drunk goblins would probably not be a good thing, she surmised.

The head table rested on a raised platform overlooking dozens of rows of tables, which were currently filled with jubilant goblins, all loudly celebrating the ascension of their new queen. Food and drink flowed freely, and the din only gained volume as the hours passed.

Olympe had snuck off with Lir immediately after the fight for the throne. She had given Alex a merry wave as Lir carried her downstream on his broad back, his tail propelling them along at a fast clip. From the mischievous glint in her cousin's eyes, Alex was sure she was now back at the Crossroads, getting up to some very un-nun-like activity with her kelpie shifter boyfriend. *Talk about a cougar,* she mused with a quiet snicker. Alex shook her head and took another sip of wine. *I better be careful,* she mused wryly, *or I won't be able to ride a kelpie back to the Crossroads without risking falling off into the raging river. Drunk kelpie driving. Sigh.*

Olympe's departure had left Grigory and Alex in joint charge of the remaining Crossroads warriors. Neither of them could refuse their erstwhile hosts' invitation to a victory celebration without risking grave insult.

Grigory, seated further down the head table, was currently flirting outrageously with a tall, attractive man to his right. Alex thought the man's name was Stefan, vaguely recalling Olympe introducing him as one of the abbey scribes during her whirlwind tour of the abbey the previous day. At the other end of the table, the lean form of Lieutenant Allard sat, back ramrod straight. The former French policeman and current undead Regenerant had massive amounts of dried blood—his own and that of those he had valiantly fought against—splattered across his starched white shirt. However, he wore it well, smiling and conversing easily in rapid French with the goblin on his right.

Alex stifled a yawn and wondered how much longer she had to

stay for politeness' sake. She didn't want to offend their goblin hosts by being the first to leave the celebration. Besides Olympe, of course. *Sigh.*

A gentle hand on her arm pulled Alex out of her semi-intoxicated musings. She turned to the goblin on her left and smiled. "Queen Modi. Thanks again for inviting us to your, um, coronation celebration—"

The little goblin grinned and patted Alex's hand. "No need to be polite, Alex. You can call it like it is. I just killed my half-brother in a bloody fight to the death and wrested the throne from his cooling hands." Modi tilted her head and smiled. "At least, that's the way I'll ensure our bards recount the noble history of Queen Modi to future generations," she murmured slyly.

Modi giggled and leaned into Alex, who knew the little goblin had polished off at least three massive pitchers of wine single-handedly. The new queen was totally sloshed.

Poking Alex none-too-gently in the ribs, Modi whispered, "No need to mention my other brother's abdication and appointment of me to the throne to the historians, right?"

Alex leaned away from the queen's wine-soaked breath and nodded. "Uh, right. I mean, you *did* fight Methol for the throne, just to make doubly sure it was yours in the eyes of your people, after all."

The goblin queen frowned and pursed her lips in consideration. "Nah. Nitus ... I mean, Grenoble abdicated and appointed me queen, fair and square. I didn't need to fight Methol for the throne." Modi's large, round eyes, suddenly sober and hard, met Alex's directly. "But I *wanted* to fight him. My brother tortured me for years, Alex. I spent more time in the dungeons than in my bedchamber over the last decade. My back bears the scars of his displeasure. That prick got what was coming to him."

Alex saw no remorse, only past pain and current triumph in the goblin queen's now-steady gaze.

"Yup," Alex replied, meeting Modi's eyes squarely. "I see what you mean, and I totally agree."

"Yes ... yes, I think you do, Keeper," the queen murmured as she searched Alex's eyes. "I know about your late father's soul death at your hands, Alex," she added, her words soft and her gaze compassionate.

Alex fought to keep the shock from her face and asked, "Does *everyone* in the supernatural world know about that?"

"Just those who matter, Alex ... on both sides of the war for this realm." With that cryptic remark, the queen stood and banged her empty pewter wine goblet on the table. "Order! Order in the room!" She shouted.

The raucous goblin crowd quieted immediately, turning respectful gazes toward their new queen. Silence soon reigned in the enormous dining hall.

Modi refilled her wine goblet and held it high. "I thank you all for joining me in celebrating our victory. We lost many good goblin brethren, but our kingdom is now free of the despotic rule of my half-brother and the malign influence of our mother, Yima. May their souls rot in the deepest bowels of the Underworld!"

Jubilant cheers rang against the cave's high ceiling.

The new queen patted the air, quieting her goblin subjects. "That said, we still have lots of work to do." She cast a fierce gaze over the assembled crowd. "Those of you who supported my brother had to know the true depths of his betrayal. You benefited from his largesse, allied yourself with his tyrannical rule, and aided his unholy alliance with Nyx's earthbound Chaos Council henchmen."

Shocked murmurs swept the room, the assembled goblins now eyeing each other with distrust.

"But I won't have anyone—you hear me—anyone taking revenge on fellow goblins," the queen commanded, slapping the table hard for emphasis. "Evil not fed starves, darkness not tolerated disburses. Neither will get sustenance or shelter in this nest any longer. Do you hear me?" Modi's command rang from the walls.

All her subject's heads nodded as one. Alex thought she heard a few sighs of relief sprinkled throughout the crowd. She wondered if Modi would truly allow her late brother's supporters to remain free as long as they committed no further crimes. She doubted evil would die so easily as that.

"However," the queen continued, a feral grin curving her thick lips, "I have spent the last decade watching the goings-on in this kingdom. I know, as the humans say of their Santa, 'who has been naughty or nice.'"

The crowd shifted and muttered, disquieted by their new queen's warning words.

A casual wave of Modi's hand brought forth several dozen royal guards, who marched with purpose into the massive dining hall. More than a dozen terrified goblins raced for the nearest exit, but the guards captured them all quickly.

The guards were not gentle when rounding up the traitors. Their screams of pain and terror would haunt Alex's dreams for weeks. She glanced up and caught the queen's pensive gaze on her. Trying to hide her distress, she muttered, "I understand why you had to do that, but still..."

Modi smiled at Alex and mind-spoke her reply. *"Yes, I think you do understand, my new friend."* The queen shook her head slowly, her expressive eyes sad. *"But please, Keeper, don't think the war for this realm is over. I'll do my bit here by rooting out the traitors in my nest, hunting down the last of the Council members allied with my late brother, and rebuilding our alliance with Olympe and her Crossroads community."*

She patted Alex's hand and spoke her warning out loud. "But you, my dear, have your work cut out for you. There will be battles and hard decisions ahead for you, I fear, and you'll need all your considerable powers to succeed against Nyx." The queen brushed Alex's cheek softly and murmured, "You and your loyal supporters will win, Alex, I'm sure of it. But only if you seek and listen to the wisdom of your elders and stop denying and stifling your divine powers will we win this war."

Overcome by the queen's stern warning, Alex merely nodded and lowered her gaze.

"She's right, you know, Alex." Larry's familiar voice mind-spoke his agreement with the queen's sage advice. *"You can't deny or suppress your divine powers any longer, Alex."* He snorted and gave his magical partner a severe side-eye. *"And you should absolutely listen to your elders—you remember how much older I am than you, right?"*

"Oh, shut up, you fur ball," Alex retorted, scratching Larry's ears affectionately. "I know you're an ancient Familiar, bud. In fact, I'm pretty sure I've seen signs of senility—"

Before Alex could finish her teasing, Larry barked and then launched himself off his chair and took off, with Grenoble in hot pursuit. The two friends raced the length of the raised platform and headed for the closest exit.

"I'll deal with your insults later, Alex. Grenoble says the chef has promised us a huge doggie bag for the trip back to the Crossroads." With those parting mind-spoken words, Larry and his partner in crime disappeared toward the kitchens.

24

___

A DREAMLESS SLEEP

The return journey was uneventful. Every single kelpie head hung low in exhaustion as the massive creatures drifted with the current toward the Crossroads. Upon arriving back at the gravel beach from which they had departed many hours earlier, Alex and her team slid off the kelpies' backs, mumbled their thanks and goodbyes, and trudged wearily up the tunnel toward the abbey, and their beds.

Alex almost made it to her room without running into anyone who might delay her much-needed rest. However, just before she turned the corner into the hallway leading to her bedroom, she heard soft murmurs ahead. Recognizing Olympe's voice, she paused. She debated turning around and finding another team member to bunk with, but Larry's side-eye and derisive snort forced her to continue toward her room.

"Good evening, Alex," Olympe said as Alex approached. She smiled down at Larry and added, "It's good to see you, too." The diminutive warrior nun lounged against the wall right next to Alex's bedroom door. Lir stood beside her, his massive human form filling the corridor and blocking any hope of a quick getaway. *Dammit.*

Olympe's smug grin and Lir's possessive hand on the much shorter woman's shoulder confirmed Alex's suspicions. Her elderly cousin and even more ancient lover had been getting it on, while Alex, Grigory, and the rest of the team had been suffering through the hours-long celebration party at the goblin nest.

"Hi Olympe," Alex replied, giving her cousin an uncomfortable finger wave. "Hope you two have been, uh…" She winced and stopped talking, not at all sure where she'd been planning to go with her comment. *Awwwkward.*

Olympe burst out laughing while Lir just smirked, humor lighting his gaze.

When she finally stopped chuckling, Olympe shook her head with a grin. "Oh, Alex, you're so funny. Your suspicions are correct. Lir and I are lovers, on occasion." The tiny woman leaned into Lir's muscular form with a happy sigh. "We've been seeing each other on and off for a few centuries. And yes, I know I look decades older than this handsome hunk of man—kelpie beside me. However, it's Lir who is robbing the cradle."

Alex glanced at Lir, who nodded solemnly, although a twinkle glinted deep in his eyes. "Olympe is a mere youngster compared to me, Keeper. I'm old enough to have witnessed Queen Boudicca's rebellion against the Romans … nice woman, by the way. Shame about her execution."

After doing some quick mental arithmetic, Alex's eyes widened. If Lir had witnessed the Celtic uprising in Britannia, that meant he was over two thousand years old. A true Elder. She probably should be a lot more respectful of the ancient shifter currently cuddling and making smoochie noises with her cousin. *Well, damn.*

Finally, Olympe parted from her handsome beau after a final lingering kiss. Lir grinned at Alex, then loped down the corridor, heading back to the river and his waiting kelpie herd. Olympe opened Alex's bedroom door and preceded her inside. Alex followed with a sigh, realizing sleep would have to wait. Her cousin obviously wanted a full report of the happenings at the goblin banquet.

～

Fifteen minutes later, Alex stifled a yawn and finished her report. "Queen Modi has already imprisoned her brother's supporters and promised to hunt down any Chaos Council stragglers hiding out in the tunnels. She told me she'll pass along anything the Chaos Council idiots reveal when they're, uh, questioned."

Alex winced, knowing the goblin queen's guards would use whatever means necessary to elicit every scrap of information from Nyx's co-conspirators. She was very sure there would be blood involved. And pain. Lots of pain. With a resigned shrug, she moved on. Such was the supernatural world she now inhabited. "Anyway, the only other thing we need to discuss is that the goblins definitely knew we were coming. Which means we must have a traitor in our midst—" She added reluctantly.

"I thought as much," Olympe replied dryly. "I have my suspicions about who betrayed us, but we can deal with that in the morning." She patted Alex's hand gently. "You look exhausted, my dear. I'll send a watcher to keep an eye on you as you sleep, since, from what you've told me, Morpheus most likely got away." Giving Alex a sharp nod, she added, "The bastard could still return and pull you—or others on our team—into a never-ending nightmare."

Alex nodded her agreement, then heaved a sigh when the door closed behind her seemingly indefatigable cousin. She stripped off her filthy clothes and threw them into the still-burning fireplace. They smelled of blood and fish, wine and sweat. After a lightning-quick shower, she fell into bed and closed her eyes. The door opened quietly as she hovered on the precipice of sleep. The gentle voice of her French police officer friend assured Alex that he would guard her well as she slept.

"That's right, you Regenerants don't need to sleep," Alex mumbled. She pulled the covers over her head, then a thought struck, shocking her awake. She sat up and gazed worriedly around her small room. "Where's Larry? I haven't seen him since we got back." Wincing, she rubbed her head, regretting the many glasses of wine she'd consumed earlier that evening. "In fact, I haven't seen him since he and Grenoble took off to the kitchen in search of a doggie bag back at the goblin nest."

Leonard smiled and lowered himself onto the upright chair in the corner. "Never fear, my friend. That Familiar of yours always lands on his paws. Larry and Grenoble arrived back at the Crossroads ensconced on the royal barge, which was loaded full of their favorite snacks and meats, by command of Queen Modi." The Regenerant snorted a laugh. "It'll be a wonder if those two don't eat themselves sick over the next few days."

Alex heaved a sigh of both relief and frustration. She needed her Familiar in top form over the coming days to help root out the traitor in their midst and capture any remaining Chaos Council attackers still at large in the tunnels underneath the abbey. She was determined to ensure her newfound cousin's Crossroads were as safe as could be, before she and her team departed.

All these were things to worry about when she woke, though. Just before Alex slid into sleep, an image from the night's battle popped into her tired mind. When she had fought Morpheus, her Keeper staff had gained a new lightning color: ebony black and glittering with power. *What the hell? Nope, not going there now,* she mused as she descended into sleep in the dark hours of the night.

～

ALEX WOKE at dawn the next morning. Her sleep had been deep and dreamless, but there hadn't been enough of it, leaving her vaguely tired, but wide awake. She drew back the covers, taking care not to disturb the small poodle asleep at the foot of the bed. Larry must have returned before dawn. He belched softly but didn't wake. Alex rolled her eyes, hoping her magical Familiar hadn't eaten himself into a food coma. *Sigh.*

"Good morning, Alex," Leonard whispered, careful not to disturb the sleeping canine. "I hope you slept well, even if not long enough."

Alex donned her thick robe against the room's chill. The fire had died down ages ago, and the abbey's ancient stone walls hadn't been designed to offer warmth or physical comfort.

"Hi Leo. I slept well, thanks to you," Alex replied. "Um, I'm up now, though," she added. She badly wanted a long shower to warm up, followed by coffee, lots and lots of coffee. "You don't need to stay."

The Revenant smiled and rose. "I'll leave you then. I'm sure you want to get your day started." The wiry, lean former police officer headed for the door. With his long-fingered hand on the doorknob, Leonard glanced back at Alex and issued a vague warning. "Today will not be easy, or free of pain for any of us, Keeper. I have a feeling..." He slipped out the door before she could question him.

And what the hell did her friend's warning mean? Alex wondered as she languished under the burning hot spray of her bathroom's powerful shower. At least the ancient abbey had good water pressure, she mused, distracted by the water's welcome heat as it loosened the tight muscles at her shoulders. Returning to her original question, she tried to parse Leonard's words. Yes, they still had a spy to root out, along with a few stray Chaos fighters hiding somewhere nearby. It certainly wouldn't be easy, but pain? The only pain she planned for the day belonged to her enemies, not her friends.

Alex resolved to use *all* the magic at her disposal—even her death magic—to ensure both her old and her new friends and family stayed safe from here on out. She shook her head, ignoring her mind's insistent murmuring about time magic. And what the hell was that black lightning yesterday, anyway? She brooded.

She turned off the water with a sigh, resolving to take a walk in the fresh air after breakfast to clear her mind. Her thoughts were running in frantic circles of responsibility, possibility, and fear of the unknown new magics manifesting deep in her soul, like weeds in a neglected garden. And the day hadn't even really started yet.

25

___

SURPRISE ATTACK

After breakfast, Alex strolled through the extensive abbey grounds, admiring the precise trimming of the box hedges and inhaling the sweet scent of roses rambling over arches that separated each section of the lovingly tended gardens. Weak early-morning sunlight highlighted the morning dew still clinging to individual blades of grass. A light mist lingered in the air. Shivering a little, she zipped up her fleece sweatshirt and slumped wearily onto one of the wooden benches placed strategically throughout the gardens.

While the walk had helped wake Alex up, it hadn't brought clarity to her thoughts. Who was she to have the divine powers of a god? What the hell was her divine grandfather thinking? She desperately wished to return to the life of a mere Crossroads Keeper, which had more than enough excitement and drama for her. Less than a year ago, before her sudden reintroduction to the supernatural world, Alex had never doubted she was fully human. There had been no other possible options. The most exciting thing to happen to her until that point had been when she told her boss at the university to stop sexually harassing his subordinates. Oh, and punched him. Hard.

Now, here she was, a lynchpin in the supernatural world. Crossroads Keeper, demi-goddess, and Envoy of the gods, with a crapload more power than any one mortal should have. Who was she to be appointed the supernatural world's demi-goddess hero? And *was* she even mortal anymore?

Alex knew her cousin, Olympe, a demi-goddess like her, was around five-hundred years old. While the warrior nun had certainly aged, it happened at a snail's pace compared to the average mortal. And Olympe's mother was a 'mere' Olympian goddess, while Alex's grandfather was a Titan, the Primordial god of death and time.

Who's to say how long I'd live—if everyone and their sister weren't out to kill me? Alex brooded. She blew out a resigned sigh. Zeus probably had a death warrant out for her for skipping his divine dinner party. Plus, Nyx had a major hate on for her, and her idiot cousin, Morpheus, had promised to kill her the next time he saw her. *Sigh.*

Alex watched a snail leave a slimy trail across one of the smooth rocks bordering the pathway near the bench. For all she knew, the snail would outlive her. *Well, shit.*

THE FRANTIC PEAL of church bells sliced through the morning air. The sound was no gentle call to prayer, but a discordant medley of alarm. Alex rose from the bench and gazed wildly around, sensing danger, but unsure from which direction it came. She called her Keeper staff and took off down the nearest pathway.

Shouts and shots rang out up ahead. She ran toward the sounds of fighting and sent a wild mental shout for help to Larry and anyone else magically connected to her. She felt worry from Conor and Tyre, but they were too far away from the abbey to help. From Larry, she felt support and, strangely, a vicious rage.

Rounding the corner of a tall hedge, Alex realized the fight was centered around the abbey's outbuildings, including the long, low-slung infirmary. More than a dozen heavily armed men dotted the surrounding roofs, spraying gunfire and arrows into the crowd below. A black helicopter hovered overhead, filled with more men firing into the battle.

The abbey's defenders, many still clad in nightgowns and obviously roused from their beds, had brought their own deadly weapons. Alex squinted as she hurried toward the deadly melee. She thought she saw a rocket launcher on the shoulders of a tall, skinny nun she recognized as one of Olympe's admin staff. A red fireball shot out of the device, followed by a lightning-fast projectile. It streaked through the sky and hit the helicopter overhead, which promptly burst into flames and tumbled to the ground. *Yup, definitely a rocket launcher*, Alex thought, as she watched the spiraling helicopter crash into a garden shed, exploding on impact. Flames roiled from the wreckage, while a plume of thick, black smoke shot into the air.

Alex shrugged, then called her magic and joined the battle. Bolts of multi-colored lightning burst from the crystal set in the staff's tip. Glittering black lightning danced and twirled with the more familiar blue and red lightning of her Keeper and necromantic magics. She aimed her staff and fired. The first fierce bolts of multicolored lightning landed like a grenade, blowing a hole in the roof of a nearby barn and sending half a dozen rooftop attackers flying.

Well, shit. Alex frowned warily at her staff, which still crackled and sparked with a trio of magical lightning bolts. She had to admit that the new black lightning was the bomb. Literally. Too bad the staff didn't have a power knob, she mused, awed at the now super-charged Keeper staff in her grip. She would have to figure out how the hell to control the black lightning or she risked killing off half the abbey's defenders.

Taking careful aim and breathing a prayer to the gods, she shot another massive blast of lightning toward the abbey's attackers. The nun with the rocket launcher had nothing on her. *Hah!*

THE BATTLE for the abbey raged forever or for an instant. Alex wasn't sure which. Between her newly super-powered staff and her well-trained team members, plus several fierce nuns with rocket launchers and a flock of other nuns wielding semi-automatic machine guns, grenades, and, weirdly, really long swords, the few attackers not killed or badly injured gave up and raced off into the night.

Alex lowered her staff and gazed around the battle zone. Her victorious team members, along with the battle nuns, were rounding up stragglers, disarming them, and marching them ... somewhere. A small group of nuns were busy treating the wounded, while others were purposefully collecting machine guns, handguns, and rocket launchers and taking them ... somewhere else. *Where the hell did these mild-mannered priestess nuns get all this heavy weaponry, and where the heck were they taking the captured attackers?* Alex wondered. Did the abbey have an armory? A dungeon? Olympe sure as hell hadn't included those in her extensive tour the other day.

"Alex, you need to come to the infirmary. Now. Use the back entrance." Larry's urgent mind-spoken voice interrupted Alex's musings. *"It's Olympe. She's badly injured."*

"What?! Where? How badly is she hurt?" Alex flung mind-spoken questions at Larry as she ran. She'd only just met her cousin, but she already loved the little priestess nun. Olympe understood Alex's magical powers, and they both shared a similar divine heritage. Heaving a sob, she raced around the long building, searching for the infirmary's back door. The front entrance had collapsed during the brutal battle, but Alex hadn't thought the attackers had breached the building. The bad guys had been too

busy defending themselves against an abbey full of angry, and heavily armed, warrior nuns.

There was no one guarding the back entrance, but Alex slowed and approached quietly. She cracked open the door and crept into a small, dimly lit anteroom from which long hallways branched off on either side. The silence inside the building was complete.

"Larry, I'm in the building. Where are you? Are you safe?" She cast out the mind-spoken plea, hoping like hell her Familiar—and the powerful new cousin she already cared for deeply—were okay.

"Follow the back hallway to the right. We're in the last room on the right," Larry replied tersely. *"And hurry."*

Alex hurried, pausing only momentarily when she reached the mangled body of the rude Infirmière Olympe had introduced her to the other day. Blood soaked the dour nurse's starched white uniform, and her eyes stared sightlessly at the ceiling. The dead woman's throat was a bloody mess. Her mangled arms and legs sported deep lacerations and what looked like multiple bite marks, as if razor-sharp teeth had savaged her.

Leaving the gruesome sight behind, Alex edged past the body and followed a trail of bloody claw and paw prints down the hallway towards her destination. She suspected the claw prints belonged to Grenoble. Despite their small size, goblins were fierce fighters. But what creature had left behind those massive, bloody paw prints? And why would Grenoble attack the nun? Suspicious dread curled in her gut.

She raced down the hallway, careful to avoid the bloody prints, and tore into the room at the end, where more blood and pain awaited her. Larry hovered over a small body sprawled on the floor at the far side of the room. Alex recognized Olympe's warrior nun outfit and her heart cracked in two. "Is ... is she still alive?" She whispered.

"Barely," Larry replied, gazing sadly down at the badly wounded woman.

Grenoble crouched on Olympe's other side. The goblin held

her pale hand gently in his claws, and tears streamed down his craggy face. He glared up at Alex and growled, "Save her, Keeper. I *know* you can do it. Use your death magic to save her."

Alex's knees gave out and she crumpled to the floor near Olympe's still form. She stroked the injured cousin's hair, her hand coming away sticky, crimson with her cousin's blood. *Oh, no.*

"Freeze time so she doesn't die while you're healing her, Keeper!" Grenoble's angry growl sounded loud in the still deathly still room. "Use your time magic, Keeper! Now!"

She gazed despairingly at the grieving goblin and shook her head in denial. "I don't have healing magic *or* time magic, Grenoble." She gazed sadly down at her injured cousin and whispered, "But I *wish* I did."

Larry padded over to Alex and placed a bloody paw on her knee. She breathed a sigh of relief when she realized the blood wasn't his, but wondered dully where he had acquired it. His paws were way too small to be the bloody ones she'd seen around the body in the hallway.

"Hurry up and freeze time, Alex. We both know you can do it," Larry demanded. The little poodle shook his head and snorted in frustration. "We both know you are capable of so much more than you are ready to believe. Do it. Now."

I could at least try, Alex admitted as she gazed down at the tiny, still woman lying in a growing pool of blood. She would try anything to save her new cousin. Bracing herself, she reached deep inside her soul—past her Keeper magic, past her death magic—even further, until she found a closed door she only half-believed existed. A scream ripped out of Alex when she opened the door. Time stopped. Black spots danced at the edge of her vision, threatening to drag her into unconsciousness, but she grit her teeth and fought it back. Once the blackness receded, Alex gazed around the small room, her eyes widening in shock at the frozen tableau. Besides herself, the only thing moving in the room was a dark shadow, which twisted and swirled lazily in one corner.

Alex watched in horror as the shadow coalesced into a human form.

Morpheus, her nemesis—well, one of them, anyway—grinned viciously at her. "Do you think that your feeble attempts to freeze time can affect me? I'm a god, for God's sake ... um, for the gods' sake." The handsome god of nightmares frowned. "I mean ... well, you know what I mean..." His words trailed off and frowned harder. "Anyway, I told you I'd kill you the next time we met. So that's what I'm here to do," he sneered.

Alex fought both dread at Morpheus's obvious power and a grin at his verbal confusion. She pursed her lips and studied the angry god dubiously. "Your mother told me you weren't the sharpest knife in the drawer. Seems like she's right."

The thunderous expression on Morpheus's face hardened further. "My dear mother betrayed her own mother by training the likes of you in death magic. Instead of helping Nyx defeat you and your ignorant allies, she has sided with the forces of 'good' ... whatever that means."

"So, you'd rather support your insane grandmother's plans to bring chaos to all the realms than support your own mother and aunts as they fight to maintain balance," Alex queried, genuinely confused by Morpheus's dedication to Nyx's nefarious cause. His mother, Clotho, was the goddess of the tapestry of life and the kindest—and most sane—of the three Fates. Alex realized then that the motherly goddess and her two quirky divine sisters had gained a place in her heart. *Huh, I guess the Fates are now heart family,* she mused wryly. *What the heck! Why not add a trio of deadly goddesses to my ever-expanding family circle?*

Morpheus scowled at her and snarled, "My mother and her sisters are part of the divine establishment. They want to maintain the status quo, but the power of the gods is slowly being eroded. We are being forgotten, and inferior species now rule in our place. These ignorant fools have no fear or reverence for our divinity."

"If you keep frowning like that, your face will freeze," Alex replied, the words popping out before she could stop them. She fought to keep her face blank, despite the fear pounding through her veins. Why, oh why, did she have to bait the god of nightmares? The little toe rag was insanely powerful, but he was also her cousin, or nephew ... or something like that. The family lines of the gods were incredibly complex, to put it mildly. *Sigh.*

Morpheus glared at her and smiled grimly. "I'm going to enjoy killing you, cousin." A massive sword appeared in his hand, its sharp blade glinting in the room's harsh overhead lighting.

Movement flickered in Alex's peripheral vision. She risked a glance around the room to see if her time magic had weakened, but everyone remained frozen in place ... except the rogue god who wanted her dead ... and the enormous black wolf sitting under the window across from her. *Wait a minute, where the hell did that thing come from?* Alex wondered, her heart racing in fear. Was this creature the source of the massive bloody paw prints surrounding the body in the hallway? Had the wolf killed the woman?

The wolf tilted its head and gazed at Alex with glowing golden eyes. The intelligence and warning in the creature's gaze deeply worried Alex.

"Icelus? What in Hades are you doing here, brother?" Growled Morpheus. "I thought you were still amusing yourself on Crete with that little nymph of yours."

Alex's eyes widened as the wolf's image blurred and a tall, muscular man, shirtless but dressed in black trousers, simply appeared in its place. She flicked her gaze between the two gods and could definitely see the resemblance. Both men were tall and muscular, with golden hair and handsome faces. But where Morpheus wore what seemed like a permanent sneer, his brother's expression was carefully blank.

"Which brother are you?" Alex asked. She racked her brain, then remembered her aunt's detailed explanation of the Oneiroi, the three divine brothers with power over the realms of sleep, dreams ... and nightmares. "Wait, you're the god of dreams, right? And you can shape-shift, too, if I remember my mythology—er, family tree, rightly." She gave the wolf shifter a small finger wave. *Why was she babbling?* She shook her head to clear her thoughts. The room now contained not one, but two powerful gods, both of whom wanted her dead. She should concentrate on that, not on trying to figure out her complicated divine family tree.

The wolf's glowing golden eyes had remained after his shift. The attractive god regarded Alex with polite courtesy. "I am Icelus, god of dreams, cousin ... or is it aunt?" The man's lips quirked in a small grin. "I can never remember the Byzantine relationships of our divine family tree," he said with a wry chuckle.

"I know, right?!" Alex blurted. She had been sure Icelus shared his brother's loyalty to Nyx, but doubt—and hope—crept in.

She frowned at the man with the golden gaze. *Should she just outright ask? Why the hell not?* "Hi, Icelus—er, cousin. Um, which side of this, er, battle ... war ... whatever you want to call it, are you on, by the way?"

Icelus crossed his arms and eyed his brother thoughtfully. "Well, I'm not on the side of our crazy grandmother, Nyx, that's for damn sure," he murmured. The god's golden gaze slid back to Alex, and he huffed a sigh. "While I've been trying to stay out of this matter, I see that is no longer an option." Before Alex could blink, Icelus blurred back into his wolf form, then leapt at his shocked brother with a menacing growl.

Morpheus managed a strangled shout, but his cry was cut off when the wolf clamped massive jaws around his neck. The god's sword clattered to the ground, but he replaced it with a wickedly sharp dagger, which he plunged into Icelus's furry flank. Blood flew, and the wolf yelped in pain, but then he closed his massive jaws and bit down viciously on his brother's neck. Deep crimson arterial blood streamed against the room's pristine white walls.

Alex eyed the battling duo, her hands clenched. She quickly charged her Keeper staff with magic, but the fight before her moved so fast she couldn't risk a shot. Since it appeared Icelus was on her side, she didn't want to risk injuring him further.

The fighters blurred as grey-black shadows coalesced and wrapped around them. Squinting, Alex thought Icelus had the upper hand, but she couldn't be sure.

A deep, foreign voice sounded in Alex's head. Icelus. *"I'm taking my brother back to Mount Olympus now, where we'll finish this fight. For now, anyway. This war is far from won, though. Good luck, Keeper. Save the nun. She's a good friend of mine."*

The swirling gray shadows winked out of sight and silence settled over the room. The only reminders of the bloody fight between the divine brothers were the crimson splashes and slashes of blood decorating the floor and walls.

Alex heaved a deep sigh and sent her staff back to the ether. The good news was that Icelus appeared to be on her side in the battle against Nyx and her co-conspirators on the Chaos Council. The bad news was that Icelus had mind-spoken to her, adding a new magical connection to the other voices in her head. It was becoming awfully crowded in there.

CLOSING HER EYES, Alex shook her head to clear it, then risked a glance around the room. She winced at the awful scene surrounding her, which was still frozen in time. Olympe's small body sprawled on the black-and-white tiles, the blood pool around her injured form creating surreal patterns on the floor's checkerboard pattern. Larry sat next to her, his frozen gaze fixed on the injured nun, one paw resting on Alex's leg. Grenoble stood, scowling, mouth wide open, caught in the middle of his command to Alex to use her death magic to heal his friend.

She rubbed her hands over her face and groaned. What did the fierce little goblin think she could do with her dangerous death magic that would heal Olympe—or anyone else? It was *death magic*, for frick's sake.

The first time she had used her death magic had been when her father had tried to kill her to further his and Nyx's nefarious plans to escape the Underworld. With barely a thought, she had incinerated her father's borrowed body and obliterated his very soul. Later, the Fates had informed her that she had narrowly avoided wiping out everyone in Hades's Underworld castle, both friend and foe, with her uncontrolled death magic.

Lucky me, Alex brooded. That fateful day, she had become the first grandchild of the gods known to inherit a Titan's Primordial power. Overnight, her death magic had made her a demi-goddess —and put a target on her back at the same time. She had worked hard over the past several months to learn how to control her death magic. Once the Fates pronounced her sufficiently trained, Alex had stuffed her death magic into a box and buried it in the dark recesses of her soul, determined never to use it again. Until now, it seemed.

She winced, recalling the glittering, ebony-black bolts of lightning that had danced and swirled around her staff, entwined with her normal red and blue magics, during the battle. It seemed her Keeper staff was now channeling death magic. She absently rubbed the swollen red skin on her palms. The damned staff had burned her hand with the vast amount of divine power it now contained. It seemed her death magic had *no* plans to stay buried. *Sigh.*

Alex brought her mind back to the frozen present and gazed sadly down at her grievously wounded cousin. Like everyone else still in the room, Olympe remained frozen in Alex's time magic— yet another divine magical power she had inherited from dear old granddad. She may have just met Olympe, but her newfound cousin had already carved out a space in her heart. Running her hands through her long, dark hair, Alex despaired. Grenoble had said she could use her death magic to heal. To save Olympe. But how?

"*Death is the other side of the coin of life, dear,*" a gentle voice whispered. "*Of course you can use your death magic to heal.*"

Olympe. Had to be. But how? Alex wondered. Time remained frozen.

"*Yes, it's me, Alex,*" Olympe said. "*I'm mind-speaking with you, since my mortal form is too weak to talk.*"

Alex gasped and crawled closer to her injured cousin, heedless of the pools of blood surrounding the still form. "Olympe? Can you hear me?" She laid a gentle hand on the tiny priestess nun's head and stroked her hair. "I'm so sorry this happened to you, cousin." A pained sob escaped her. "What can I do to help?"

A wry chuckle sounded in Alex's mind. "*First of all, you can stop trying to ignore and bury your divine magics. All magic has its uses, even death magic, my dear.*"

Alex nodded at her cousin's words, reluctantly accepting the truth of them. She was a demi-goddess, dammit. She needed to 'woman up' and stop whining at the fickle finger of Fate. An unwilling laugh escaped her lips. Her cousins, the Fates, certainly were fickle—and kind of crazy—but the divine trio accepted their death magic and had attempted to teach her to do the same. It wasn't the Fates' fault if Alex's sole focus during their training sessions was to master her death magic just enough to control it and bury it deep in her soul, never to be seen again.

"How do I heal you, Olympe?" Alex asked, determination threading her words. She really had to stop compartmentalizing her magic and denying the divine powers she inherited ... especially the ones that frightened her. "Tell me what I need to do to save your life, cousin," she pleaded.

Olympe's eyes cracked open slightly, seemingly by force of will alone. The injured woman studied Alex, her gaze full of wisdom and pain. "*Open the doors in your soul, Alex—all of them—including the one behind which you have barricaded your death magic. Throw away the locks, the boxes, everything. Then embrace all your divine magics. You won't be whole until you do, my dear.*" The diminutive priestess nun sighed and closed her eyes. "*Take it from someone who knows.*"

Not knowing what else to do, but willing to follow her mentor's advice, Alex closed her eyes, gritted her teeth, and opened herself to the full force of the divine magics she kept buried deep in her soul. All of them. Instead of the searing pain she thought she'd feel, a lightness enveloped her heart. Rivers of magical power surged past the mental barriers she used to suppress her more terrifying powers. The blue of her Keeper magic merged with the red of her necromantic magic, while the pale, clear river of her time magic flowed into and along with both. Then came her death magic. From the very depths of her soul, a glittering ebony river swirled up, then into and around her other magics. Thin streams of other colors—yellow, green, and purple—joined the now-raging river of her powers, until the flow resembled a magical rainbow.

Dimly, Alex wondered what magics the new colors represented, but she resolved to deal with that another time. Now, she wanted ... needed, to heal her cousin. Forcing open her eyes, she squinted at the dazzling light show filling the room. A rainbow of magic danced and swirled in the air, reflecting dazzling colors on the walls and ceiling. Her eyes widened in wonder at the brilliant display of magical powers. Her powers. The same glittering rainbow of colors wove around her hands, where they now rested on Olympe's unmoving chest. Alex watched in awe as one strand of magic separated itself from the others. Black death magic flowed out, spreading itself over Olympe's still form. Once it completely covered the injured woman, the glittering ebony magic snapped and sparked for several long moments before morphing into a gently glowing, radiant gold.

Holy shit! Alex's jaw dropped as she watched her magic do its thing, seeming to need no active input from her. Tears fell as she realized her mistake. There was no way to suppress any of her magics. Not if she wanted to be whole and to help her growing heart family defeat Nyx's forces of chaos. She couldn't deny her demi-goddess powers any longer. She would need them all if her side was going to win the war against chaos.

Alex felt Olympe's chest move under her hands. She gasped and studied the prone woman with hopeful trepidation. There. Another breath. Her cousin was alive! *Great goddess, I guess death magic is good for more than just killing the bad guys,* she mused, overcome with awe.

After several tense minutes, Olympe slowly opened her eyes, which sparkled with clarity and humor, and tried to smile up at Alex. The tiny nun's voice entered Alex's mind, gently chiding her. *"It would make things easier if you released your time magic, my dear. I'm finding it hard to talk, considering the stillness imposed on me by your greater power."*

"Oh. Shit. Sure," Alex stuttered. She concentrated and found she could pick out the transparent time magic from the rainbow river of colors still swirling around the room. With a thought, she commanded the magic to release its hold. And it did! *Holy crap! Maybe I'm getting the hang of this,* she mused.

The room instantly burst into sound and movement, momentarily disorienting Alex as the previously frozen scene disintegrated into noise and chaos.

"You need to heal her. Now!" Grenoble shouted as he stalked toward her.

Larry crouched protectively next to Alex. "She'll heal Olympe, Grenoble, I swear, as long as you don't eat her first. Then I'd have to eat you, you idiot," the pink-eared poodle growled.

Olympe sat up with a joyous laugh. "It's already done, you two." She placed a restraining hand on the furious goblin's arm. "Calm down, Grenoble. It's over. Alex froze time and healed me."

Slowly, the squat goblin turned his head toward his old friend, his enormous eyes morphing from anger to brilliant joy. He wrapped her in a tight hug, his shoulders heaving with silent sobs. "You're alive. You're okay. Thank the gods that worthless Keeper cousin of yours finally got her magical shit together."

Olympe patted Grenoble on the back with one hand and stroked Larry's fur with the other. "I'm fine, you two. I'm okay." She finally drew back from the goblin's tight embrace and fixed him with a stern eye. "Oh, and Grenoble, can you please stop insulting my cousin, considering she's the most powerful demi-goddess in history, and the woman who just saved my life?"

The goblin hung his head and muttered something under his breath before nodding reluctantly at Olympe. "I'm very glad she healed you, my friend." Grenoble's large, luminous eyes turned to regard Alex. "And I'll try to stop insulting you, Keeper. But I make no promises."

Alex grinned at the growly little green guy. "That's good enough for me."

26

GOODBYES & GODDESSES

Dusk had fallen by the time they had cleared up the extensive damage from the abbey battle. Everyone had pitched in to help, including Alex and her team. Major building repairs would have to wait for another day, though. Rocket launchers—and Alex's newly super-charged Keeper staff —sure could make massive holes in walls and roofs.

Olympe, back to her normal self after her near-death experience, thank the gods, had called an after-action meeting for the following morning, then instructed everyone to have an early night. Alex was happy to obey; she ate a quick dinner and fell into bed directly afterwards, immediately falling into a dreamless sleep.

Way too early the following morning, Larry served as the bearer of bad news. When he jumped on the bed and licked Alex's face, she covered her head with a pillow and groaned. "Go away, dog breath. I'm not done sleeping."

"I hear you," Larry replied. "But what your priestess warrior nun of a cousin wants, she gets. And Olympe wants a meeting to discuss yesterday's attack." He dug at the covers and nosed at

Alex's pillow. "Meeting starts in twenty minutes, dudette. If you want a shower beforehand, you'd better rise and shine."

Alex groaned and swatted sleepily at the pink-eared poodle barking in her ear. "All right, all right. Can you tone it down, dog-breath? I'm coming."

"So is Christmas," Larry snarked, but he stopped harassing Alex and scampered back as she crawled reluctantly from the bed. "You look like crap," he added helpfully.

Not bothering to reply, Alex trudged into the bathroom and studied her image in the mirror. She had to admit that the furry asshole was right; she looked like crap. Shrugging, she turned on the shower and stepped in. *At least I'll be clean, even if I look like something the dog dragged in*, she muttered as the shower's hot water pounded her awake.

Larry's muted voice floated into the bathroom. "You're too big, Alex. I couldn't drag you anywhere..."

"Oh, shut up, you furry little menace," Alex growled.

Larry barked a laugh. "Listen, I brought you a croissant and an orange juice. They're on your bedside table. I'm gonna head back to the kitchen because Henri is saving me and Grenoble some pancakes. I'll see you at the meeting."

Alex turned off the shower and sighed at the sound of Larry's paws snicking on the wooden floor as he raced out of the room. She couldn't stay mad at her magical Familiar. He may be a pain in the ass, but he *had* brought her breakfast.

CONVERSATIONS SWIRLED around the large conference room. Alex rubbed her tired eyes and tried to concentrate. Despite drinking several large mugs of coffee from the urn someone had thought-fully provided, she was still exhausted. With a supreme effort, she refocused on the meeting, studying the tall, skinny nun currently standing in front of a massive whiteboard, an old-fashioned wooden pointer clutched in her skeletal hand. A pale blue floral dress hung on the woman's thin frame, while a fuzzy, royal blue sweater, several sizes too large, enveloped her. The only sign of her nun status was a short white veil pinned around the woman's head, from which frizzy blonde hair peeked out.

The nun used her pointer to tap a hand-drawn chart that took up most of the whiteboard. "We have twenty-five of the attackers confined in the dungeon, Keeper Olympe. Another six were seriously wounded and are currently being treated in the infirmary." She moved the pointer to highlight a more sophisticated printed graph taped to one side of the whiteboard. "We have accounted for all of our weapons and returned them to the armory." Giving Olympe an apologetic glance, she added, "I'm afraid we'll need a top-up on the armory budget to replace the large amount of ammunition we used yesterday."

Olympe smiled kindly at the speaker. "No worries, Sister Ann. We can find money in the budget to cover the ammunition restock, I'm sure. Please coordinate with Guardian Grigory to order replacement supplies." She pointed an admonitory finger at the man sitting to her left. "And make sure you get the better brand of bullets for the machine guns, Grigory. The last batch you purchased wasn't up to the usual standards."

The burly Guardian nodded solemnly at his Keeper's instructions, leaving Alex to wonder just how many gun battles her cousin's abbey had experienced ... and how many more the indefatigable warrior nun foresaw in its future.

Sister Ann cleared her throat and continued her report. She grimaced and said, "Unfortunately, seven of our people sustained injuries in the fighting, but none of them required a stay in the infirmary. All are back to work—"

"All but one," Grigory interrupted, his face a mask of anger. "Last night's attack revealed the traitor in our midst." He gazed around the room, his eyes flinty. "As some of you know, we've suspected for a while that there is—was an informant among the

Crossroads staff. During the recent skirmishes at the Crossroads, the attackers seemed to know precisely when and where to attack."

"We increased the guards in the Crossroads cave after each attack." The Crossroads Guardian flicked an apologetic glance at Olympe and heaved a pained sigh. "Since the attacks all originated from the tunnels near the Crossroads, that's where I concentrated our defensive forces. However, I should also have increased the guards around the abbey perimeter. That was a failing. My apologies, Keeper."

Olympe placed a comforting hand on Grigory's arm. "No need to apologize, my dear. We all make mistakes." She shrugged philosophically. "Including me. I should have been more diligent in examining the minds and hearts of everyone in our community. If I had, I might have discovered the traitor before she—"

"Before she drugged the guards at the abbey's back gate and opened the portcullis, allowing the attackers entry into the abbey grounds before dawn yesterday," Grigory growled.

All traces of sleep gone, Alex leaned forward, eyes wide. Who was the traitor? She suspected a certain someone—and she was about to find out if she was correct.

Whispers and speculation swirled around the room, the volume increasing until Olympe raised her voice and called for quiet. Silence immediately descended, and all eyes turned expectantly to the tiny warrior nun.

Olympe smiled at her attentive audience, but grief dulled her normally bright blue eyes. "I want to thank everyone who helped defend the abbey and the Crossroads yesterday, as well as those who organized the cleanup response in the aftermath. We are a very tight community and a supportive one. It strikes at the heart of our community when one of our members betrays us." She shook her head with a sigh. "We may never know why our sister betrayed us, although I have my suspicions, which I will not discuss in this meeting. That said—"

Grenoble, who had been growling under his breath since the conversation about the traitor started, launched himself from his chair. The goblin landed on the conference table next to Olympe, his razor-sharp claws gouging the table's glossy surface.

"The traitor was Sister Reine, the Infirmière," he stated. Amidst gasps of horror, the little goblin explained. "I was doing my early morning rounds when I spotted her coming up the path from the back gate and slipping into the infirmary's back door. There was no reason for her to be out that early, or to be anywhere near the abbey walls. I headed over to question the guards and found the portcullis up and the gates wide open. The abbey's guards were unconscious, and dozens of attackers were heading over the bridge. I fell back and mind-called Grigory, who raised the alarm. Then..."

He paused and cast a questioning glance at Olympe. She shook her head and patted the distressed goblin on the back. "That's all everyone needs to know, my friend. Thank you."

Grenoble's thick lips turned down, grief floating in his enormous eyes. With a nod and a grunt, he scrambled back to his chair as the room erupted in angry murmurs.

Everyone quieted when Olympe clapped her hands. "The rest of the story can be told another time. Or not," she stated firmly. "The bottom line is that, thanks to all of you, we fought off yesterday's attack on the abbey and defended our Crossroads."

She smiled warmly at Alex. "Thanks also goes to my newest cousin and her team for their valiant help yesterday. Together, we have vanquished the current threat to our Crossroads." The warrior nun's eyes tightened, and she raked a determined gaze around the room. "However, the war against Nyx and her Chaos Council is far from over. She'll try again. At another Crossroads. At another time. We must be diligent and remain prepared to meet her evil *wherever* it next arises."

Olympe's gnarled Keeper staff appeared in her hand, the ancient wooden rod towering over her tiny form. The warrior nun handled the large staff easily. Banging her staff loudly on the flag-stones, she shouted, "Praise to the triune of our patron goddesses! Power to the Crossroads!"

The room erupted in chants and cheers. "Praise Hecate! Praise Demeter! Praise Persephone! Power to the Crossroads!"

LATER THAT DAY, Alex sat in Olympe's small sitting room, suppressing a yawn. She had eaten and drunk too much at the celebratory meal after that morning's meeting. Her bed called to her, but so did her own Crossroads, along with her heart family. Despite her argument with Conor, she missed him and didn't like how they had left things between them. She had been away for too long. After the blood, tears, and revelations of the past few days, she needed to hug her heart family. And make up with Conor.

Smiling tiredly at her newfound cousin, Alex sighed and suppressed another massive yawn.

Olympe returned Alex's smile, but remembered pain clouded her eyes. The older woman spoke softly, "Thank you again, Cousin Alex, for your help over the past few days. I know that your experiences here have stretched your spirit and soul in new and uncomfortable ways. However, it is well past time for you to embrace *all* your magic, my dear." A determined grin curved the priestess warrior nun's lips. "The supernatural world needs you at full power if we are to defeat Nyx and her divine conspirators and disband the Chaos Council."

"I know, I know," Alex muttered. Her hands gripped her chair's carved wooden arms so hard her knuckles whitened. "I get it. I really do. No more 'head in the sand' about my ... uh, scarier magical powers," she vowed.

Larry, seated at Alex's feet, his warm, furry body resting supportively against her legs, wagged his tail and added his two cents. "It's about damn time, partner!" The little poodle flicked an apologetic glance at Olympe. "Um, sorry for the swear words, ma'am."

Olympe gave a rich laugh. "Oh, Larry, you *do* remember that I'm not really a nun, right? I don't give a hoot about swear words, sweetie." She grinned slyly down at the canine Familiar. "In fact, I've used more than a few in my time, dear ... especially over the last week."

EVERYONE STARTED as the door flew open and a goddess swept into the room. "No, don't stand and no bowing, please," Demeter sang, before plopping down in the nearest chair with a groan.

"Um, we weren't—" Alex started, then she clamped her lips shut. Probably not a good idea to tell a goddess she hadn't been intending to stand, let alone bow. *The gods really needed a lesson in humility*, she mused. *Riiiiiight. Like that was gonna happen.*

Olympe studied Demeter with raised brows. "Are you well, Mother? You look exhausted."

"Ugh. I'm fine, no thanks to my idiot brother, Zeus," Demeter drawled. "I've spent the last several days trying to convince him that delaying his damn dinner ... or at least not killing those who couldn't attend on his chosen day—which was today, by the way—wouldn't harm his street cred."

The goddess slouched lower in her chair and rubbed her tired eyes, but a triumphant grin peeked out underneath. She lowered her hands and gave Alex a slightly scary smile. "I did it! Of course! Who's the best goddess? Me! I'm the best goddess!" Demeter launched herself out of her chair and did a victory dance, singing, "I'm the best damn goddess ever! Go, me!"

Olympe and Alex exchanged wary glances, then turned their gazes back to the dancing goddess, who was now doing something that resembled twerking. Alex stifled a giggle, and Olympe snorted.

"Mother, what are you doing? That dance, um, is rather undignified for a goddess, don't you think?" Olympe indicated Demeter's abandoned chair. "Would you care to sit down and explain yourself clearly? Obviously, you come bearing good news."

The happy goddess reluctantly discontinued her weird version of twerking and collapsed back into her chair with a laugh. "Oh, the news is better than good, Daughter," she replied with a grin. Demeter leaned forward and said, "So, here's the scoop."

The goddess explained she had convinced Zeus to postpone the dinner until all his invitees—specifically Alex and Demeter—could attend. After Demeter had informed her brother of the plot to assassinate guests at his event, the god had spent several days raging and overseeing an investigation into the matter. Just as Zeus's investigators prepared to give their report to a temple-full of gods and goddesses, Morpheus and Icelus had tumbled out of the Mount Olympus Crossroads and into the temple, still engaged in the deadly brawl that had begun in the Grenoble Crossroads' infirmary. Once the guards separated the brothers, Zeus demanded answers, and the truth came out, including about the attacks on my Crossroads.

Demeter gave a shark-like smile. "My idiot brother is finally at least listening to what I've been telling him for ages: that Nyx's aspirations to escape her prison in the Underworld threaten not only humans and supernaturals, but all the realms—including Mount Olympus." She snickered and rubbed her hands in glee. "Morpheus is now cooling his heels in the Mount's dungeon, while Icelus and a select few others—including you, Alex—will be the guests of honor at the banquet, which has officially been rescheduled for tomorrow night."

Olympe clapped in delight. "It sounds like Nyx overplayed her hand this time. Her grandson, Morpheus, is in leg-irons, and Zeus is riled enough, hopefully, to join the fight to protect the realms."

"Well, we'll see about that," Demeter cautioned. "My brother still questions the extent of the conspiracy and doubts that there are other gods besides Morpheus in league with Nyx." The goddess shrugged philosophically. "Typical male ego. Zeus refuses to believe anyone, least of all a disgraced goddess currently locked away at the edge of the Underworld, could organize a full-scale rebellion amongst 'his' gods and goddesses," she muttered, rolling her eyes in frustration.

"Tomorrow night?" The two words in Demeter's explanation that struck the most fear in Alex's heart were 'banquet' and 'tomorrow'. "Zeus has rescheduled the banquet for tomorrow night?"

Demeter gave Alex a sly grin. "Yes, Keeper. Tomorrow night, we storm Zeus's palace on Mount Olympus in our best evening togas, sip wine with the gods, and work to unmask the traitors."

In a tiny voice, Alex whined, "But I've never worn a toga and I'm just a demi-goddess."

The goddess waved away Alex's protest. "Near enough, Alex, near enough. You have the blood and Primordial magic of Chronos, the most powerful Titan in existence, flowing through your veins." She narrowed her eyes and studied Alex consideringly. "And I think I've got just the toga for you."

After the merriment of her arrival, Demeter's expression sobered. She fixed Alex with an intense gaze, uncharacteristic gratitude in her lovely eyes. "Alex, you have my heartfelt thanks for dropping everything to help sort out the dilemma at my daughter's Crossroads. Within a few days, you and your team helped depose the despotic goblin king, who was in league with the Chaos Council attackers. The new goblin queen has banished the Chaos Council contingent and pledged renewed friendship with Olympe and the Grenoble Crossroads. During the attack on the abbey yesterday, I hear that you and your team fought bravely."

The goddess smiled warmly, her usual reserve gone. "I have also been told that you used your divine powers over death—and life—to heal my daughter after she was grievously wounded in the battle. I am grateful, Keeper ... Alex. Thank you."

Alex's eyes had widened during Demeter's speech. She realized how rare it must be for a goddess to express gratitude, let alone to thank a mere mortal for their actions. "Um, you're welcome, ma'am—er, Demeter."

The goddess smiled at Alex and murmured, "I owe you one, Keeper."

Alex smoothed her face and hid her shock. She wasn't too sure having a goddess 'owe you one' was the blessing it seemed, but that was a problem for another time. *Well, crap.*

27

MOUNT OLYMPUS

The Grenoble Crossroads had a direct connection to the Crossroads on Mount Olympus, so the journey through the ley lines didn't take long. The direct link didn't surprise Alex. She imagined Demeter had orchestrated the connection to ensure she could visit frequently, allowing her to stay in close touch with her demi-goddess Keeper daughter.

The Fates—with the likely exception of Atropos—were thrilled to welcome Alex to their mansion set high on the slope of Mount Olympus for her stay. Even the normally stern Atropos gave Alex a slight smile upon her arrival. The wicked gleam in the woman's eyes worried Alex, though. The goddess of death had something planned; of that, Alex was sure.

After enduring her divine cousins' enthusiastic greetings and eating a multi-course dinner laid on in her honor, Alex bowed out of the welcome party as soon as she could gracefully do so. The events of the last week had taken their toll. Tomorrow was Zeus's banquet; she needed to be rested and ready for whatever craziness the divine celebration brought her way.

When Alex had discreetly requested to be excused from the

party, Atropos had been unexpectedly helpful, immediately offering to lead the way to her assigned guest room. The sly grin Atropos wore as she ushered Alex down the mansion's maze of hallways would have worried Alex if she weren't so exhausted. As long as the damned room had a bed, she'd be happy.

Alex couldn't find fault with the elegant guest room to which her cousin led her; it was large, well-decorated, and had a massive four-poster bed piled high with fluffy pillows and embroidered throws. With a final mysterious smile, Atropos departed quickly, leaving Alex alone in the room. Larry had remained at the party, but had promised to be along shortly. The greedy little poodle had already put away a hefty meal, but he had mumbled that he wasn't quite finished. *As if he'd ever truly be finished when food was on offer,* Alex mused with a tired grin.

She hoped her magical partner wouldn't take too long to appear; she felt nervous here on her own. The rest of Alex's team had not accompanied them to Mount Olympus. Instead, they had traveled back home, leaving her and Larry to journey into divine danger on a mountain full of gods on their own. Demeter had been insistent Alex wouldn't need their help, assuring Alex that she would be well-protected. The goddess had snickered and told Alex that, since she would stay with the renowned Fates, not even a rogue god would mess with her while under their roof—not if they valued their immortal lives. Alex had recalled Atropos and her ancient and deadly scissors of Fate, and had to agree. *Sigh.*

Too tired to explore the rest of the room, Alex climbed onto the comfortable bed with a relieved sigh that ended in an enormous yawn. It had been a very long day. Through the open French doors at the foot of the bed, a tapestry of white-hot stars glittered high above. The lack of light pollution on Mount Olympus gave the sky a dark brilliance she had never seen before.

She snuggled into the bed's soft blankets with a satisfied sigh. Just as her eyes closed, the door opened quietly. She sat up, eyes wide and heart pounding, but Larry's familiar form immediately calmed her. The silent servant, who had let the little poodle in, gently closed the door, leaving the two of them alone.

The bed dipped as Larry jumped up. Frowning at her magical Familiar's smiling, furry face, Alex asked, "Why aren't you tired? You couldn't have gotten any more sleep than I did last night—and you were up earlier than me, as well."

Larry grinned and nudged her hand with his nose. "I'm just happy that Demeter let me come with you." A shadow passed over his eyes and a slight growl rumbled deep in his chest. "I didn't want you to face your first trip to Mount Olympus alone. That asshole Morpheus might be chained up in the dungeon, but there are other dangers here .... traitors, too. You need a defensive wingman at your side, Alex. This place can be deadly at the best of times."

Larry's normally optimistic nature quickly reasserted itself, and he grinned. "Besides, I hear Zeus puts on a truly magnificent spread at his banquets." His pink ears perked up. "It's all-you-can-eat, you know. And I can really eat. I can't wait for the banquet tomorrow night."

Alex rolled her eyes and rubbed her Familiar's soft, pink ears. "Your stomach is a bottomless pit, you fur-ball," she told him with a wry smile.

Relaxing back onto the bed, she sleepily studied the detailed scene painted on the gold-trimmed ceiling overhead. Dozens of people cavorted across a pastoral scene full of rolling hills, rivers, and farmland. Fresh-faced shepherdesses stroked their tame goats, while groups of picnickers reclined on blankets dotted across gently rolling fields.

Alex's eyes closed, lulled toward sleep by the peaceful scene overhead—until realization dawned. Her eyes popped open, and she gazed up at the painted ceiling in amused horror, a furious blush rising on her cheeks. Those goats had goaty legs and hooves —but human torsos. The shepherdesses weren't stroking the goats' ... well, they were, but certainly not the heads she originally thought she saw. Okay, they were stroking different, X-rated, and very long heads. And the various clumps of people on the multitude of blankets spread across the scene weren't picnicking. They were ... *Oh. My. God. Atropos, that sneaky goddess, has put me in the porn bedroom,* Alex mused wryly. She gasped when one of the painted centaurs turned his *actual* head and winked at her, then returned his lascivious gaze back to the buxom maiden who was stroking... um, well, you know.

No wonder Atropos had that wicked gleam in her eyes when she offered to show me to my room, Alex reflected with a surprised chuckle at the stern goddess's sly joke. It looked like even the powerful goddess of death had a sense of humor. Pulling her embarrassed gaze from the pornographic goings-on overhead, she snuggled under the covers, cuddling Larry closer with an amused snort, vowing not to mention the pornographic ceiling with seemingly sentient painted goat-men and writhing orgies to her hosts. Maybe this was a typical ceiling decoration among the gods. Who knows? If so, she didn't want to embarrass herself by asking for a different room with a less X-rated ceiling. Plus, if putting her in the only room with an animated porno ceiling was Atropos's idea of a joke, she didn't want to give the annoying— and incredibly deadly—goddess the satisfaction of getting a rise out of her.

Larry whispered, "I can feel your embarrassment, Alex. We're mind-connected, remember?" He licked her face and huffed a snicker. "Yes, I've seen the porno ceiling. And no, porno bedroom ceilings are not the 'norm' amongst the gods, although the older goddesses do like to have at least one such room, in which to entertain their, uh, toy boys."

Alex grimaced, slightly nauseous at the thought of her millennia-old maiden cousins cavorting on the bed under the X-rated ceiling with younger, virile men with six-pack abs, tousled hair, and bedroom eyes. She threw off the covers and launched herself off the bed, eyes wide. "Don't ... just *do not* say anything else, Larry.

That's just—I've totally lost my appetite, and I'm not even sure I'll get it back by tomorrow night's banquet. Eeew."

She eyed the bedcovers suspiciously and muttered, "Let's hope the servants cleaned—"

Larry snorted a laugh, then rolled over on his back and wriggled around on the covers. "Dog nose here, remember? The covers and sheets are perfectly clean, Alex." He gave her an amused side-eye. "Whatever the Fates have gotten up to in here—"

Alex held up a hand and shook her head. "Don't ... just *do not* say anything else, Larry. My mind already needs a shower just thinking about it." After a brief hesitation, Alex approached the bed and slipped back under the covers with a jaw-cracking yawn. She was too tired to worry about her divine cousins' past sexual escapades in this very bed. As sleep dragged her under, she could swear she heard faint laughter from the figures on the ceiling.

A SOFT BUT persistent knock woke Alex early the next morning. She cracked open her eyes and sat up, momentarily disoriented, and gazed around the unfamiliar room. Then the previous day's events came rushing back. That's right, she was on Mount Olympus in her cousins, the Fates', mansion. Involuntarily, her eyes traveled to the ceiling, where the gods, centaurs, and assorted other creatures still cavorted in X-rated bliss. The same centaur from last night winked lasciviously down at her. *Ugh.*

Another, more persistent, knock brought Alex's gaze back to the main part of the room, which glowed with quiet ostentation. White marble floors reflected the early morning light, while elaborately carved chests and elegant furniture was arrayed around the large bedroom.

A very firm knock on the door sounded, and a perky female voice asked, "Miss Alex, it's Calliope, the maid. Can I *please* come in? I have your breakfast."

Alex hastily pulled the covers up to cover her extremely skimpy nightgown. *What the heck was I thinking when I packed this thing?* She wondered idly. She called out, "Uh, sure. Come on in, Calliope. Sorry it took me so long to reply."

The door opened soundlessly, and a short, curvy woman with a mass of barely tamed fiery red curls and bright, sky-blue eyes entered the room carrying a massive tray piled high with food. She smiled merrily at Alex and bobbed a curtsy. "No worries, ma'am. I hear you had a busy day yesterday. However, you have a visitor waiting for you downstairs, so I thought I'd better bring up something for you to eat while you get dressed."

"A visitor?" Alex replied, her eyebrows raised questioningly. As far as she knew, no one on Mount Olympus except the Fates knew that she and Demeter had arrived late the evening before. The Mount's Crossroads had been quiet, staffed by just two guards, who had both bowed low to Demeter and silently waved them through. On their journey through the sleeping city, they had seen no one but the carriage driver and some feral cats slinking between narrow alleyways, and heard nothing but a barking dog or two.

"I'm Calliope, ma'am, and I work for Clotho," the woman informed Alex as she carefully placed the laden breakfast tray on a table near the French doors. "She asked me to look after you while you're here." The bubbly maid grinned, anticipation sparkling in her large blue eyes. "After this, if all goes well, Clotho says she'll promote me to work as her personal assistant. Finally. I'm getting really tired of the maid thing." Calliope blushed and added, "Sorry, ma'am. That's way more information than you need. I'm always being told I have a tendency to run off at the mouth." The lively woman widened her eyes comically and placed a restraining hand over her lips.

Alex snorted a laugh. "No worries, Calliope. I've been told the same thing about my overactive mouth. Many times." She climbed out of bed and hurriedly donned her dressing gown while the maid's attention was on setting up her breakfast.

Once satisfied with the table's arrangement, Calliope turned and gave Alex a conspiratorial grin before a shadow crossed her face. "Come, we must hurry and get you ready. Heli will get ... impatient if you keep her waiting too long." The irrepressible maid's sunny smile soon returned. "Demeter sent her to take you shopping for a formal toga to wear at the banquet tonight."

Alex nodded absently as she glanced around the room. She didn't see Larry anywhere. Where had the furry little weasel gone?

As if expecting Alex's question, Calliope said, "I let Master Larry out early this morning. He's already gone for a walk and had his breakfast in the kitchen, ma'am." The maid chuckled. "When I left the kitchen, he was deep in negotiations with the chef for a second breakfast."

Alex laughed and rolled her eyes. "Of course he is, the furry little chowhound." Enticing scents drew her toward the table, her eyes widening in pleasure. Fluffy croissants filled a woven basket, while little clay pots of jam, honey, and butter huddled together on a silver tray. Fresh orange juice and, thank the gods, a pot of coffee was placed to one side, while a covered plate sat in front of the table's only chair.

The maid whipped the cover off as Alex sat. A full English breakfast filled the plate to bursting. With her mouth watering, Alex picked up her fork and dug in. Larry wasn't the only food-obsessed member of their magical duo, she admitted to herself.

Calliope bobbed her head respectfully and said, "I hope this breakfast is satisfactory, ma'am. The chef cooked you an English breakfast, along with some French croissants, as he knows you've traveled here from France, via England, so he thought—"

"He thought right, Calliope. Please give the chef my compliments," Alex replied as she scooped strawberry jam onto a flaky croissant. She smiled at the bubbly, talkative maid and added,

"Thank you for bringing me breakfast, Calliope. I really appreciate it."

"Oh, it's no trouble, ma'am. Really," Calliope murmured. She smiled and bobbed another curtsy.

Alex stifled a sigh and mentally rolled her eyes. She was used to doing most things herself, and she sure as hell wasn't used to this level of subservience from anyone. "Please call me Alex. Ma'am is for old ladies," she begged. When the maid nodded hesitantly and dropped into yet another curtsy, Alex hastily added, "And no more curtsies, please. I'm not royalty, Calliope."

The maid's eyes widened in shock. "Oh, no, you're much more than that ma'—, er Alex. You're the demi-goddess who has saved two Crossroads so far and who went into Hades itself to imprison the evil goddess Nyx, with an army of undead Regenerants at your command."

Before the woman could do any more fan-girling, Alex cut her off. "I'm just me, Calliope. Alex. A relative of the Fates, your employers. Can you please just treat me like a run-of-the-mill guest? Or, better yet, a visiting friend? Your friend, even? Please?"

Calliope's forehead wrinkled slightly as she considered Alex's request. Then a huge grin spread across her expressive face. Her eyes twinkling, she nodded decisively in agreement. "Yes, Alex. I think I can do that ... friend."

The cheerful maid whirled to face the wardrobe and flung it open. "If you could please hurry and finish eating, Alex, we need to get you ready for your shopping excursion." Calliope flicked quickly through the dozens of tunics and wraps filling the massive wardrobe. "Clotho took the liberty of having some clothing delivered yesterday when she heard you were coming. She figured you wouldn't have anything appropriate to wear on Mount Olympus."

Alex sighed and sipped her coffee. She had a suitcase filled with the clothes she had traveled with for her trip to the Grenoble Crossroads, but it contained practical outfits suitable for the job at hand, which was to battle the bad guys. She wasn't happy to admit it, but knew that hard-wearing pants, t-shirts, and leather jackets were almost certainly not appropriate attire for the city of the gods.

After finishing the last of her truly excellent coffee, Alex grimaced, then joined Calliope by the wardrobe, hoping her cousin had included at least a few things she wouldn't be too embarrassed to be seen dead in. Not that death wasn't a distinct possibility on this trip, she mused. *Banquet with the gods, indeed.*

28

RETAIL THERAPY

Alex had insisted on a quick shower before letting Calliope prepare her for the day. The maid had plaited Alex's thick, dark hair into a heavy braid before pinning it around her head with jewel-studded golden pins, then fluttered around, straightening and smoothing Alex's clothing.

Once Calliope stood back with a satisfied nod, Alex studied herself in the full-length mirror. Clotho's discerning eye for Olympian fashion pleasantly surprised her. During their time in San Antonio, Clotho and her two sisters wore nothing but voluminous pristine white togas, which Larry had informed Alex were of an old-fashioned style, even for Mount Olympus.

However, Alex's wardrobe contained several dozen well-cut tunics in a variety of deep colors and rich fabrics. Once belted, the royal blue tunic the maid had chosen draped nicely to her ankles. A Greek key pattern, embroidered in gold, edged the tunic's square neckline, while the narrow leather belt Calliope had wound around her waist glittered with tiny amethysts in the same shade as the tunic.

Pulling several pairs of sandals from the wardrobe, the maid held each one up to Alex's outfit before choosing a dark blue pair.

"Here, put these on, Alex. We must hurry. Heli is surely getting impatient by now." She flicked an apprehensive glance at Alex and murmured, "Heli is ... um, difficult, at the best of times."

Alex sighed as she studied the sandals, already dreading meeting the apparently impatient and unpleasant Heli. She frowned at the multitude of footwear in confusion, realizing she had no idea how to put any of them on. Long strips of embroidered ribbon and leather, fastened to a flat leather sole, made up the entire collection. "Um, how..."

Calliope smiled and waved Alex into a chair. "Here, let me put them on for you." She fitted the leather soles to the bottom of Alex's feet, then expertly wrapped the attached ties up her legs, almost all the way to her knees, before tying everything off in a neat bow. "Stand up and see how they feel, Alex," she directed, as she rose and moved back, studying Alex with a satisfied smirk.

Alex stood and took a few test steps. The sandals were surprisingly comfortable, while the loose tunic swirled softly around her ankles. *I could get used to dressing like this,* she mused, then snickered. Greek tunics embroidered with gold thread, jewel-studded belts, and knee-high wrap sandals would look more than a little out of place in modern San Antonio, and were even a little too much for the supernatural city hidden within.

Calliope grinned approvingly at her. "You look amazing!" She grabbed Alex's arm and hurried her new friend out of the room. "Time for you to go toga shopping."

THE MAID LED Alex quickly through a maze of opulent hallways, finally stopping before an elaborately carved door Alex thought might be near the main entrance. She'd been so tired last night she couldn't remember much about the mansion's layout.

Calliope opened the door and ushered Alex through. "Alex, meet Heli, Demeter's personal assistant. Heli, this is Miss Alex, demi-goddess and Crossroads Keeper," she said briskly. After bobbing a general curtsy, the maid quickly departed, leaving behind an uncomfortable silence.

Alex smiled tentatively at the stern-looking woman seated near the window. All she could say about Heli was that she looked very gold. The thin, wiry woman had deeply tanned golden skin, strange, golden eyes, and flaxen hair, while a rich-looking pale gold tunic hung on her thin frame. She suppressed a sigh at the sour expression and pinched lips marring the woman's long face. Shopping with this battle-ax would *not* be fun.

Forcing her smile to remain in place, Alex strode forward and held out her hand. "It's nice to meet you, Heli. I understand you're taking me toga shopping this morning?"

Heli raked Alex from head to toe with a condescending gaze. She wrinkled her nose and stared at Alex's outstretched hand as if it were a dead fish. "Oh, that's right, handshaking is an Earth custom, isn't it?"

The unpleasant woman rose and grasped Alex's hand in a limp handshake, letting go quickly. "We'd better get going," she snipped. "Or there'll be nothing good left in the better toga shops. Everyone wants to look their best for Zeus's banquet this evening." Heli flicked a dismissive glance at Alex and curled her lip. "I'll do the best I can, however..."

Alex interpreted Heli's unspoken words. '*...however, I'm not sure how I'm supposed to make this tall, curvy country bumpkin look presentable.*' She narrowed her eyes, thinking fast. She had no desire to have this unpleasant woman help her choose a toga for the banquet. Heli obviously had a chip on her shoulder about being asked to dress a mere demi-goddess and would probably put her in the most hideous, outdated, and ugly toga she could find, telling Alex it was all the rage. *Just nope.* She needed to make a good impression tonight. Her life might depend on it.

Heli sniffed and headed toward the room's open door. Before she reached it, Alex implemented her hastily thought-up plan.

She held up her hand to stop the woman's progress. "Just a minute, Heli. Shouldn't I have a maidservant as an escort for our shopping trip? After all, my cousins, the Fates, are very important goddesses here on Mount Olympus. We wouldn't want their friends to think the Fates weren't offering me the respect and courtesy due a close family member, would we?"

Alex suppressed a grin at the fury in Heli's eyes. "I'm going to ask Calliope to accompany us today, if it's all right with you." She raised her brows and eyed the irate woman inquiringly, refusing to look away as Heli fumed.

After a tense moment, Heli looked away and replied stiffly, "Of course, Keeper Alex, you may bring a companion. It shall be as you wish."

Alex practically skipped into the hallway, where she caught the attention of a passing servant and asked her to send Calliope to join the shopping party. The older, silver-haired woman curtsied and hurried away to relay Alex's request.

Heli joined Alex in the hallway, her glare still firmly in place. "I'll tell the carriage driver to expect an extra person," she snapped as she yanked open the heavy wooden front door. "Your maid can sit with the driver," she added spitefully, her golden toga snapping as she strode out into the morning sunshine.

Alex stared after the golden nightmare and shook her head with a thoughtful frown. "What the hell is that woman's problem?" She muttered.

A familiar voice behind Alex answered her mumbled question. "Heli is one of Zeus's many fully human daughters, my dear." She turned quickly and smiled at her favorite divine cousin, Clotho. The matronly goddess wore her normal voluminous, pristine white toga, while her silver hair, wrestled into a thick braid, trailed down her back.

The kindly goddess smiled at Alex, then flicked a glance out the still-open door toward Heli, who was now glaring at Alex from the waiting carriage. Clotho sighed quietly and explained. "Heli inherited no magical power from her divine father, not even a drop, Alex. She takes after her mother, a human who is a mere servant in one of Zeus's many palaces. While Heli longs for acknowledgement from her father, having no magic means it will never come, I'm afraid."

Clotho breathed a frustrated sigh, her wise gaze pinning Alex in place. "On Mount Olympus, just as on Earth, one's inherited status and power level—or lack thereof—often governs the course of one's life, don't you agree, dear?"

Alex frowned, but nodded reluctantly. "I, uh, never asked for my magical powers—"

Clotho snapped, "This isn't about you, Alex. Heli has her own burdens to bear. Have they made her sharp? Yes. Could she handle herself better ... treat people better, especially those she resents so bitterly, like you? Also, yes."

The goddess placed a gentle hand on Alex's shoulder. "Be kind to her, dear, no matter how much you want to take her to task for her harsh manner."

Alex's gaze slid guiltily away from Clotho's knowing look. "Okay. I'll treat her with respect, even if she doesn't offer me any in return. I'm sorry, Clotho."

"No need to apologize, Alex. You are a good person," Clotho murmured, patting Alex's arm gently. "We all make snap decisions about people without knowing their circumstances, but we must remember that their burdens are not the same as ours."

Before Alex could reply, Calliope came rushing down the hall before sliding to a stop in front of Alex, breathing heavily. "I'm sorry for the delay, but I had to change into something presentable for our shopping excursion." The maid bobbed a quick curtsy to Clotho. "Ma'am."

Clotho laughed as she ushered them both out the door. "Go. Have fun, girls. Buy beautiful togas."

Calliope halted, glancing at her employer with a frown. "You mean buy *a* beautiful toga ... for Alex. Right?"

"No, Calliope, buy yourself a toga as well. I've decided you'll be attending the banquet tonight as Alex's personal assistant," Clotho said, grinning at the shocked maid. "If Demeter will have a personal assistant at this evening's function, then Alex should, as well."

Calliope nodded mutely, then gave Clotho a fierce grin and hurried after her new mistress—even if only for a day.

ALEX STUDIED herself in the dressing room's full-length mirror with a sigh. This was the fifth toga she had tried on in this shop, which was the third one they had visited that morning. She had lost count of how many simpering store clerks she'd met and how many togas the women had stuffed her into. So far, both Heli and Calliope were agreed; they had not found the perfect toga for her. Yet. She was surprised that the two very different women had agreed on anything, and shocked that Heli, despite her brash manner, truly seemed interested in finding Alex a suitable toga, rather than sabotaging her sartorial efforts.

Someone whipped aside the curtain covering the dressing room, startling Alex. A grinning Calliope stood in the opening, eyeing her with approval. "This may just be 'the one,' Alex. It fits you much better than anything else you've tried on. Plus, the color along the border really suits you. It matches your green eyes perfectly."

Alex glanced down and fingered the toga's fine material. A wide strip of emerald green fabric edged the toga's many folds. Unicorns and other fantastical creatures embroidered in fine gold thread pranced, crawled, and slithered across the silken border, while sparkling jewels glittered along its length. The unicorns had rubies for eyes, blood red against their snowy white coats. Appropriate, Alex mused, recalling the herd of fierce unicorns she had fought alongside in her first battle. She had been shocked to discover that unicorns were not the shy, gentle 'horses with horns' that legends portrayed, but enormous, fierce creatures who enjoyed a good fight more than anything. She had known then that human mythology bore little resemblance to the supernatural truth. That realization had both terrified and amazed her. It still did, every day.

"Can we say we've found 'the one', then?" Calliope asked, her eyes hopeful. "I think this toga looks stunning on you, Alex. The green border really sets off your eyes."

Alex agreed with a nod. At least they could cross one item off their shopping list. Calliope had told her she would also need matching sandals, a cashmere stole, hair adornments, jewelry, and more, but they couldn't shop for those until they found the right toga, so they could coordinate colors, fabrics, and jewels. *Sigh.*

Grinning, Calliope steered Alex out of the dressing room and into the shop's elegant customer lounge, where Heli reclined regally on a pillow-strewn chaise lounge. Servants fluttered around her, pouring the dour woman wine and serving her snacks.

Heli glanced casually at Alex, then did a double take, her eyes narrowed in consideration, thin lips pursed. "Well, I think we've performed the impossible: found a toga that doesn't look half bad on you and that won't embarrass your divine family at the banquet tonight," she drawled.

Alex clenched her jaw and merely nodded. There was no point in responding to Heli's venom. It just made the unhappy woman smile when Alex reacted to her biting words. "So, we'll get this one, then," she replied blandly.

Heli waved her hands at the shop assistants in dismissal and rose from the couch. "That'll do. Now, you'll need to shop for the finishing touches." She wrapped her shawl around her thin shoulders and added, "I can see you both have things well in hand. I'm going to leave you two to it." Heli strode from the shop, her parting words floating over her shoulders. "I have far more important things to do today."

Calliope and Alex grinned at each other in delight. "Finally," Calliope breathed. "I was beginning to wonder if I'd spend this evening in the dungeon for slapping that obnoxious bit— uh, woman, instead of attending the banquet."

Alex snickered and rolled her eyes. "Me too, girlfriend."

Now that it was time to pay for her first purchase, Alex realized she had not given a thought to how she would do this. She eyed the salesclerk, who was busy wrapping the toga, worriedly. Would they accept an earthly credit card? Probably not. She had barely any cash on her, and, based on the exclusivity of the store, she knew what little she had probably wouldn't buy a single hair clip, let alone a formal toga and all the accessories. Her American dollars weren't the right currency, she was sure.

Calliope correctly interpreted Alex's concern and assured her that Clotho was picking up the tab for the shopping excursion. Alex nodded mutely, heaving an internal sigh of relief and resolving to pay her cousin back after the event. Somehow.

The two new friends spent the rest of the morning loading down the carriage with bag after bag of beautiful—and extremely expensive—clothing and accessories, including a lovely toga and all the trimmings for Calliope, as well. *Go big or go home,* Alex mused with a smile.

"Are you hungry, Alex?" Calliope asked. "I don't know about you, but I'm starving, and I know just the place for lunch."

Lunch? Alex's stomach growled in response.

29

LUNCH, INTERRUPTED

Alex sighed and sipped the light, fruity wine Calliope had ordered when they first sat down. She resisted rubbing her sore feet, instead gazing around the enormous room at the other diners, all of whom lounged on long, low chaise lounges, which surrounded large tables of a similar height. Dozens of serving staff hurried between the tables and the kitchens, ferrying jugs of wine, water, and food that looked and smelled amazing. Alex's stomach growled loudly, making her dining companion laugh.

"The food will be here soon, I promise," Calliope said with a grin. "My older brother is the head chef here. He'll take care of his baby sister ... and you, of course. My doofus of a brother knows I'll tell our mom if he keeps me waiting too long. Then he'll be eating burned food at home for weeks."

Alex laughed, protesting, "But he's a chef. Can't he cook his own food?"

"Not in our mother's kitchen, he can't," Calliope replied, rolling her expressive eyes. "No one is allowed in there but my mother and our long-time cook, who is totally loyal to my mother above all of us mere children, even if many of us are now adults."

A pang of sorrow pierced Alex's heart. She grew up with a cold, distant mother who had always treated Alex like an inconvenience—when she thought of her at all. Other than her kindly stepfather, who had died when she was a young adult, Alex had always thought she had no other family. However, less than a year ago, a legacy from a long-lost aunt had propelled Alex into the bosom of a loving heart family which had been mourning her loss for years—ever since her conniving, non-custodial mother had kidnapped her as a child.

Calliope sensed Alex's change in mood and apologized. "I'm sorry, Alex. I don't know what I said that upset you—"

Alex pulled herself out of her bitter memories and smiled at her new friend. "Don't apologize," she assured her. "It's nothing you said. Not really." She grinned and clinked her drink against Calliope's. "Here's to big, happy families, like yours."

Silently, Alex thanked the gods for her newly discovered and ever-growing heart family. Maybe it hadn't been what she had wanted when she had first arrived in San Antonio to settle her aunt's estate. She had been determined to wind up her aunt's affairs and leave town as soon as possible, longing to return to her quiet, independent, and family-free life. Things had not turned out as she had planned—and she was thrilled they hadn't, even if her new life came with danger, too many responsibilities, and more magical power than she knew what to do with.

"HERE'S YOUR FOOD, LADIES," said a handsome, smiling man in a white chef's hat and apron. His smile widened to a grin, and he tipped his head to Alex before flicking an exasperated glance at Calliope. "If my sister gets too annoying, you have my permission to dunk her in the closest fountain."

Calliope gave her brother a mock glare. "Chion! What are you doing serving our meal? You're the head chef," she chastised.

Grinning, she added, "I thought they kept you locked in the kitchen so the lonely matrons don't see your handsome face and swoon into their soup bowls."

Chion's dancing eyes belied his scowl. "You know very well, sister, that this is my restaurant, and I can do as I wish." He grinned sheepishly and murmured, "Plus, the last woman that fainted totally wasn't my fault."

Alex watched the sparring siblings with a smile. She had to agree with Calliope, though; her brother *was* incredibly good-looking. With a riot of curling blond hair, brilliant blue eyes, chiseled cheekbones, smooth olive skin, full lips, and a dimple in just the right spot on his chin, Calliope's brother was heart-stoppingly handsome. And he looked nothing like his short, curvy, red-headed sister. *Hmmm.*

Chion turned a brilliant smile on Alex, dragging her out of her musings. "Ignore my sister, ma'am. I apologize on her behalf. She's the baby of the family and hasn't yet got the maturity—" Chion's teasing apology cut off when Calliope kicked her brother's ankle. Hard. "Oww! That hurt, brat!"

Calliope grinned unrepentantly at her scowling brother. "Did it? Oh, I'm so sorry, but I haven't got the maturity to know that a good kick to the ankle would hurt." She gave Alex a merry wink and picked up her wine, then put it back down with a gasp.

"Oh, I'm so sorry, Alex. Excuse my manners!" Pink-cheeked, she gestured at her attractive sibling. "This is my brother, Chion. Chion, meet Alex. She's cousin to the Fates and a demi-goddess in her own right—"

Before her new friend could spout off all of her supposed achievements, Alex interrupted. She held out her hand and said, "It's nice to meet you, Chion. Your sister has, uh, told me so much about you." *Not.*

Chion grinned and shook Alex's hand with a firm grip. "I'm sure she told you there would be hell to pay at home if I didn't serve my baby sister and her guest well and with all speed." He removed the golden domes covering their plates with a flourish and murmured, "Enjoy your meal, ladies."

Alex watched the confident man stride back toward the kitchen, turning female heads along the way, then gave her attention to the food on her plate. She groaned and grabbed her fork. "This food smells wonderful, and I'm starving!"

Calliope, her mouth already full of her older brother's amazing cooking, gave Alex a closed-lip grin and nodded in agreement.

The two friends ate their delicious meal in companionable silence.

Toward the end of the meal, a short, compact server approached carrying a folded piece of paper, which he discreetly handed to Alex. "I'm so sorry to interrupt, ladies, but there's, uh ... a lady who'd like a word with you, ma'am." He gazed at Alex expectantly.

Alex frowned at the server, then opened the folded paper he had handed her and read the note it contained.

Meet me in the private dining room. Send your new friend home with an excuse. I'll explain everything when you get here. ~D

Suppressing a resigned sigh, Alex realized that 'D' could only be one person, er, goddess. Demeter. Nothing good ever came from meeting demanding goddesses in restaurants, she brooded, remembering the time when Demeter's divine daughter, Persephone, had stormed into her uncle's pizza restaurant, interrupted her date with Conor, and demanded Alex stop an imminent royal coup in the Fae realm—which the promiscuous goddess may or may not have instigated. She sighed, wondering why Demeter was using cloak and dagger methods to meet with her, but she dared not avoid the goddess's imperious summons.

"What does the note say?" Calliope asked, studying Alex with raised brows. "Should I call my brother out here to deal with things?"

Alex shook her head and patted the air. "No worries, Calliope. There's a, uh, friend in the private dining room who wants to have a chat with me." She forced a calm smile. "You go ahead and take the shopping back to the house. My friend will give me a ride home, I'm sure."

Calliope frowned, her worried eyes on the note still in Alex's hand. "But you don't know anyone on Mount Olympus. Do you?"

"It's someone I know who visits my Crossroads regularly," Alex explained. "She's good friends with my Aunt Maia. No worries. Really. I'll see you at home in a little while."

After giving Alex a searching look, Calliope reluctantly agreed. Still suspicious, she told Alex, "Okay, but if you have any trouble at all, just flag down a server and ask for my brother. He'll sort things right out."

Alex smiled at her new friend. "I will. You can count on it."

Calliope sighed and rose from her couch. "Don't be too long, Alex. You'll need to rest before we get ready for tonight's banquet. And we really can't be late."

"No worries. I'll make sure this doesn't take too long," Alex assured her, before rising and following the server away from the table.

30

OF MEETINGS & MUSTACHES

The server led Alex the length of the elegant dining room and behind a massive potted palm that hid an unobtrusive door. He knocked diffidently, then ushered Alex into a private dining room before closing the door softly behind her.

The dining room was almost empty ... except for the two people seated at opposite ends of a massively long dining table. Both stared appraisingly at Alex. She recognized the woman; her guess had been right. Demeter lounged on a comfortable but upright dining chair, sipping wine with a sly smile.

Alex studied the large man at the far end of the table. Despite the sunlight streaming in from a series of massive windows lining one side of the room, shadows partially obscured the man's face. She gingerly approached the table, hoping for a better look at the mystery man.

"Oh, stop it with the theatrics, brother," Demeter snapped. "Alex needs to know who she's talking to, you fool."

Alex narrowed her eyes and studied the man more closely. She could tell he was tall, even seated. Shimmering golden curls cascaded down to brush his wide shoulders. Thick, muscular arms revealed golden skin. She got the impression of a square face, tall forehead, large nose, and full lips from what she could see behind the shadows swirling around the man's face.

Demeter slapped her hand on the table and growled, "Knock it off, Zeus. Now. Let her see your face, you idiot." The goddess turned her gaze to Alex and gestured to a chair beside her. "Come, child. Sit next to me so we can chat."

Alex smoothed her face, keeping hidden her shock at facing not one, but two powerful Olympian gods. *Freaking Zeus!* What the hell did he want with her? This couldn't be good. Pasting on a smile, she approached the grinning goddess at the far end of the table.

Demeter poured a goblet of wine, placing it on the table next to Alex with an enigmatic smile. "Sit, Keeper, and have some wine. You'll need it," she murmured.

Breathe, Alex reminded herself. *Don't let these scheming gods get to you.* She suppressed a sigh and admitted that wasn't happening, especially since she now seemed to be the 'go-to' person when any of the friggin' gods had a problem. She plopped down on the chair next to Demeter, swigged a gulp of the surprisingly excellent wine, and turned her gaze to the god at the far end of the table, barely containing a yelp when she realized the table had shrunk drastically and changed shapes since the last time she looked. The three of them were now seated around a cozy, round café table set for three.

Holy Hades, Alex mused, nearly overcome by the chief god's powerful presence, especially now that he sat so close to her his knees brushed hers under the tiny table. She focused her eyes on Zeus's still-shadowed visage and fiddled with her wineglass, waiting not-so-patiently to find out what the gods wanted from her this time.

"Ouch! Who kicked me?" Zeus complained. "That hurt."

"It was meant to, brother. Now drop the shadows and join the party," Demeter demanded, her delicate golden brows lowered in irritation. The goddess's lovely face lightened, and she gave Alex a wry grin. "Not that my august brother's face is any prize, mind you. Especially not with that ridiculous fake mustache he's got plastered under his lip."

Alex gazed expectantly at the god seated way too close to her. She figured even Zeus wouldn't want to anger his powerful sister, and she was right. The shadows abruptly faded, revealing a classically handsome face—golden curls toppling over a high forehead, sharp cheekbones, and thick eyelashes a girl would kill for—all just as she pictured it. Well, except for the enormous, raven-black mustache reposing under the golden-haired god's rather large nose. She stifled a disbelieving laugh, turning it into a cough.

"I know, Alex," Demeter snickered. "He looks ridiculous with that ... that dead ferret glued to his face." The goddess rolled her eyes. "My brother thinks that monstrosity makes a good disguise, allowing him to walk around Mount Olympus unrecognized. *As if.* He even wears the damn thing on his jaunts to the earthly realm, if you can believe it. Says everyone treats him like a celebrity if he's not in disguise. Poor thing."

Alex flicked her eyes between the two divine siblings, seeing not only the resemblance between the two but also the deep affection they had for each other. She realized that, despite Demeter's earlier inference that Zeus would harm his sister for not attending the banquet, the only one in real danger of that had been—and still was—Alex.

"Um, well..." she stuttered, unsure how to respond to Demeter's teasing without offending Zeus.

"No need to say anything, Keeper," Zeus said, smoothing the massive mound of hair above his lips. "I know way more than my sister about disguises. The mustache looks amazing, right?"

"Yep. Amazing," Alex assured him, trying not to wince. *Not.*

"Now that we've got my brother's mistake of a mustache out of the way," Demeter said, "we should get down to business." The goddess studied Alex appraisingly. "You're probably wondering why I requested to meet with you in private and why my annoying brother is present."

"Well..." Alex began.

Zeus stopped messing with his mustache and leaned forward, his suddenly intense gaze pinning Alex in place. "You're here because my sister tells me I need to pay more attention to the size and extent of the divine rebellion allegedly going on under my nose."

Demeter snickered and sipped her wine. "There's way too much going on under your nose, brother."

Zeus touched his furry mustache and flicked his sister an annoyed glance. Then he returned his intense blue-eyed gaze to Alex. "Tell me, Keeper, is my harpy of a sister right? Is Nyx really planning to stage a coup from her prison at the edge of the Underworld, right under my nos—um, right now? Do you truly suspect the connivance of some of my gods in this coup?" The god rolled his eyes, adding, "Other than Morpheus, of course, who's always been a grandmama's boy and a royal pain in my ass. And what's this I hear about a nefarious group supposedly working with Nyx called the 'Chaos Council'?"

Nodding encouragement at Alex, Zeus said, "Talk to me, Alex. Pretend I'm not a god."

Alex nodded mutely. *Yeah, right.* The man was most definitely a god. Still, she straightened her shoulders and started her explanation. It was high time someone woke up this egotistical and oblivious god before his kingdom—and the rest of the realms—descended into divine chaos, while the fool fiddled with his fake mustache.

SOME TIME LATER, Alex finally finished her impromptu explanation. Thankfully, Zeus had been a good listener, only interrupting to clarify a point and nodding when he understood.

"So that's about it, I think," Alex said as she reached for her wineglass. Convincing a doubting god that he risked his divine kingdom—and so much more—by keeping his head buried in the sand was thirsty work. She risked a glance at Demeter, who had remained silent during her speech. The goddess had merely sipped her wine and nodded once or twice in agreement.

"Did I miss anything?"

"No, child," Demeter replied, gracing Alex with a small smile. "You did well."

The goddess eyed her brother with pursed lips, absently moving her wineglass in a slow circle on the table. "*Now*, do you believe me, brother?"

Several fraught moments passed while Zeus considered the two women before him through narrowed eyes, an enigmatic expression on his handsome face.

The god finally sighed, his wide shoulders sinking in defeat. "Yes, I believe you, sister. It's ... I just ... I mean, well, I guess I haven't realized that our divine sister, Nyx, poses a genuine threat to my kingdom, let alone to any of the other realms," he admitted. "After all, we all got together and locked her chaotic ass up at the far side of the Underworld millennia ago. Things have been relatively quiet since."

Demeter snorted a laugh. "Only *you* would say things have been quiet the last few thousand years, brother. While the rest of the gods have had their hands full with history and happenings, you've been too busy sleeping around and suffering the consequences meted out by your harridan of a wife to pay attention." The irritated goddess met her brother's sheepish gaze and asked, "When's the last time Hera tried to kill you, anyway?"

Zeus shifted in his chair and looked away, absently stroking his extremely fake mustache. "Last month's mushroom soup tasted a little funny..." he murmured. After a tense pause, he waved a dismissive hand. "And it's not like my wife doesn't sleep around, too."

"Did it ever occur to you, brother, that Hera sleeps around to get back at you for your many, many affairs?" Demeter patted Zeus on the shoulder with a sigh. "I'm afraid your marriage troubles are a topic for another time, brother. Right now, we must plan a strategy for tonight's banquet so we can unmask the traitors and throw them all in the dungeon." The powerful goddess sipped her wine and shrugged philosophically. "Or we could just kill them all. That would work, too."

Almost as an afterthought, Demeter flicked a glance at Alex and added, "Oh, and perhaps we could save this one's life while we're at it. Hopefully."

Both gods turned considering gazes on Alex, who was still reeling from Demeter's casual mention of the very real threat to her life at that evening's banquet.

"Uh, maybe I could just skip the banquet—"

"NO," both gods shouted simultaneously.

"Okay. Just asking." Alex sat back with a defeated shrug and sipped her wine, tuning out as the divine siblings discussed strategy and considered which gods they knew they could count on—and those whose loyalty was in question. She recognized some divine names, but many, many others she had never heard of before. *And here's yet another example of the total inaccuracy of the human version of Greek mythology,* she mused.

As she sipped the last of her wine, Alex realized the conversation going on around her had drawn to a close. She looked up to find both Demeter and Zeus studying her appraisingly.

"What?" She asked, nerves shivering up her spine. "Um, did I miss something?"

Demeter's lips curved into a sly smile. "Not much, my dear. Just the part where you need to save the day."

Alex just barely refrained from banging her head on the table. *Sigh.* "Alright, what do you want me to do?"

"Bring *all* your divine powers tonight, Alex," Zeus counseled her, a grim smile playing on his lips. "We may need them." The king of the gods shifted uneasily in his chair. "Especially if your—um, grandfather, Chronos, decides to show up."

Well, hot damn.

DEMETER SPENT the carriage ride back to the Fates' mansion counseling Alex on divine banquet etiquette. "Don't forget: you must stand when a full god enters the room, but not for anyone lower than that. And don't forget to hold your wine goblet in your left hand, while eating only with your right..."

Alex listened to the goddess's instructions with an internal sigh. After the meeting they had just attended, where battle plans and life and death were the chief topic of conversation, which hand to hold her wineglass in seemed exceedingly unimportant.

"I'll send a guarded carriage for you tonight, Alex. Don't forget to bring your new friend, Calliope," Demeter said with a sly smile. "We've got exciting plans for her."

That off-hand comment woke Alex out of her musings. She glared at Demeter and growled, "Calliope will *not* be a human sacrifice tonight, or anything like that. I absolutely forbid it."

Demeter raised her eyebrows and gave Alex a warning glare. "I'll overlook your disrespect this once, child, but watch your tone with me. You may be a powerful demi-goddess, but I can still squash you like a bug."

Alex gulped and nodded as an icy trickle of dread slid down her spine. "Sorry, ma'am. It won't happen again."

"Of course, your new friend won't be a human sacrifice, Keeper," Demeter huffed. The goddess rolled her eyes and added, "We don't do that kind of thing. Well ... not anymore, at least. Who do you think we are? A bunch of ancient, immortal savages?"

Don't say it. Don't say it. Alex counseled herself as she strove to keep her opinion off her face and out of her reply.

"No, ma'am. Not at all," she replied blandly.

The carriage pulled to a stop on the gravel drive in front of her cousins' elegant manor house. Alex spotted Calliope madly waving at her from under the portico. She gave the goddess a wary side-eye and risked her wrath by repeating her earlier command as a plea. "She's my friend, Demeter. I don't want to see her hurt tonight. Please."

The beautiful goddess merely smiled and replied, "Then you'd better bring your A-game, my dear."

Her shoulders drooping wearily, Alex sighed and nodded in silent assent. She stepped out of the carriage without another word when the driver opened the carriage door.

"There you are!" Calliope enthused, her face crinkling with a welcoming smile. "It's been hours, and I was starting to worry." Alex found herself enveloped in a crushing hug. "Next time you get a secret message like that, I'm not leaving you, no matter what you say," she whispered. Releasing Alex, the maid stepped back and studied her with concern. "Are you really okay?"

Alex forced a smile and nodded. "I'm fine, Calliope. Just tired. Do I have time to take a nap before we get ready for the banquet?"

Calliope stared thoughtfully after the departing carriage before turning a sunny smile on her new friend. She nodded at Alex and said, "Of course, there's time for a nap. Olympian banquets don't start until well after dark." Grabbing Alex by the hand, the maid pulled her inside. "Oh, and I've sorted out all your purchases and had your formal toga brushed and ironed. I've put a small snack in your room to tide you over until tonight. And I told Larry—he's back in your room, by the way—that he better not touch your snack, or I'll tell the chef to cut his food rations."

Bemused, Alex let the happily chattering woman usher her down a labyrinth of hallways until they reached her guest bedroom.

"Now get some rest, then have something to eat, Alex," Calliope commanded. "I'll be back in a couple of hours to draw your bath."

"I can do that by myself," Alex protested.

"Nonsense," the woman assured her. "I've already rounded up several volunteers from among the maids to help get you ... us, ready for tonight." She grinned, her big blue eyes sparkling with excitement. "I'm going to a divine banquet! I can't believe it! It's gonna be so much fun!"

Alex nodded silently, then shut the guest room door with a relieved sigh, leaving her bubbly friend in the hallway. She sure as hell wasn't counting on the 'fun' part. If they both got through Zeus's infernal banquet with their lives, she'd be happy.

31

LARRY REVEALS A SECRET

A low noise startled Alex awake. She struggled with the twisted bedcovers and sat up, her bleary eyes straining to make out anything in the growing gloom. When a furry face appeared six inches from her nose, she yelped and scrambled back until the bed's carved headboard stymied her retreat.

"It's only me, Alex. No need to freak out." Larry snickered and wagged his tail, his tongue hanging out in a canine grin. Then he sobered and added, "Time to rise and shine, dudette. There's ... uh, have a couple of things we need to discuss before your chatty new friend and her hoard of helpers show up to get you ready for tonight's banquet."

Alex glared at her canine Familiar and pushed him away. "You scared the crap out of me, fur-face! Couldn't you just tap me with your paw, like you usually do? Noooo, you've got to get right in my face and bark, you jerk," she complained.

Larry rolled his eyes, retreating to sit at the end of the bed with a huff. "I tried to wake you up gently, sleepyhead. But you were sleeping like the dead. Listen—"

"Stop. Just stop," Alex interrupted. She held up a warning

hand and climbed wearily off the bed. "I'm still not awake, bud. Lemme just use the facilities."

"Then can we talk?"

"Then we can talk."

ALEX KNEW she needed to let her magical partner have his say. She couldn't hide in the bathroom forever, anyway. When she reluctantly opened the bathroom door, she spotted her furry Familiar lounging hopefully on the rug under the table by the window. Her stomach rumbled with hunger when she recalled the snack Calliope had left for her.

"You better not have eaten my food, fuzz-butt," Alex grumbled, before pulling the silver dome off the tray. She smiled when the tray revealed a nicely arranged assortment of finger food, including tiny flatbreads, bowls of olives, slices of cheese, and plump dates.

"I wouldn't do that to you," Larry replied with a snort. "I know how you get when you're hangry."

Alex gave the little poodle a disbelieving smile. "You're telling me that Calliope's threat to tell the chef to cut your food rations had absolutely *nothing* to do with you leaving this food alone?"

Larry tried on an innocent look, but then grinned up at Alex. "Her warning might have had something to do with your untouched snack," he admitted. He yawned, stretched, and climbed out from under the table. "But she didn't say that you couldn't share some of it with me ... best friend."

"Suck-up," Alex said without rancor as she sat down to eat. She offered him a slice of cheese, which disappeared in one quick bite. "Slow down, bud, or you'll take off my finger. There's plenty here for both of us."

The two friends enjoyed their meal in companionable silence.

Not long after the last crumb left the plate, Larry jumped on the bed and sat facing Alex, a somber look overtaking his furry face. Apprehension raised the hair on the back of Alex's neck. Larry's normal chipper snark and sass were nowhere in evidence; whatever her Familiar had to say must be serious.

"Spit it out, Larry. Whatever it is, it can't be that bad."

"Oh yes, it can."

"Oh no, it can't—" Alex stopped herself. "I'm not playing that game. Out with it, fur-face," she demanded.

Larry nodded, then straightened up, placing his front paws together, as if sitting at attention. "What I'm about to tell you needs to remain between you and me, Alex. I've been keeping it to myself, but you really need to know, since my secret might just give us an advantage at tonight's damned banquet. But no one must ever know what I'm about to tell you—unless it can't be helped." The suddenly serious poodle lowered his gaze to the blanket and whispered, "Plus, what I've got to say might ... uh, change your mind about me. I just need you to know that I'd never do anything to harm you, Alex."

Concerned, Alex rose and moved to the bed. She sat next to her uncharacteristically intense Familiar and placed a gentle hand on his back. "Larry, whatever you have to tell me won't change my mind about you. You're my magical partner and my best friend. Nothing can change that, bud."

"We'll see," Larry muttered cryptically. He gazed intently at the bedspread, as if engrossed in the fabric's warp and weft. "Remember, after the battle to save the abbey, when I mind-spoke to tell you that Olympe was badly wounded and asked you to come to the infirmary?"

"Yeeees," Alex drawled, wondering where this was going. "I came running." Memories of the bloody scene in the infirmary flooded her mind. "I passed Reine, the Infirmière, lying in the hallway." She grimaced and rubbed her eyes, as if she could erase the sight of the dead woman from her memory. The nun's throat had been viciously torn open; gaping wounds had covered her arms and legs, and a lake of blood had pooled around her body. "She was ... um, very dead."

"Do you remember seeing the paw prints in the blood?" Larry asked softly.

Alex's eyes widened at the memory. "Yes! There were these huge paw prints all around the body, and a bloody paw print trail led down the hallway, toward—"

"Toward the room where you found me, Grenoble, and Olympe," Larry stated.

Alex absently stroked her Familiar's back, offering them both comfort as she recalled the grisly scene. "I thought ... well, I really didn't give the paw prints too much thought. I was still buzzed from the battle and wanted to get to Olympe as fast as possible to see if I could help." Dread curled in her stomach, and her hand clenched in the little poodle's soft fur. "What are you trying to tell me, Larry?"

"They were my paw prints, Alex," Larry replied softly. He raised sad eyes to meet Alex's and whispered, "I'm the one who killed Reine."

"What?!" Alex gasped, her eyes wide with disbelief and shock. She softened her tone and said, "Larry, those paw prints were massive. No offense, but your mini-poodle paws are way too small to have made those prints. You couldn't have ... why would you..." Her protestations trailed off as she studied Larry's carefully blank expression. "Explain. Now, please."

"First, let me tell you why, then I'll tell you how," Larry replied. He shook his head growling softly, as if the memories he'd stirred up disturbed him as much as Alex. "During the battle, Grenoble and I were scouting around the back of the infirmary to see if any of the bad guys were hiding in the woods behind it when we heard a scream. It sounded like Olympe, so we booked it through the infirmary's back door to see what was going on."

He closed his eyes and rubbed a paw over his face, as if to wipe away the horror he and Grenoble had found inside the infirmary.

"We found Olympe on the floor in the back room, covered in blood. Reine stood over her with a knife, about to deliver a killing blow. We both attacked the traitor, but she got away. I told Grenoble to stay with Olympe. Reine ran, but she didn't get far. I … um, finished the job in the hallway."

Stunned, she eyed the little poodle doubtfully. "But the paw prints … they were massive. How could you—"

"I could because I had to, Alex," Larry replied simply. "I couldn't let Reine kill Olympe or get away and warn the attackers." He huffed a frustrated sigh. "I'm so, so sorry."

"Don't apologize for doing what you had to do, bud," Alex murmured. She shook her head and rubbed a reassuring hand down Larry's tense back. "Reine deserved her fate for what she did." She frowned down at her lapdog-sized Familiar in confusion. "But how…"

Larry eyed his magical partner and licked his lips. "What I'm about to say is the really important bit. And it's why I'm telling you what really happened that day." He growled low and flicked Alex a glance. "You know I'm an eternal animal Familiar, right? After each assignment, my soul returns to the Underworld, where I'm issued a new job, a new magical partner … and a new physical form."

He rolled his eyes, frustration coloring his next words. "And, of course, since my case manager at DEAF—that's the Department of Eternal Animal Familiars, and yes, the acronym is fitting—well, he and I don't get along. I think Mort's a total waste of space, and he knows it. Mort, uh, tends to 'get even' with me for my smart mouth by giving me the most ridiculous physical form he can think of—"

Alex snickered; she couldn't help it. "That totally explains your current poodle incarnation." She burst out laughing, eyeing Larry through tears of mirth. "Boy, you must really have pissed your case manager off to rate the pink ears and tail, though."

Larry curled his lips in a sheepish grin, nodding in reluctant agreement. "Well, Mort shouldn't be such a dick all the time. I can't help it if the guy is such a lazy, incompetent oaf." He snorted and shook his head. "But that's not important right now. What *is* important ... and is something the idiots at DEAF have yet to discover, is that some powerful Familiars like me can shift into any previously assigned form—if the need is great enough. We try not to do it unless it's life or death, and we've all taken an oath not to reveal our secret to anyone, so the official drones at DEAF don't find out and shut down this magical loophole out of pure spite—" his words trailed off into an annoyed whine.

"I won't say a word, Larry," Alex promised solemnly, honored that her Familiar trusted her enough to reveal such an important secret. She placed her hand over her heart. "I promise on my life."

"Thanks, Alex," Larry muttered with a sigh of relief. "I appreciate that."

"Soooo, tell me. What former form did you take that day at the infirmary?" Alex couldn't help asking, her curiosity piqued.

Larry shook himself, as if throwing off the seriousness of their conversation. "In my last magical gig, I had the body of a massively muscled, midnight black Rottie-Pit mix." He snickered, as if at an inside joke. "I was a real junkyard dog. That canine body was my favorite physical form in centuries, and I really hated giving it up."

"Wow," Alex breathed, her eyes wide as she considered the small white poodle with bright pink ears seated next to her. "So that explains the huge paw prints."

"Yep." Larry squinted up at Alex, his gaze filled with worry. "That explains the huge paw prints around Reine's body, all right." He hesitated, then added, "The main reason I'm telling you this now is because I'm afraid my junkyard dog form might need to come out and 'play' at tonight's banquet if things get dicey."

Alex smiled down at her anxious Familiar and gently tugged on one of his fluffy, bright pink ears. "I don't blame you for doing what needed to be done during the battle at the abbey, Larry. I'll never blame you for that, whatever happens tonight, or in the future."

After a tense moment, the little poodle sighed and settled down on the bed, his warm body pressed against Alex's thigh. He laid his head on her leg with a soft growl of contentment. "Thanks for understanding, Alex. You're the best."

She ruffled Larry's ears affectionately. "Just remember that the next time you and Grenoble come up with some hair-brained scheme that could get you both into trouble."

"No promises," he mumbled, adjusting his head so Alex could scratch under his ears. "But I'll keep it in mind."

A BRISK KNOCK on the door startled them both from their moment of contentment.

Larry jumped off the bed and scrambled underneath it. "I'm outta here. I'm not letting those ladies primp and prod me into a total fluff-ball for tonight's banquet."

Alex chuckled at her Familiar's irritated protest. "Don't think I won't tell Calliope where you're hiding, bud. You could use a good bath and blow-dry."

"Traitor."

"Scaredy-cat."

"Don't you dare call me a cat!"

The sharp knock came again, and Calliope's muffled voice sounded through the heavy wooden door. "Alex, are you awake? Can we come in? It's time to get ready for the banquet."

"Come on in, guys. I'm ready for you," Alex called, not even trying to keep the reluctance out of her voice.

32

BATTLE AT THE BANQUET

After several long hours of bathing, primping, prodding, dressing, hairstyling, makeup, and Alex didn't know what else, the gaggle of giggling maids Calliope had recruited to prepare them both for the banquet finally pranced out of the room. Alex stood in front of the full-length mirror, considering the stranger before her. She had never been much of a fashionista. A decent, clean outfit, a brush of mascara, and a touch of lipstick were usually the extent of her party preparations.

She almost didn't recognize the elegant woman gazing back at her from the mirror. Her thick, dark hair swirled in intricate loops around her head, each braid glittering with gold thread strung with sparkling gemstones. Strategic curls hung loose on each side of her face and tickled the back of her neck. Kohl-lined eyelids made her eyes sparkle like emeralds, while the rest of her makeup was discreet, merely enhancing her natural attributes, including her high cheekbones, full lips, and determined jawline. The toga she wore draped around her curves flatteringly, while the gold-ribboned sandals Calliope had insisted she buy that morning peeked out from underneath the lavishly embroidered hem of her under-tunic.

A reluctant smile curved Alex's lips. She might not be looking forward to Zeus's divine—and very possibly deadly—banquet, but her outfit sure slayed. With a pang of disappointment, she realized she wished Conor were attending the banquet with her. She missed him.

Movement behind her caught Alex's attention. Her eyes met Calliope's admiring gaze in the mirror.

"You look like a goddess, Alex," her new friend breathed reverently. "Truly, you do."

"Demi-goddess," Alex corrected, not willing to accept the promotion, even if only as a compliment. No way did she want the power or responsibilities of a full-fledged goddess. *Just nope.*

She turned to her friend with a smile. "You look marvelous, too, girlfriend." Calliope wore a light blue tunic almost the same color as her eyes. Green dragons twined along the wide embroidered edges of her toga, each sinuous creature breathing fiery scarlet flames that complemented the petite woman's red hair.

Calliope smiled, a deep blush coloring her cheeks as she shook her head. "Thanks, Alex, but I'm just your lady-in-waiting tonight. You're the star of the show. The guest of honor."

Alex sighed, anxiety roiling in her stomach. She had no desire to be the guest of honor at a divine banquet—or anywhere else. She just wanted to go home, make up with Conor, sort out the ghost war situation, and manage her Crossroads, but she suspected that tonight's banquet with the gods would nix those small dreams forever.

～

TRUE TO HER WORD, Demeter's luxurious carriage awaited Alex and Calliope in the courtyard. The three Fates, each dressed in different gem-colored togas, would take their own carriage. After hasty goodbyes, attentive guards helped the Fates into their carriage, which soon clattered down the cobbled driveway into the night.

Demeter's carriage featured two handsome, heavily armed warriors, each of whom perched on a small ledge that ran along the back of the vehicle. The goddess stuck her head out of a curtained window and waved a peremptory hand, beckoning Alex and Calliope forward. "Hurry up, you two. We don't want to arrive late. That's almost as bad as not arriving at all." She snickered and added, "And we all know how Zeus feels about that."

Alex shivered, recalling the foul-mouthed cherub who had appeared at her Crossroads recently to present her with an invitation to tonight's banquet. Attend—or die—was the main takeaway from that unpleasant experience. The cherub had casually mentioned his quiverful of arrows tipped with poison for the 'no' replies.

As she and Calliope arranged their togas on the bench opposite Demeter, Alex couldn't help asking, "Uh, will Zeus's messenger cherub, Momus, be attending tonight's party?"

Demeter gazed at Alex, her eyes glittering with humor in the carriage's dim light. "Gross little creatures, cherubs, aren't they?" The goddess snickered and shook her head. "Cherubs are just one more thing that humans got wrong, historically speaking. I really can't help laughing whenever I see those Renaissance paintings depicting cherubs as sweet, innocent little babies with wings, sent to bring the blessings of God. You'd think butter wouldn't melt in their mouths."

Alex grinned at the goddess, feeling her anxiety lessen. When Calliope couldn't contain a snort at Demeter's observations, Alex allowed herself a snicker.

"Cherubs are all foul-mouthed, nasty little bastards, if you ask me," Demeter snipped. Soon, all three women were helplessly giggling at Demeter's accurate, if profane, description of the cherub species.

◡

THEIR CARRIAGE soon arrived at Zeus's palace, along with hundreds of other carriages and palanquins, in a confused swirl of activity. As the trio alighted, servants quickly cut through the crowd and swept Alex and her party past the long line of guests still awaiting entry.

"Follow me, please," demanded a haughty servant dressed in a golden tunic. He ushered them through the castle's massive entryway into an enormous, high-ceilinged lobby. "Come this way and hurry up. You are all to be seated at the head table with his highness, King Zeus."

Alex caught Demeter's knowing gaze. The goddess rolled her eyes. "My brother is going through a 'king' phase right now." She leaned close and whispered, "And don't forget ... you've never met him or his mustache before."

Suppressing a grin, Alex hurried after the fleet-footed servant as he led them down one glittering hallway after another, until they finally spilled into an immense room with a ceiling so high the light from thousands of candles arrayed in lofty chandeliers barely reached the floor.

If one word could sum up the banquet hall, it would be 'gilded,' Alex thought as she gazed around in amused disbelief. Glittering gold leaf covered almost every surface: floors, walls, mirrors, window-frames—even the towering marble columns supporting the ceiling sparkled with gold veins. Gleaming jewels hung from the golden chandeliers and adorned the gilded candelabras scattered around the room.

"Elvis called, and he wants his decorations back," Alex murmured to herself.

"Sorry, what did you say?" Demeter asked.

"Oh, nothing," Alex muttered. She forced a smile, overwhelmed by the extravagant decor and the extraordinary divine power she felt emanating from the guests already milling around the room. "I didn't say anything," she reiterated. *And if I have my way, I won't say anything at all this evening,* she mused. That would probably give her and Calliope their best hope of making it through Zeus's damned banquet alive.

The arrogant servant ushered them toward a raised platform at the far end of the enormous room. Alex spotted a tall, heavily muscled man lounging on a—you guessed it—gilded throne positioned in the middle of the long head table that ran the length of the platform. Thick, golden curls cascaded down the man's back and were held in place by a thin golden diadem. His olive skin glowed from within, while a firm jaw, high cheekbones, and full lips gave him conventional good looks. The obnoxious mustache Zeus had worn for their secret meeting earlier in the day was, thankfully, missing. The god's luminous emerald eyes contained so much power that Alex stopped dead when they fixed on her.

Demeter placed an unobtrusive hand under Alex's arm and urged her forward. "Never let them see you sweat, my dear," the goddess murmured. "Especially not my bro—uh, I mean, the High King of the gods, as he has taken to calling himself."

Demeter's mocking words calmed Alex's racing heart. She forced herself to meet Zeus's gaze, refusing to lower her eyes as she stepped onto the raised platform and approached his throne. She dipped her head slightly to acknowledge the god, still not breaking their mutual stare.

Demeter made the introductions. "Hello Zeus. Please meet Keeper Alex and her companion, Calliope. They are both thrilled to be here this evening, as am I."

Alex pursed her lips to prevent a grin. Hopefully, Zeus missed the barely concealed sarcasm in his sister's words.

After a tense moment, Zeus's lips curved into an approving smile. He winked and gestured Alex to take a chair on his right. "Welcome, Keeper Alex. Please join me. We have reserved a chair next to us for our guest of honor this evening." He chuckled and patted the chair. "Come. Sit, Alex. After all, it's not every day we welcome a new demi-goddess into our midst."

Alex finally lowered her gaze from that of the powerful god, but not before seeing a merry twinkle lurking in his eyes, as if he'd recently learned a secret about Alex that amused him greatly. *Damn it.* She'd had enough of secrets and really didn't want to deal with any more. After all, with each new secret revealed, her workload increased, as did the danger swirling around her and those she loved. *Fuck-balls.*

A NOT-SO-SUBTLE PUSH from Demeter propelled Alex toward the chair next to Zeus.

"I'll sit next to you, Alex," the goddess murmured, so I can referee. "Calliope will be seated at the end of the table, with the other assistants."

Alex sank into the chair next to a god who used the royal 'we' when speaking of himself. High King Zeus, indeed. She breathed a sigh of relief when Zeus's attention switched to a petite, slender woman with sly eyes who swayed her way toward the head table. Alex could swear she heard Zeus suppress an annoyed growl before smoothing his features and rising to greet the beautiful newcomer.

"Hera, my lovely wife," Zeus murmured as he took the goddess's hand and kissed it. "So glad you could break away from your ... activities to attend tonight's banquet."

Hera gave her husband a thin smile before quickly withdrawing her hand and rubbing it on her toga. "I wouldn't miss tonight's event for the world, husband." The lovely goddess flicked Alex an enigmatic glance and murmured, "It will be ... interesting to see what develops, don't you agree?"

Zeus's eyebrows rose at the dark undercurrent in Hera's seemingly innocuous words, but he didn't challenge them. He merely pulled out the smaller throne on his left and helped his wife into it.

After seating Hera, Zeus pointedly turned away from her and toward Alex with a smile. Alex risked a glance over Zeus's shoulder at Hera and shivered at the malicious gleam in the powerful goddess's gaze.

Zeus could be quite charming, Alex admitted, as the King of the Gods engaged her in polite conversation. Soon, her nerves receded, and she enjoyed the rich red wine a server had unobtrusively poured for her.

Larry brushed against Alex's feet under the table, where he had retreated and curled up quietly while everyone was talking. *"Don't worry, Alex,"* he mind-spoke his encouragement. *"You've got this."*

"Thanks, Larry," Alex whispered, leaning down to run a hand over her Familiar's head.

ALEX JUMPED when Zeus abruptly stood and clapped loudly. Luckily, she had just set her wineglass on the table so she could pet Larry, or she'd have spilled it on the crisp, white tablecloth. Silence immediately descended as all faces turned toward their king.

"Attention, honored guests!" Zeus boomed, his voice effortlessly reaching everyone in the vast room. "We thank you all for graciously agreeing to attend tonight's banquet in honor of our newest demi-goddess." He took Alex's hand and pulled her to her feet. "We are thrilled to introduce our newest family member to the citizens of Mount Olympus. Please welcome Alexandria: Crossroads Keeper, Priestess of Hiereiai, and Olympian demigoddess!"

The room erupted in polite applause. Her cheeks blazing with embarrassment, Alex gazed around the room. She observed varying expressions in the crowd, ranging from happiness (her aunt Clotho was grinning widely) to polite interest, to barely masked anger and even outright hatred. *Seems not everyone was thrilled to welcome a new demi-goddess,* she mused. She took careful note of those who appeared the most unhappy. They might just be on Nyx's side in the dark goddess's never-ending machinations designed to overthrow order and ensure chaos reigned supreme.

As the audience's applause died down, shouting in the hallway outside the banquet hall could be heard.

"Move aside and let us in!"

"We have the right of entry!"

Heads turned toward the entryway, and the massive dining room quieted. Angry scuffles and the ring of swords being drawn sounded loud in the room's sudden stillness. As if by a hidden signal, several dozen of the banquet attendees sitting closest to the door jumped to their feet, drew their weapons, and rushed toward the guards preventing the crowd in the hallway from entering the room. Suddenly, snorting, stamping hooves, and an enraged bellow echoed from the dining room's high ceiling as a massive black bull charged into the room, forcing the guards away from the door. Multiple attackers followed the bull's charge, forcing the guards to retreat further.

Fierce fighting quickly spread around the massive banquet hall as the gods chose sides. Swords clashed and arrows whizzed through the air. Explosions rocked the room as powerful gods fought with magic. The gigantic bull charged unerringly through the chaos toward the raised platform supporting the head table.

Zeus waved his arms and bellowed orders, but the cacophony swallowed his words.

Alex called her Keeper staff and quickly charged it with her various powerful magics until the crystal at the staff's tip crackled with multi-colored lightning. But who should she fight? Amid the chaos, and not knowing friend from foe, Alex's urge to act was stymied ... until she spotted Morpheus creeping along in the wake of the massive black bull still pounding his way toward the head table. Her table. *Well, fuck.*

Suddenly, an enormous black dog shot out from under the table and charged toward the angry bull, growling and barking. *"It's me, Alex! The big black dog is me!"* Larry's worried voice sounded in Alex's mind. *"Please don't hit me with those crazy lightning bolts you've got shooting from your Keeper staff!"*

Alex's jaw dropped. Her fluffy little poodle Familiar had morphed into a massive, muscular, and midnight black junkyard dog, just as Larry had said he could. She tasted fear as she gazed in horror at the charging bull. The damn thing was bigger than an SUV. Even at Larry's enhanced size, he was no match for that creature.

Larry's body glowed with golden power as he launched himself onto the bull's back and bit down on his thick neck. The bull bellowed and shook himself, but Larry clung on, jaws working as he savaged the enraged animal's throat.

Alex shook her head, realizing that she had to trust her Familiar to do his job. She had other villains to fry. Literally. Aiming her staff at the silent figure still lurking in the bull's shadow, she let her magic loose. Multicolored prongs of lightning blazed from her staff and quickly found their mark. Morpheus screamed in pain, his body rigid as Alex's magical lightning surged through him. A stray lightning bolt hit the bull in the rear, causing it to buck madly, dislodging Larry from his back.

Larry landed nimbly on the floor before twisting himself around and under the beast, where his massive jaws ravaged the creature's exposed belly. Alex spotted a trio of blocky, brown canine heads on the beast's far side. The new dogs joined Larry's attack, allowing Alex to breathe a sigh of relief. Four dogs just might take that monster bull down.

She spared a glance up and down the head table. The only ones left were Zeus and Demeter, who had each taken a side and were fighting to keep the attackers off the raised platform. Where the hell did Hera go? Alex wondered as she raked the melee with her gaze. She watched with wide eyes as Zeus's snarling wife brandished a sword at Atropos, several tables away. The powerful goddess of Fate could beat Hera in the bitch department hands down, Alex knew. Atropos viciously snipped her ancient, bloodied scissors of Fate and eyed Hera with determination.

Zeus spotted the standoff and shouted, "Don't end her, Atropos! We need her alive. My wife obviously has answers about the opposition that we will need!"

Atropos flicked an annoyed glare at Zeus, but nodded in understanding. She quickly sidestepped Hera's sword swing, closed her scissors, then turned and stabbed the goddess with them on her now unprotected side. Hera screamed in pain and dropped her sword. The other two Fates closed in. Clotho touched a gentle hand to Hera's head and the injured goddess's body jerked, fell to the floor, and stilled. Lachesis produced sturdy ropes from under her voluminous toga and bound Hera's immobile form.

Alex sighed with relief. The Fates had subdued one of the most dangerous of the divine traitors. She turned her gaze back to the still-raging battle, her eyes widening with shock at the arrow whizzing straight toward her. She ducked, narrowly avoiding the deadly projectile, which swoshed by her head with a vicious twang.

A smoke-roughened voice carried over the noise of battle. "Fuck it! First time I've missed in eons. I won't miss my next shot, Keeper!"

Dammit. Alex recognized that voice. It belonged to Momus, the messenger cherub she and the others had been joking about a short while age. That winged asshole was trying to kill her. Demeter was right—cherubs *were* nasty little bastards.

~

IF ONLY I had time to take aim, Alex thought desperately as she crouched behind the table, *I could end that flying fucker.*

Suddenly, the world stilled. Nothing moved. All sounds had ceased. Alex risked a glance over the table and saw a frozen tableau of horror. Both attackers and defenders were frozen in place. Swords had stopped short of their targets, and arrows had stilled in mid-flight. *It wasn't me!* Alex shook her head in denial. "*I didn't do it this time!*" She protested with a groan of dismay.

"Yes, actually you *did* do it, my dear." A deep, masculine voice spoke near Alex's shoulder. "You stopped time with merely a thought, as you have done at least once before, Alex. Your time magic is almost as powerful as mine," the voice murmured thoughtfully.

Alex swung around to face the person who had crept up on her, unheard. Her staff crackled with magic, eager to lash out at the speaker, but she hastily moved it aside, unsure if she faced friend or foe.

"Don't creep up on me like that, you moron. I could have electrocuted you!" She growled.

A flicker of pride glinted in the tall man's gaze, and his amused smile widened. Alex frowned, studying the man—er—god before her. He was unusually tall, with a broad, muscular build. A thick braid of silver hair hung over one shoulder. The god's long face and gaunt cheeks gave him a funereal air, but his eyes glowed with life and power. Sooo much power.

Alex firmed her lips but couldn't keep angry words from bursting forth. "And just who the hell *are* you?" She winced, gripped her staff tightly, and muttered, "Oh, and ... uh, which side are you on?"

The large god roared with laughter. "Oh, I can certainly tell you're one of mine, alright. With all that attitude, and with the power to back it up."

"One of your ... what?" Alex asked suspiciously. "And you still haven't told me your name." She quirked a brow in query.

"My apologies, Alex," the god replied. Strangely, a fleeting look of disappointment flashed in his eyes. "I thought you might recognize the family resemblance. My name is Chronos. I'm your—"

Alex gasped and swayed. "You're my grandfather," she whispered.

Chronos winked at her and grinned slyly. "Close, but not quite," he murmured. Heaving a mighty sigh, the Titan sat heavily on Zeus's abandoned throne and gestured for Alex to retake her seat. "Come. Sit, child. We have a lot to discuss."

33

FROZEN IN TIME

Alex rolled her eyes and slumped into her chair. She resisted dropping her head onto the table or chugging the rest of her wine. Just barely.

In the ringing silence, she and Chronos gazed around the massive banquet hall. Everyone and everything remained frozen in place. Wine poured from a jug never reached the glass; faces had frozen in lines of savage laughter or fierce frowns of annoyance; another one of the cherub's deadly arrows was headed straight for her heart, but hovered in mid-air a few yards away from its target. Alex figured she could step aside before time unfroze and let the arrow whizz harmlessly by when chaotic motion returned to the room, but that wouldn't really solve anything. Momus surely had a few more demi-goddess killing arrows in that tiny quiver of his. And that foul-mouthed fool had good aim.

"I can't believe Zeus wants me dead," Alex murmured, glaring at the nasty little cherub currently frozen in mid-air, a cigarette hanging from his lips, which were curved in a malicious grin. "Why didn't he just have the little bastard kill me back at the Crossroads when he delivered the dinner invitation?"

"Because Zeus is not the one who wants you dead, Alex," Chronos replied, his voice neutral. He flicked a glance at the handsome, powerful god frozen in place at the end of the platform. "My son, Zeus, is many things, but subtle is not one of them."

"Then who?" Alex spread her arms wide in frustration. "Who in this room besides that asshole cherub and my 'dear' cousin Morpheus—oh, and most likely Hera—wants me ... specifically me, dead?"

Chronos pursed his lips and avoided her gaze. He fingered the end of his braid thoughtfully. "Who here wants you dead, child? Less than you think, but more than I'm comfortable with," he murmured, flicking a glance toward Hera, who was bound and frozen in place, with three angry, frozen Fates glaring down at her. "Hera is definitely on the *'wants you dead'* list. But the Fates seem to have her well in hand."

Alex smiled at her cousins, her affection for the dangerous—and more than slightly crazy—goddesses of Fate warming her heart. She glanced toward the formerly rampaging bull, now frozen in place, with four ... no two ... frozen dogs hanging off its bloodied carcass. Wait. She frowned and counted. There were four dog heads, but only two dog bodies. *What the heck?*

Turning a stunned gaze on the Titan at her side, she said, "Um, unless I'm seeing things, one of those dogs has *three* heads."

"Oh, the dog with the three heads is Cerberus, dear," Chronos replied with a grin. He nodded at the massive junkyard dog with only *one* head, formerly known as Larry the small white poodle, and murmured, "It appears your Familiar has been out making furry friends while you were toga shopping ... and secretly meeting with my son, Zeus, earlier today."

Alex's eyebrows quirked up in surprise. "I guess my secret meeting with Zeus isn't so secret, after all, since you seem to know all about it."

"I'm the one who suggested he meet with you, Alex," Chronos replied. "I told my son a few home truths as well. The oblivious fool needs to know who his friends are, and so do you." The Titan frowned, worry floating in his emerald eyes. "You're both going to need all the allies you can gather," he added cryptically.

Alex ignored her grandfather's cryptic warning and returned to the topic of the three-headed dog. "If that's Cerberus, isn't he—it, supposed to be guarding the gates of the Underworld?" She asked, genuinely confused.

The god's shoulders shook with silent laughter. "I understand that Hades and Persephone are on the outs at the moment, so Hades brought Cerberus as his 'plus one' to the banquet this evening." He shrugged and added, "I may have suggested that he do so."

Alex frowned thoughtfully. "I thought Hades and Persephone were getting marriage counseling?"

"Oh, they are," Chronos replied with an evil grin. "But apparently it's not going so well."

Grimacing, Alex recalled her meeting with Hades several months earlier, after the battle in the Underworld, when the big lug had begged her for marriage advice. She had recommended marriage counseling. *Oh well.*

Then Chronos's intimations caught up with her. She turned a suspicious gaze on her wily grandfather. "Soooo you told Zeus to meet with me, and you recommended Hades bring his monstrous dog tonight..."

The ancient Titan gave her a sheepish smile but remained silent.

"You're the one who organized this banquet, aren't you?" Alex accused. "Did you know that Nyx's co-conspirators would attack tonight?" Her eyes widening at Dier audacity, she snapped her mouth shut before getting herself into any more trouble. What she really wanted to ask her grandfather was, 'Whose side are you on?'

Chronos gave Alex a cheesy grin and answered her unspoken question instead of the ones she had asked out loud. "I'm on *your* side, of course, my dear." Then he waved a hand at Zeus. "And his side. And on the side of all my children but one." His gaze clouded, and he murmured softly, "Nyx." The Titan bowed his head and heaved a massive sigh.

Alex felt reluctant compassion for the Primordial god's obvious distress. She resisted reaching out, not sure her divine grandfather would welcome her sympathy, especially when she had practically accused him of scheming with Nyx. "I'm sorry," she whispered.

The Titan fiercely shook off his grief, his braid flapping wildly from side to side. "Six out of seven isn't a bad average," he muttered cryptically.

Chronos returned his gaze to the frozen room. When he spotted a charred, blackened body next to the gravely injured bull, he turned a proud gaze on Alex. "I see you've fried my traitorous grandson, Morpheus, with that special blend of magical lightning you can channel through your Keeper staff."

Alex gulped. "Um ... yes?" She flicked a panicked glance at the blackened body of her nemesis and blanched at the horrific scene. "He keeps popping up like a bad penny, trying to kill me. Is he, uh, really dead? Am I going to be in trouble for killing a god?"

"Oh yes, Alex, Morpheus is very, very dead," Chronos assured her. "And no, you aren't in trouble for doing what you had to do to protect yourself and others." The Titan regarded Alex with a gaze that gave nothing away. "Even gods can be killed with the right kind of magical firepower. Which you, my dear, have in spades."

Alex buried the horror she felt at her actions during the battle to deal with later—she was getting good at that—and studied her divine grandfather for a hint of his true feelings, but the powerful Titan had a truly excellent poker face. "Have you ever joined my Aunt Maia for one of her weekly poker games?" She asked impulsively.

Chronos chuckled and nodded, his lips curving in a regretful smile. "I've joined Maia's card games more than once, Alex. Your aunt is a real card shark."

Alex fought to keep a gleeful grin off her face. "Took you for a few bucks, did she?"

"More than a few, Alex," he replied with a dry chuckle. "Why do you think your aunt is—was richer than Croesus while she lived?"

Frowning in thought, Alex recalled her shock when the attorney had read Maia's will, informing her she had inherited a massive fortune, along with a pirate's chest of jewels, plus the Crossroads and its estate, from her late aunt. The smooth-mannered attorney had intimated that Maia's massive wealth was merely part of a Crossroads Keeper's rightful inheritance, along with the Crossroads, its temple, and the estate lands surrounding it. She wondered just how much of her fabulous wealth Maia had earned at the card table.

Chronos shifted in his chair, snapping Alex's thoughts back to the present.

"Never fear, my dear. I never gambled more than I could afford. And yes, you are right: Keepers gain substantial wealth as part of their Crossroads inheritance once they assume their role," the Titan said. "But your aunt's—now your—fortune is several times greater than average. Your aunt had an excellent accountant ... and a terrific poker face."

Alex merely nodded her understanding, then shook off her musings. She suspected the crafty Titan was trying to distract her with talk of inheritances and high-stakes card games. But she had questions. Soooo many questions. And she knew her divine grandfather had answers. Leaning forward, she met the Titan's wily gaze, determined to get those answers.

"Spill it, gramps," Alex growled. "Did you ask Zeus to hold this banquet so you and I could meet? Why didn't you just visit me at my Crossroads? Did you know the bad guys would use this event as a chance to attack? What's this whole thing really all about?"

Chronos narrowed his eyes in warning, then relaxed back into his chair with a gusty sigh. "I'd thank you to speak in a more respectful manner to your elders, child. Especially when said elder is a Titan, as well as your, ah ... relative."

"Sorry. Not sorry," Alex muttered truculently, her arms crossed and brows lowered. "You've been pulling the strings behind the scenes for ages, haven't you? What's your end goal in all this, Chronos?"

There was a deadly pause, during which Alex feared she'd gone too far in demanding answers from the most powerful Titan in existence—who just happened to be her grandfather—when she belatedly realized that their familial relationship might not save her from his divine wrath.

But Chronos merely shrugged and shook his head with a dark chuckle, then reached forward and patted Alex's hand gently, a deep sadness in his penetrating gaze. "You are so much like your mother, my dear, that it's a joy to see."

WHO'S YOUR DADDY?

Deep anxiety roiled Alex's stomach. She vaguely remembered being told that Chronos had had an affair with her paternal witch of a grandmother. The same witch who had spelled her to forget the magical world and her role in it after her jealous mother had kidnapped her as a child. But a witch, while magically powerful, couldn't capture the heart of a Titan. Could she?

Chronos rolled his eyes and snorted. "No, Alex, a mere witch could not capture my heart," he asserted firmly.

His answer confirmed Alex's theory that her divine grandfather could read her mind ... and that her ancestry might be even more obscure than she believed. Fear slithered through her veins. She swallowed roughly and whispered, "Who was she, then? Who was my grandmother?"

"Your grandmother isn't important right now. Your mother is," Chronos replied blandly. He hesitated and gazed at Alex intently, as if waiting to see if she understood his broad hint.

Oh no. Just noooo, Alex thought in growing horror as a fearful option occurred to her. She slammed her hand on the table, startling them both. "Just tell me, Chronos. Just tell me—the whole truth, this time." She frowned and muttered, "It's about damn time someone told me the unvarnished truth."

Chronos sighed and nodded reluctantly. His ancient emerald gaze revealed the Primordial god to be every millennium of his vast age. "You're right, child. It's high time you knew the truth. Especially since you're almost certainly the only one who can stop my wayward daughter, Nyx, before she destroys us all."

THE TITAN DREW A DEEP BREATH, then told the truth, which absolutely blew Alex's mind.

"I'm not your grandfather, Alex," Chronos said. The Titan's deep green eyes, so like her own, gazed softly at her. "I'm your father." He patted the air when Alex opened her mouth to protest. "Just give me a minute and I'll explain. Hmmm. How to put it concisely? Okay, here goes. You know the mythology surrounding my reign on this very Mount, correct?"

Alex frowned, delving into distant memories from her college mythology classes. "Um, you and the other Titans all lived here on Mount Olympus. As the first Primordial god, you were divine royalty and ruled the Titans." Alex gazed thoughtfully around the enormous banquet hall, with its still-frozen tableau of a battle, interrupted. "You lived here, right? This place must have been your palace before it was Zeus's."

Chronos followed her gaze around the glittering, overly ornate banquet hall and snorted. "This monstrosity? Never." He patted his chest in mock outrage and declared, "*My* palace had so much more style and elegance than this ... this overdecorated McPalace that Zeus brashly erected on the bones of my former home."

Alex snickered, very glad that someone else besides her saw the glittering gaudiness of Zeus's enormous palace. "It *is* all a bit much, isn't it?" She murmured.

"I think my son might just be compensating for something,

don't you?" The Titan replied with a wry grin. "I don't really blame him, though ... not when you take into account that harridan of a wife of his, Hera."

In a moment of full accord, father and daughter lapsed into a companionable silence, both idly studying the still scene before them.

Finally, Chronos shook off his lethargy and threw Alex a sideways grin. "Here's the unvarnished truth, my daughter. My wife, Rhea, and I had seven children, not six. You are that seventh child."

Alex's jaw dropped, stunned into silence. Her worldview shifted, and she closed her eyes as dizziness overwhelmed her, making the room tilt and spin.

"Here, drink this," Chronos murmured. He wrapped Alex's hand around a half-full goblet of wine.

Eyes still closed, her thoughts whirling, Alex drank. Once her mind cleared, the implications of Chronos's latest revelation sank in. So far, this conversation was not going at all the way she had thought it would.

She blew out a heavy sigh and cracked open her eyes. Studying the god sitting next to her thoughtfully, she sounded out her thoughts. "If my mythological memory serves me correctly, you and Rhea never got along. You were jealous of your own children. Believing they would be powerful enough to overthrow your rule one day, you ate every child your wife bore, until Zeus, whom Rhea hid from you until he was old enough to do what you had feared ... throw your Titan ass off Mount Olympus."

The more Alex had said, the wider Chronos's grin had gotten, until he finally barked a loud guffaw. "Oh, Alex. I'm so happy the misinformation campaign we Titans put in place several millennia ago is still working so well." He snickered and rolled his eyes. "Rhea and I ... Zeus threw my ass off Mount Olymp—" Chronos collapsed into helpless giggles, which only increased when he spotted Alex's confused frown.

Alex poured herself more wine, then sipped at it and waited. She would get answers out of this ancient, crafty supposed father of hers if she had to wait all night. "Whenever you're ready ... dad ... feel free to correct me."

Chronos finally sobered enough to speak. He shrugged philosophically. "Truth be told, Alex, all the Titans—including your mother and I—had long been tired of ruling from on high. We wanted a way out ... to retire, if you will. So, we got together and planned our escape." The Primordial god of Time smiled at the memory. "Your mother and I put it about that a prophecy was made, which revealed that my children would overthrow me one day. So, in fear for my throne, I immediately ate them all." His lips curled in a disgusted grimace. "Who eats their kids? Gross. Anyway, after spreading that rumor, we hid all our children until they became adults. We raised them in secret and trained them to rule—to prepare for a handover—not a takeover. When Zeus and our other Olympian children were ready, Rhea and I gathered up the other Titans, and we all simply ... retired, handing over the keys to Mount Olympus to the next generation."

Alex's eyes had widened in wonder at Chronos's revelations. "But what about the other Titans? Surely, they all couldn't have been happy being forced into retirement with you."

"Why do you think we came up with that ridiculous story about me eating our children?" Chronos replied blandly. He idly picked some lint off his toga and flicked it away. "We couldn't reveal our plans until our children were old enough to take the reins ... until they were powerful enough to band together and kick that moribund lot of Titans off the Mount, if any of them fought me on their forced retirement. Plus, don't forget, the other Titans had been busy in the children department over the years, as well. Their many Olympian offspring were more than happy to side with mine in the proposed change of leadership, when the time was right."

The Titan gave Alex a smug grin. "Once presented with the

choice of a smooth transition into an earthly retirement or fighting off a bloody uprising led by their passel of ungrateful adult children, the last of the holdouts finally agreed to retire—if not gracefully, at least without a fight."

"Ooooohhhh. I get it," Alex murmured as understanding dawned. She eyed the crafty god admiringly. "Sounds like you and Rhea played the long game. Basically, you both spent decades orchestrating a change of ownership on Mount Olympus ... and planned it in such a way as to avoid a bloody coup attempt." Frowning thoughtfully, she asked, "But where are all the other Titans now? I mean, they've had a couple of millennia of living in retirement. Are any of them still around?" Fear lanced through her, setting her heart racing. "Do any of them dream of reconquering Mount Olympus and returning to power?"

Chronos gave Alex a smug grin. "Nope. None of them are at all interested in returning to power. They have all settled happily into their retirement, as I knew they would." The Titan flicked Alex a glance and chuckled, but his gaze revealed an ancient exhaustion. "Don't forget, child, we Titans, especially the Primordial ones like me, had ruled since the dawn of time ... millions of years. We were tired. Our game was slipping. It was high time for new blood to take over. Thus, our children, the Olympians, were born and trained, and the, er ... change in management plan was success-fully executed."

"What are the other Titans doing now?" Alex asked, not merely out of curiosity. Despite Chronos's assurances, she wondered if any of the out-of-work Titans still dreamed of their glory days and might even consider supporting Nyx's takeover bid.

"You want to know they are now? Well," Chronos drawled, eyes up as he tapped his chin. "Let's see. Oceanus runs a dive shop in Cabo. Hyperion has an observatory on one of the Hawaiian islands ... can't remember which one. When he's not studying the heavens, he's surfing—badly, from what I hear." He sniffed and shrugged. "The others are here and there around the world, happily enjoying their well-deserved retirement."

Despite herself, Alex was fascinated. Actual Titans living on Earth as 'ordinary folk', indistinguishable from their human and supernatural creations—except for the whole immortality thing. She pulled her mind back to the task at hand and heaved a sigh, knowing she had to ask, but positive that bringing up his rogue daughter would spoil Chronos's good mood. "I know you said you raised your children to take over running Mount Olympus, but what about Nyx? She's, uh—"

"She's an evil, nasty piece of work, you mean?" Chronos finished her sentence, disappointment darkening his eyes. "Rhea and I always said that six out of seven of our kids turning out okay was a pretty good average. Nyx, well..." The Titan shrugged helplessly, his large, tanned hands raised in surrender.

"Nyx is the goddess of Chaos, right?" Alex mused. "And she wants to conquer all the realms, release her chaotic powers, and rule the ruins," she stated bluntly.

"Why do you think we Titans helped Zeus imprison Nyx in the Underworld all those millennia ago?" Chronos asked with a heavy sigh and a rueful shake of his head. "Rhea and I ... well, we knew she was a bad seed from almost the moment she was born."

Silence descended, during which both father and daughter considered the existential danger their chaotic, and more than slightly psychotic, family member presented.

ALEX FINALLY SHOOK herself and pressed on with her questions. "You heard about Nyx's latest escape attempt, right? She made it all the way to Hades's castle and almost convinced that lumbering oaf of a god to support her plans."

"Yes, I heard about that," Chronos replied. "However, knew that I had an ace in my pocket." The Titan turned glittering eyes on her. "You, Alex. You are that ace, my child." The Titan—her father—grinned proudly. "You easily finished off your earthly father, took control of his Regenerant army, and used them to bundle Nyx back to her prison at the edge of the Underworld, where your undead army guards her still."

Alex held up a hand. "Wait … so, you've known about my death magic *and* my time magic, all this time?" She considered Chronos's revelations regarding her divine paternity. "Sooo, if you're my biological father, and your wife, Rhea, is my mother, then I assume you guys gave me up for adoption as a baby? That would mean Helen and Talon aren't my real parents, correct?" For some reason, this conclusion made Alex feel less awful about destroying her supposed father's soul during the battle in the Underworld. At least the dark necromantic mage who had tried to kill her wasn't her real father.

However, she had seen her original birth certificate; it listed Helen and Talon as her biological parents. There had never been even a hint that she had been adopted. She tilted her head and raised her brows at the Titan who had just told her he was her real father. "If you and Rhea are my biological parents, then how— when did you? Um, yeah. I think you need to explain yourself, bud."

Chronos chewed his bottom lip, and studied Alex with a thoughtful gaze. "How do I explain this so that you'll understand it?" He muttered quietly.

"Just pretend I'm ignorant of the birds and the bees," Alex replied, rolling her eyes at him. "If even half the mythology surrounding the reproductive habits of the gods is true, I'm thinking the birds and the bees process might be much more … um, flexible for divine beings than it is for everyone else, correct?"

Chronos chuckled and gave her an amiable grin. "That's true. Okay, then … here goes. Rhea and I made the switch at your conception." He shrugged philosophically and added, "The process we used was kind of like a mix of your modern IVF and surrogacy ... plus magic. And gods."

Alex's father shifted uncomfortably, a faint blush rising on his gaunt cheeks. "Do we have to talk about this? I thought I had finished explaining the birds and the bees several thousand years ago, when your older brother Zeus reached puberty."

"Oooohhh. Ew. Um, okay then," Alex stuttered. She frowned in confusion. "But how is that even possible?"

"Original gods," the Titan replied succinctly. "There's not much we can't do." He gave Alex a sly grin.

Alex's thoughts whirled as she processed things. "But wouldn't Helen—my, uh, birth mother—realize the truth if ... when she found our DNA didn't match? Weren't you worried about that?"

"Nope," Chronos replied, his eyes twinkling mischievously. "We made sure you had enough of your ... er, foster parents' DNA to hide your divine origins."

"I suppose this means I'm not really a Crossroads Keeper from a long line of Keepers," Alex mused. "Then what the hell am I?" She fingered her goblet and drained the last of her wine to calm her nerves.

"You *are* a true Keeper, Alex," Chronos assured her. "You carry enough of both Helen and Talon's DNA so that your birth mother's Keeper heritage and your father's mage heritage are very much a part of your birthright."

The Titan gripped Alex's hand gently, his gaze intent on hers. "But you are also so, so much more than either of them, my child. You are a full-blooded goddess ... the youngest child of the two most powerful Titans in existence." The ancient god fixed Alex with a stern, paternal glare. "My daughter, we'll need every drop of the Primordial divine power flowing through your veins to defeat your sister, Nyx, or she'll eventually consume all the realms with her dark desire to rule creation in chaos."

"Nyx is ... my sister," Alex muttered. An icy chill skittered up her spine.

"Yep. Nyx is your sister," Chronos agreed. He patted her knee reassuringly. "Don't forget, you must visit her prison in the Underworld soon, so you can reinforce your necromantic power over the Regenerants who guard her." The Titan winced and added, "I've heard she's made some converts amongst your army of undead. Unless you show up soon, there just might be a revolt."

"Well, shit," Alex muttered. "I thought I was done with the Underworld."

"Not by a long shot, my dear."

AFTER SEVERAL LONG MOMENTS, during which Alex considered the life-altering enormity of what Chronos—her divine father—had revealed, she had one only one question left. "One more thing," she asked shyly. "Um, all your other divine children are several thousand years old, at least. I'm just pushing thirty. How…"

Chronos burst out laughing, his ancient emerald eyes, which were so like Alex's, lighting with glee. "You were our 'surprise' baby, my dear. Rhea and I had thought our child-bearing years were well over a thousand years behind us. However, when Rhea started throwing up every morning and having weird food cravings, we knew." Alex's divine dad grinned and patted her arm. "And we don't regret having you for a moment."

"Not that either of you actually *had* me," Alex murmured, with a sarcastic roll of her eyes. "You made someone else handle that part."

"For an excellent reason, though, daughter," Chronos insisted. "If Nyx had discovered she had a younger sibling powerful enough to defeat her, do you really think you'd have made it through your childhood years?" He shook his head firmly. "Rhea and I went with our tried-and-true method. We hid you until your powers came in. Now, however, it's your time to shine, my youngest child."

"Yeah, right," Alex muttered. She ran her hand over her face and grimaced. Everyone seemed to have much more confidence in her abilities—magical and otherwise—than she did. *And dammit ... now I find out that I'm a full-fledged goddess?* She brooded. There went the last of her plans to suppress the Primordial magic she had kept locked away deep in her soul and to avoid the responsibilities that came along with such vast divine power. Her dreams of being nothing more than a mere Keeper and letting someone else handle all the divine machinations and end-of-the-world stuff moved impossibly out of reach. *Dammit.*

"The thing is, you *are* that 'someone else,' Alex," Chronos said, reading her thoughts yet again. "Besides, your mother and I have a lot of faith in you." The Titan slapped his thighs and rose. "But that's enough for now, daughter, don't you think? How about we get this party restarted?" The god gently pushed Alex out of the trajectory of Momus's deadly arrow. With a wave of his hand, the Father of Time brought the chaotic scene back to life.

35

BETRAYAL CLOSE TO HOME

The fierce battle resumed, and the cherub's arrow whizzed harmlessly by Alex before hitting the stone wall behind her and clattering to the ground. Momus frowned, eyeing his bow in confusion. "Missed again, dammit. I knew I should never have bought a bow from that idiot brother-in-law of mine," he muttered. "It's gotta be the fucking bow—"

Alex smiled grimly, quickly recharged her staff, and let loose at the distracted cherub before the little asshole could send another death arrow her way. A pained bellow from the injured bull startled her into discharging more power than she had intended at Momus. The deadly cherub disappeared in a puff of grey ash seconds after the full force of Alex's multicolor magical lightning reached him.

"Try to leave some of the bad guys alive, daughter," Chronos huffed as he, too, shot magical bolts around the massive banqueting hall. "We need to press them for their knowledge of the insurrection."

Alex nodded, disturbed by his intentions, but understanding the need. "You mean torture them, right?" With a pained grimace, she pulled back some of her power, trying to split her lightning into smaller bolts, intended to disable, instead of disintegrate their attackers.

Chronos pursed his lips and said, "Torture is such an ugly word, don't you think? We'll ask nicely first, my dear. I promise."

THE COMBINED power of Chronos and his Olympian offspring soon subdued the rogue gods. The fierce battle had blackened and bloodied the brash golden glitter of the enormous banquet hall. Dozens of overturned tables had spilled their contents, and broken glass crunched wetly in the morass of food, wine, and blood underfoot.

The badly injured bull lay unmoving under the clenched jaws of Cerberus and Larry, who remained in his enormous, pitch-black junkyard dog form. The bull snorted, rolling its furious red eyes as Alex approached. Hades was on his knees on the massive beast's other side. The god of the Underworld was petting and crooning to his canine plus-one. The muscular canine loosened the jaws of one of his three heads and licked his master. The other two heads remained fastened to the bull's bloody neck, mere inches from the creature's carotid artery. Somehow sensing how close to the jaws of death he hovered, the bull stayed perfectly still, although mad fury raged in his glowing, crimson eyes.

Larry, his razor-sharp teeth still fastened on the bull's neck opposite his new canine friend, rolled his eyes at Alex. "Okay, we've got him down. Now what do we do? Do we kill him?" He growled, his words muffled by the hold he had on the bull's throat.

Alex jumped when Zeus replied from beside her. The god had approached on silent feet.

"No, Larry, you can't kill this beast," Zeus said, gazing sadly down at the enormous black bull. "He was ... uh, a gift from the king of Crete, a relative of mine." The god gave Alex a grim smile. "And of yours, sister."

Alex merely nodded at Zeus's acknowledgement of their sibling relationship. She assumed she was the last to know, as always. *Sigh.*

"If we can't kill him, what do we do with him then? Obviously, someone has turned this guy to the dark side. He was fighting alongside the attackers, remember," she murmured as she gazed down at the immobilized bull. Her eyes narrowed as she noted the sentience in the enormous creature's enraged eyes. "He's ... not entirely a bull, is he?" She asked, suddenly awfully certain of the intelligence she saw in the bull's eyes.

"He's the freaking Minotaur, Alex," Larry growled, his deep voice rough with fatigue. "Don't you know your Greek mythology? You better learn it fast, girlfriend, since you'll be living it from now on."

"Well, shit," Alex whispered with a heartfelt sigh. She turned to Zeus, her eyebrows raised. "Sooo, this guy's not just a gift, is he? He's an actual relative of yours ... ours."

"Yep," Zeus replied succinctly. He shrugged and muttered, "It's um ... complicated."

"Oh, I'm sure it is," Alex replied with a heartfelt groan. "Someone once told me that everyone on Mount Olympus was related, in one way or another. They sure as hell weren't wrong."

"Nope," Zeus replied, his gaze still focused on the injured Minotaur. "They weren't wrong." He gestured to several guards hovering nearby. "Has anyone found the Minotaur's golden halter?"

One guard hesitantly approached and held out a length of embossed golden leather. "We found it, Your Majesty. It was, uh..."

Zeus snatched the halter from the guard's hands and leaned over the bull. "It was in Hera's pocket, I assume," he muttered as he fastened the golden halter around the bull's head.

"Yessir," the round-eyed guard replied carefully. He saluted smartly, then retreated to huddle with his buddies, all of whom eyed the Minotaur nervously.

"You can let go in a minute," Zeus instructed the dogs. "This halter subdues the Minotaur to the will of whoever holds its lead rope."

The injured Minotaur bellowed in outrage as the halter's magic snapped into place. Cerberus and Larry let go and jumped away moments before the massive creature rolled and lurched to his feet. The angry bull's muscles quivered, but he stood completely still, gazing at those around him with eyes full of incandescent rage.

Chronos, who had been quietly directing the guards regarding the disposition of the subdued attackers, strode over to join the group gathered near the Minotaur. Eyebrows raised, the Titan flicked his gaze around the ruined dining hall, then grinned wryly at Zeus. "*Now,* do you believe me, son? You have to admit that Hera's up to her pretty neck in this whole sorry mess with Nyx."

Zeus hung his head, then nodded slowly. "Yes, Father, now I believe you." The disconsolate god heaved a sigh. "I suppose I've known she hasn't been ... uh, been good for a while. But I thought—"

"You thought your wife's treachery was merely marital, son," Chronos counseled his despondent offspring. "No husband wants to believe his wife is conspiring with his mortal enemies."

Alex's eyes widened as she realized just how cunning her Titan father truly was. The wily god had never given her a direct answer when she asked him if he had orchestrated the banquet or if he suspected that the rogue gods would target the event, causing Hera to reveal the extent of her treachery.

Obviously, the scheming Titan's strategic planning had been at play in that evening's fiasco. To bring home to Zeus just how much of a threat Nyx and her divine co-conspirators posed, in both a figurative and a literal sense, Chronos had orchestrated that evening's battle. She eyed her divine brother's increasingly angry expression and admitted that their father had masterfully achieved his goal.

HERA SCREAMED when the Fates released her from her immobilizing bonds. The distraught goddess ran to Zeus and fell to her knees, pleading with her betrayed husband not to imprison her. However, Zeus had finally had enough of his wife's treachery.

"Lock her in a cell reinforced to hold divine beings," Zeus instructed the guards tersely. The grieving god shook his head as he watched the guards march his still-protesting wife from the massive dining room.

"I could cut the bitch's lifeline if you want," Atropos offered, with a meaningful snip of her gory scissors. "Even end her soul, if you're so inclined," she added with an anticipatory grin.

Zeus shook his head with a sigh. "She used to be so different," he murmured softly. "What the hell happened?"

"Oh, Hera's always been a first-class bitch," Atropos stated baldly. "You've always just closed your eyes to it, you big idiot."

"Because I loved her," Zeus said simply.

Atropos rolled her eyes. "Because she's good in the sack, more like," she muttered.

Alex reddened at Atropos's plain speaking. The bold goddess of Fate may be right, but it probably wasn't wise to hammer home just how much of a raging bitch Hera was to the god who fell in love with her millennia ago.

Chronos clapped his hands sharply to end the brewing dispute. "All right, that's enough, everyone. We're all finally in agreement that Hera is a piece of work. We must now force answers from her and the rest of the traitors if we're to save all the realms from Nyx's chaotic rule." The Titan patted Zeus on the shoulder and added, "Don't worry, son. I'll question Hera myself. I'm sure I can get answers from her without hurting her. Much."

"I don't care what happens to her from now on," Zeus growled, shaking off his father's hand. "Just do what needs to be done." With a curt nod to Alex, the frustrated god strode from the room.

Chronos pursed his lips and gazed thoughtfully after his son. "I knew it would be hard for him to discover the extent of the rot in his kingdom—and in his own home—but still..."

Clotho, always the kindest of the Fates, smiled gently at the dispirited Titan. "Don't worry, my dear. Zeus will be fine. He just needs some time to process things."

The goddess bustled over to Alex and took her arm. "Come, dear, let's get you back to the villa." Glancing around the destroyed dining room, Clotho murmured, "Now, where has your new assistant gotten to? Oh, there she is, over by Demeter. Let's head over there." The motherly goddess hauled Alex across the room. Casting a backward glance at the massive junkyard dog, who stood with his paws resting in pools of the Minotaur's congealing blood, the goddess called, "You, too, Larry. Come along now. It has been an exhausting evening, and everyone needs to get some sleep before heading home in the morning."

36

HOMEWARD BOUND

Early morning sunlight streamed in the window when Calliope pushed open the bedroom's wooden shutters. Alex groaned and pulled the bedcovers over her head to block out the dazzling light. "Just a few more minutes, please," she begged.

Larry whined, "I'm starving, Alex. The chef says he won't feed me second breakfast until you come downstairs for your first one."

Alex poked her head from under the covers and gave her Familiar, now back in his pink-eared poodle form, a squinty-eyed glare. "You mean to tell me you've already eaten one meal, and I have to drag myself out of bed so you can have a second one?"

"Yup." Unrepentant, Larry grinned at her from his spot at the foot of the bed and wagged his pink tail. "Besides, there's a whole crapload of people downstairs who want to say goodbye before we leave."

Alex groaned again and buried her head under her pillow, which Calliope quickly snatched away.

"Rise and shine, boss," the cheerful woman sang. "It's a new day for us all."

Heaving a put-upon sigh, Alex dragged herself from the

warmth of her bed. She shot an irritated side-eye at the interlopers. "Beat it, you two. I need a shower before I face the day."

The steaming mug of coffee on the bedside table cheered her immensely. She snagged it on the way to the bathroom.

ALEX HAD JUST FINISHED DRYING her hair when her phone dinged. Hope surged, and she hurried out of the bathroom. Perhaps Conor had broken his phone silence to wish her a safe trip home. Her shoulders slumped when she realized the text message was from her estranged mother.

I know what you did last night, Alex. You've made some dangerous enemies. We need to talk. Call me.

Alex hadn't gotten a text from her mother since her overnight visit to London what seemed like ages ago, even though it had been less than a week. She hadn't replied to any of the half a dozen text messages Helen had sent over the past several months, hoping her mother would get the message and leave her alone. She had nothing to say to the woman who had tried to kill her as a toddler, then kidnapped her a decade later, all in an attempt to gain Alex's Keeper inheritance for herself. Just nope.

She smiled grimly, recalling her 'birds and bees' conversation with Chronos the previous evening. At least Helen wasn't her real mother. Mostly not. Kind of. Rolling her eyes at the complexity of her biological origins, Alex swallowed the lukewarm dregs of her coffee and strode out the door. Might as well get the goodbyes over with so she could head home to her heart family. And to a possessive Hellhound Barghest that better get over his attitude before she was done with him, at least on a personal level.

BREAKFAST WAS EXCELLENT, but the goodbyes were tough, as they usually are.

Clotho hugged Alex one more time, dabbing tears away with the long sleeve of her tunic. "You'll call us when you get home, my dear? Just to let us know you made it safely?" The stout goddess pushed a bulging bag into Alex's arms. "Here you go. I had the cook prepare some food for your return journey."

Lachesis gave Alex a birdlike peck on the cheek. "There are four of everything in the bag, Alex, even though only the three of you are traveling today." The diminutive goddess smiled nervously and fingered the edge of her toga. "You know I like nice, even numbers."

Larry wagged his tail happily. "Don't worry, Lachesis. More food is always better. I'll eat the leftovers." He eyed the large bag hungrily. "In fact, I could eat now."

The pink-eared poodle's food obsession broke the room's gloomy atmosphere, and everyone laughed at the little chowhound. Even the stern-faced Atropos unbent enough to quirk her lips a fraction.

Demeter, who had been hovering at the edge of the room, approached Alex to say her farewells. The goddess leaned close and whispered, "We have much to discuss, sister. But not here." She flicked a glance at the others and murmured, "Let's meet at Hecate's place in the In-Between once you are settled back at the Crossroads. I'll text you."

Alex nodded, hiding a wince, both at the goddess's casual acknowledgement of their newfound sibling status and at the mention of texting. She was beginning to loathe demanding texts from imperious family members.

It took a long time for everyone to say their goodbyes and even longer before the luggage was packed and last-minute instructions had been issued. It was early afternoon by the time Alex and Larry could depart ... with an extra traveling companion.

Clothos had watched with a teary smile as Demeter formally

appointed a thrilled Calliope as Alex's new Assistant Keeper. "You'll need her help, Alex," the goddess had murmured while everyone celebrated Calliope's good fortune. "You've got more responsibilities than ever, sis."

Alex merely sighed and nodded at Demeter's whispered words, knowing they were true.

THE RETURN TRIP through the Crossroads ley line system took almost a full day. Alex and her traveling companions had overnighted at the London Crossroads. The following morning, they each enjoyed a full English breakfast—Larry's idea—then set out for home.

37

I'LL ALWAYS STAY

Alex lurched dizzily out of the San Antonio Crossroads. Ley line travel disoriented her every time. Putting a hand to her nauseated stomach, she trudged out of the temple and squinted at the substantial crowd gathered in the courtyard. It seemed like half the town had turned out to welcome her back. She hid a wince at the noise as everyone shouted and clapped riotously.

"Oooh, look," Larry crowed. "They've even put up a Welcome Home banner for me." He flicked a glance at Alex. "I'm sure it's meant for you, too. Maybe."

Alex smiled down at her grinning Familiar. She knew he was teasing her just to ease her nerves at the unexpected press of excited people after their long and tiring trip. "Thanks, Larry," she murmured. "How about we both share the welcome?"

WHAT SEEMED LIKE HOURS LATER, Alex finally extricated herself from the exuberant gathering. She had searched in vain for a glimpse of Conor, her heart sinking when she didn't find his face in the welcoming crowd.

Maia, the first to greet Alex, had merely hugged her niece with a sympathetic smile, then gathered up Calliope and introduced her to everyone as the new Assistant Keeper. Alex watched her gregarious aunt's ghostly form maneuver Calliope through the curious crowd. Things would be all right, even if Conor wanted to cool things off between them. But they still had to work together, so they needed to hash things out. *Friends would work,* Alex brooded. Hopefully, they could still be friends.

She ignored her aching heart and trudged wearily through the garden toward her apartment off the mansion's side courtyard. Larry had met up with Grenoble at the welcome home party. The two miscreants had agreed the party wasn't over yet, so they stayed behind. There *was* still an enormous amount of food left over, after all.

As Alex rounded the garden's precisely clipped hedges, the staircase to her small studio apartment came into view. A tall, familiar, and very handsome man lounged at the bottom of the steps. Alex's heart sped up as she approached, but she worked to keep her emotions off her face. She drew to a halt several meters away. Knowing Hellhound Barghest shifters could smell emotional reactions, she didn't want this one to scent her sorrow ... or her attraction.

Conor gave Alex an easy grin, but his stiff pose revealed his discomfort. "Welcome home, sweets," he said. "I hear you handled things on your mission with your usual amount of skill and diplomacy ... and with absolutely no need for my help."

Alex blew out a slow breath. She refused to fight with him. She just wasn't up to it right now. "I'm tired, Conor. Can we talk about this later?"

He shrugged and nodded. "Sure thing, sweets," he murmured as he prowled forward and drew her into a tight hug. "I missed you," he growled. "I'm glad you're home safe."

At first, Alex stiffened at his embrace, then she sank into it with a sigh. She couldn't deny her feelings for this frustrating man any longer. She loved him. However, until they came to an agreement about her need for some level of independence and Conor proved he could control his overprotective instincts, she couldn't reveal her feelings.

"Barghest here, remember?" Conor murmured as he nuzzled her ear and dropped small kisses along her neck. "I can smell your sadness ... and your attraction." Then he drew back with a confused frown. "No, it's more than attraction..."

Alex stepped out of his embrace and shook her head. "Not tonight, Conor. I know we need to have a conversation about this ... thing, between us, but I'm seriously not up to it tonight."

Conor relented and gave her a crooked grin. "How about I draw you a hot bath and bring you some tea? Then you can fall into bed ... with or without me."

"Sounds like a plan," Alex replied wearily as she climbed the steps to her apartment. Once they reached the landing, she studied Conor's face, suddenly unsure of the situation. However, she risked asking a question. "Can we ... just. Can you stay? Just to sleep, though. For tonight. Until we have time to talk—"

Conor pushed open the door, then took her hand and led her into the room. He smiled softly and whispered, "I'll stay, Alex. I'll always stay."

38

THE WOMAN IS A GODDESS

Pale pre-dawn light suffused the sky the following morning when Alex received a summons from Hecate. She sat up and rubbed her eyes as the goddess's command echoed in her head. Hecate had no need for a cellphone, Alex brooded, when she could easily mind-speak with her oath-bound Keepers. And probably anyone else she had a mind to.

Conor lay still next to her, his even breathing suggesting sleep. When she glanced over, she saw his eyes were open and fixed on her, warmth filling his amber gaze.

"Morning, sweets," he murmured, giving Alex a slow smile. "Sounds like you've gotten Hecate's divine summons, too."

Surprised, Alex asked, "You heard Hecate? I thought she was speaking only to me."

"Nope. She wants me there too, for some reason." Conor threw the covers back and sat up. Alex couldn't help her gaze from traveling to his bare chest and flat stomach. She suppressed a sigh. They had slept in the same bed last night, but that was all. Conor's presence had been a huge comfort, but the emotional distance between them still existed.

Connor's sly grin as he slid out of bed informed Alex that he knew she'd been ogling his bare chest. She pulled her gaze up to his face and rolled her eyes. "Don't get any ideas, bud. We still need to have a serious conversation about our relationship before ... well, you know."

With a wink and a nod, he agreed. "Understood." His gaze turned serious. "We'd better get a move on. Goddesses as ancient and powerful as Hecate definitely don't like to be kept waiting." Strolling toward the bathroom, he added, "I call dibs on the shower ... but you're welcome to join me."

The pillow Alex threw at Conor fell short. "We're not going there until we have our talk, remember?"

Alex heard the too-confident man snicker, then the shower came on.

With a flap of the dog door, Larry bounded into the room. "Hurry up, slowpoke! We had better not keep Hecate waiting."

"So I hear," Alex murmured as she stroked her Familiar's fluffy head. "You got her mind-call, too, huh?"

"Yup. She's called pretty much everyone, including the posse members. We're supposed to meet her in the barn arena for a sit-rep," Larry explained. He leaned his head into her hand. "Hey, partner, while you're waiting for the shower, can you get that spot behind my ears I like?"

She obliged, her thoughts on the upcoming meeting. If Hecate had called the posse together and wanted a full report, it was likely that everyone would soon know about her newly discovered fully divine status. She wasn't sure she was ready for that—or if she would ever be. With a shrug, she climbed off the bed and headed to her closet; time to choose a power outfit to go with her promotion to goddess status. Alex admitted to herself that there was no point in trying to avoid her divine heritage any longer, especially since her divine father, Chronos, had informed her that their side would need every bit of his youngest daughter's divine power to win the war against her sister, Nyx, and that power-hungry goddess's Chaos Council co-conspirators. *Sigh.*

A sharp ding from her phone informed Alex she had received a text message. Her stomach sank; she just knew it was another text from her mother—or rather her human, um, birth mother—whatever. She decided to call the woman Helen from then on. Despite the enormity of the revelations about her true parentage during the talk she had with Chronos on Mount Olympus, Alex was actually relieved that Helen wasn't her true mother. She had yet to meet Chronos's wife, Rhea, her real—er, original mother. But the ancient and powerful female Titan must be a better option to call 'mom' than Helen. *Right?*

Conor interrupted Alex's musings when he walked out of the bathroom with nothing but a fluffy white towel wrapped around his slim waist. She couldn't help her gaze from traveling appreciatively over his lean but muscular physique. He threw her a smug grin, then crossed the room and picked up her cell phone from the nightstand. "I thought I heard you get a text message, sweets."

Alex's eyes widened, and she attempted to grab her phone before Conor read her sort-of mother's text. "Give me that—"

Conor's thunderous frown as he studied the phone told her it was too late; he had seen the message. She hadn't told him about the texts from Helen, hoping that the scheming woman would tire of sending them if she never replied. Plus, the situation with her mother was something Alex wanted to handle on her own.

With a quick flick of his fingers, Conor accessed the rest of the text messages Helen had sent over the past several months. His accusing gaze met Alex's worried one, and he growled, "Why am I just finding out now that your mother has been sending you ominous texts for months and repeatedly demanding that you contact her?"

Alex's gaze slid from Conor's furious one. "I don't have any intention of speaking with her," she stuttered. "And I didn't want to bother—"

"You didn't want to bother me?" Conor turned away and threw his clothes on with quick, sharp movements. "You wanted to handle Helen yourself? Right? Just like you want to handle everything else yourself these days," he snarled, before striding to the door and flinging it open. His amber gaze was a strange mixture of sad and angry. "When will you learn you are not alone, Alex? Not only is there no need for you to be, but your insistence on having so-called independence puts your friends and family—and the rest of the freaking world—in extreme danger!"

Alex dropped her gaze and heaved a sigh, grimacing at Conor's angry muttering, which receded as the irate Hellhound shifter stomped down the stairs. Unheeded tears tracked down her cheeks. Conor was right, and she knew it. She thought she had already dealt with her desire to 'go it alone', but it was something she had done all her life until just a few months ago upon rediscovering her heart family and her Keeper heritage. She snorted a sad laugh, recalling Olympe's earlier, half-jesting words, 'Old habits are hard to break'.

Larry pushed his warm body into Alex's legs and gazed up at her, his chocolate brown eyes both wise and understanding. "Independence isn't a bad thing, Alex. But neither is inter-dependence. You know, granting others not just heart space, but head space, too. Allowing others to help you with things that require a combined effort is the smart thing to do ... even if you're a freaking goddess."

Alex nodded slowly. She thought she had been doing so well since her return to the supernatural world. She had rediscovered her long-lost heart family, immersed herself in learning about the supernatural world, and was finally getting comfortable with her new role as a Crossroads Keeper. But Alex had to admit that she'd been stubbornly avoiding taking ownership of her growing magical powers and her widening responsibilities to her new world. She had been asserting her independence partially to avoid these further responsibilities. However, that was no longer possible. Or safe. *Crapola.*

As soon as Alex entered the large barn used for posse meetings, she flicked a nervous glance at Hecate. Stone-faced, the strikingly beautiful goddess reposed on a massive throne-like chair positioned in the middle of the riding arena. Demeter and Persephone lounged in similar chairs on Hecate's right side. Alex's eyes widened when she saw a fourth chair positioned to Hecate's left. The throne-like chair was as massive and anciently elegant as the other three. And ... it was empty. *Oh no.*

Avoiding any decision about where to sit, Alex turned to face the audience. The posse members seated on stepped risers gazed at her attentively, many faces smiling in welcome. She suppressed a sigh of relief when she noticed the ghosts were all seated together again. It appeared the truce she had helped negotiate before leaving for the Grenoble Crossroads was holding. Crazy Sam flew low over Queen Elizabeth's head, making an irritating buzzing sound. The ancient ghostly queen swatted him away, looking merely annoyed instead of enraged. *Progress*, Alex mused.

Billy the Squid had spread his fifty-plus foot length against the far wall. He rumbled a greeting to Alex, waving several of his thick tentacles in enthusiastic welcome. Two tentacles held up a massive Welcome Home banner.

Alex's heart warmed; she smiled and waved back at the gigantic squid. Billy sported bright new construction-site orange headgear. The human-sized hat, which perched precariously on the enormous squid's pointy head, featured a towering fan of wispy blue feathers stuck in its crimson braided-leather hatband. "Love your new hat, Billy!" She called.

"Thanks, Alex. It's my new favorite!"

Grenoble squatted on the lowest riser next to his best friend,

Larry. The goblin's mottled green skin glowed in the arena's harsh fluorescent lighting. He grinned at Alex, showing off a mouthful of razor-sharp teeth. Grenoble bowed his head and placed a hand on his chest, as if giving her an unspoken oath of support. Hiding her shock, she merely nodded at the former goblin king. She recalled the time right after she had first met the toddler-sized goblin—when she had needed Larry to convince the fierce little guy not to devour her as a snack. *More progress.*

Alex spotted the ghostly form of her aunt seated in the front row next to her beau, Alan. Since Maia's harrowing experience in the Underworld, her body appeared almost solid, like that of a much older spirit. The ghost and her half-fae boyfriend were sweetly holding hands. The very-much-alive attorney hadn't been willing to accept his lover's death as the end of their relationship, so there the two sat, a happy, if slightly odd, couple. Maia's face bore a happy grin. She blew Alex a kiss and mouthed, "I'm so proud of you, my dear."

Alex smiled affectionately at her aunt, then cast her gaze over the rest of her posse members. *Since when did they become 'my' posse members?* She mused. However, deep in her heart, it felt right. A strident voice cut across the massive arena, startling Alex out of her musings.

"Alex, come here and take your rightful place at my side," commanded Hecate.

Unnoticed, Conor had moved to stand at Alex's side. He rubbed her back and murmured, "Better do it, sweets. You don't want to make that angry goddess any more pissed off than she already looks."

Suppressing a heavy sigh, Alex reluctantly approached the massive throne-like chair at Hecate's side and gingerly perched on the edge of the seat.

"Sit back, Keeper," Hecate instructed. "We have a lot to discuss ... including those texts from your human half-mother you've been hiding from me." The goddess fixed Alex with a narrow-eyed glare and growled, "After that, you can share with us the results of your endeavors at the Grenoble Crossroads and also reveal your divine status ... sister."

"I haven't been hiding Helen's texts," Alex protested. She rolled her eyes and reluctantly repositioned herself in her seat until her back rested against the carved wood of the ancient throne. It was just like Hecate to begin with the one thing Alex was ashamed of, instead of lauding her for the successful mission against the Chaos Council at the Grenoble Crossroads and for her part in the decisive win at the battle on Mount Olympus.

Demeter sat forward and placed a restraining hand on Hecate's, which clung, white-knuckled, to the arm of her chair. "Now, sister, perhaps we should start with the positives. Alex and her team ended the attacks against the Grenoble Crossroads." The goddess gave Alex a thankful smile. "She also saved my daughter's life, and her Familiar rooted out and killed a traitor hiding at the heart of one of our Crossroads."

Hecate snorted and shook her head, but she loosened her death-grip on the arm of her chair. The gaze she turned on Alex still sparkled with anger, but pride and approval lurked there as well. "You and your team did well, Alex. Thank you for ending the attacks on the Grenoble Crossroads and for saving the life of your niece, Olympe."

Alex nodded silently, accepting Hecate's praise. She kept the startled realization of her real relationship to her new friend, Olympe, off of her face. The revelation that Chronos was Alex's true father meant that the ancient Crossroads Keeper wasn't her cousin, but her niece. Oh boy, everybody was sooo right. All the gods were related ... often in more ways than one. *Well, dammit. Then why—*

"Why do I call you 'sister'?" Hecate murmured, plucking the question out of Alex's confused mind. The lovely goddess's lips curved in a reluctant smile as she gazed at Alex, her eyebrows raised in mocking inquiry. "You are a sister to *all* of Chronos's Olympian offspring, Alex ... and that includes me."

Alex's eyes widened as she puzzled over her complicated family tree. "Oh ... okay. Yep. I think I understand, ma'am," she said.

"Don't you dare ma'am me!" The goddess snapped. "You can call me by my given name. Or sister. Those are your choices."

"Yes, ma—er, Hecate." Alex didn't think she'd ever feel comfortable calling the ancient goddess her sister. *Well, crap.*

Persephone, who had been so quiet Alex had almost forgotten her presence, leaned forward and grinned at Alex. "Welcome to the family, Auntie Alex! And don't you dare call me ma'am, either, or I just might have to smite you."

Demeter chuckled at her daughter's words. Then she spread a warning gaze among the seated goddesses, her eyes lingering on Alex. "There will be no smiting between the four of us. We must concentrate on defeating Nyx and her confederates and not on fighting amongst ourselves. Agreed?"

A chorus of yeses came from the other three goddesses, including the newest one.

THE POSSE MEETING TOOK HOURS. Planning the trip to the Underworld to reinforce Alex's control over the army of Regenerants guarding Nyx took up most of the morning. Exhausted and hungry, Alex asked Conor to step in and facilitate discussion of the last few items.

The handsome Hellhound Barghest shifter flashed her a grin full of warmth and mischief. "Sure thing, sweets." He turned his attention to the agenda fastened to the clipboard she had handed him and checked off the next item. "Only a couple more things to go, folks. Next, we need to address some communication issues..."

Alex suppressed a groan. The next agenda item was obviously

Helen and the ominous text messages she had been sending Alex ... and that she had been keeping to herself. *Well, damn.* She really should have gotten through that agenda item before handing the meeting over to Conor, so she could control the narrative.

Nah. She admitted to herself that she had indeed been wrong to hide the text messages. After all, she had a team of willing and capable posse members, plus a passel of powerful gods in her corner. Together, they faced an existential threat to their world from an insane and powerful goddess. Since Helen, Alex's kind-of mother, was almost certainly aligned with the Chaos Council, Nyx's earthbound group of co-conspirators, she really shouldn't have ignored the text messages.

Alex realized she would need all the help she could get for the coming battles, so she sucked it up, stood up, and issued an abject apology for withholding important information. She pledged to be a better posse member ... and a better goddess.

PERSONAL PIZZA

The chandelier hanging above their table rocked dangerously. Alex blew an irritated breath and eyed the grinning ghost perched amongst the light fixture's wrought iron branches. "Listen, Sam, I know you're excited to be back on your regular haunting schedule here at the pizza restaurant, now that the ghost truce is in place, but could you please go haunt another table? Please?"

"It's Crazy Sam to you, girl, and don't you forget it!" The ghost gave the chandelier a final mad swing, then launched himself into the air. He grinned slyly at Alex and gave Conor a thumbs up. "I hear you two lovebirds need to do some making up," he cackled. The ghost's parting words floated over his shoulder as he swooped across the restaurant's large dining room. "And then you can get to the making-out part. Wooohooo!"

Alex felt a blush creep up her neck. She eyed Conor apprehensively and muttered, "Don't you dare say a word, bud."

Conor sipped his wine to hide his grin. "Gonna be kind of hard for us to talk this thing out without words." He put down his wineglass and placed his hand over Alex's. "It's been a busy few days planning our return trip to the Underworld. I'm glad we finally have a chance to talk privately. I think—"

The server arrived in an aromatic cloud of garlic, cutting Conor's next words off. The wiry man expertly slid a massive pizza, bubbling with cheese, onto the pizza stand resting in the center of their table. "Enjoy," he murmured, then discreetly whisked himself away.

"How about we eat this thing out instead, guys?" Larry's muffled words came from under the pristine white tablecloth. "Talking can wait. Strike while the pizza's hot, I say."

Alex shoved Larry gently out from under the table with her foot. Giving her magical partner an amused glare, she told him, "Listen, fur-face. I thought you agreed to eat on the terrace with your pal, Grenoble?"

The small, pink-eared poodle grinned unrepentantly up at her. "But I can't eavesdrop on your make-up talk from the terrace." He snickered and added, "But I sure as heck plan to make myself scarce for the second part, though ... the make-up sex."

Conor, a faint blush coloring his cheeks, glared down at Larry and growled, "Beat it, hound, or I'll tell Vinnie to make sure the cook burns all your pizzas to a crisp from now on."

"Aw, guys," Larry whined, "there's no need to be like that. Alright, I'm going. I'm going." He padded slowly away, mumbling about blackened pizza and sacrilege.

Conor slid a piece of pizza onto Alex's plate, then helped himself to a slice. He smiled at her, his gaze filled with warmth and heat. "Larry's a pain in the ass, but he may have a point. How about we eat and run? Save the talking for later?"

Blushing, Alex nodded her agreement, then bit into the delicious pizza.

～

Join my VIP Reader's Club newsletter for the latest information about upcoming releases, bonus content, discounts, and more.

For more information about my books, along with purchase links, please visit my website at:

www.samanthablackwoodnovelist.com

Reviews are always appreciated. *If you enjoyed this book, I would be grateful if you could spend just five minutes leaving a review on your favorite book vendor's website.*

- Woofs & Wags, Samantha Blackwood

ALSO BY SAMANTHA BLACKWOOD

The Crossroads Keeper Series

Prequel - Larry's Familiar Tale

Book 1 - Hecate's Heir

Book 2 - Persephone's Problem

Book 3 - Demeter's Dilemma

Book 4 - Hades in Hot Water - Coming Soon

Book 5 - The Chaos Council - Coming Soon

Book 6 - Nixing Nyx

The Kitchen Witchery Series

Book 1 - The Maple Muffin Murder

Book 2 - The Lemon Croissant Corpse

Book 3 - The Damson Danish Death - Coming Soon

Join my VIP Reader's Club to receive a free copy of Larry's Familiar Tale, the prequel to the Crossroads Keeper series, and to receive news about upcoming releases, bonus content, Larry's Life Blog, multi-author book fairs, reader discounts, and more.

For more information about my books, newsletter signup, and purchase links, please visit my website at:

www.samanthablackwoodnovelist.com

ABOUT THE AUTHOR

Samantha Blackwood writes witty, humorous novels in the urban fantasy, supernatural, and paranormal mid-life cozy mystery genres.

She lives near the beach in sunny Portugal with her husband and their pack of rescue dogs. She has worked professionally with dogs for most of her life and proudly claims the title of 'Crazy Dog Lady.' Her friends and family don't disagree...

Of course, she couldn't imagine not including dogs in her writing, so there's at least one sassy, snarky canine character, based on one of her own dogs, in each of her books.

For more information, please contact the author.
www.samanthablackwoodnovelist.com
sam@samanthablackwoodnovelist.com

Find her on social media.
Facebook.com/samanthablackwoodnovelist
Instagram.com/samanthablackwoodnovelist
Pinterest.com/samanthablackwoodnovelist

9 781955 624169